Expensive People

Expensive People

JOYCE CAROL OATES

VICTOR GOLLANCZ LTD · LONDON
1969

575 00302 2

The story, "The Molesters," which is Chapter 14 of
Part II of this book, was published in *The Quarterly
Review of Literature*, Volume XV, Numbers 3/4.

Printed in Great Britain by
Lowe & Brydone (Printers) Ltd., London

for Kay Smith

part I

1

I was a child murderer.

I don't mean child-murderer, though that's an idea. I mean child murderer, that is, a murderer who happens to be a child, or a child who happens to be a murderer. You can take your choice. When Aristotle notes that man is a rational animal one strains forward, cupping his ear, to hear which of those words is emphasized—*rational* animal, rational *animal*? Which am I? *Child* murderer, child *murderer*? It took me years to start writing this memoir, but now that I'm started, now that those ugly words are typed out, I could keep on typing forever. A kind of quiet, blubbering hysteria has set in. You would be surprised, normal as you are, to learn how many years, how many months, and how many awful minutes it has taken me just to type that first line, which you read in less than a second: I was a child murderer.

You think it's easy?

Let me explain the second line. Child-murderer is an "idea." I am writing this memoir in a rented room, ignoble enough and smelling of garbage, and outside in the street children are playing. Normal, like you and everyone who chances upon these sweaty words of mine, the children are making noise. Normal people always make noise. So it crosses my desperate, corrupt, cobwebbed mind, my flabby, cringing mind, that those noises could be silenced in the way I once silenced someone else. Already you are struggling and tugging with your distaste, eh? You're tempted to glance at the back of this book to see if the last chapter is a prison scene and a priest visits me and I either stoically refuse him or embrace his knees manfully. Yes, you are thinking of doing that. So I might as well tell you that my memoir will not end in any such convenient way; it isn't well rounded or hemmed in by fate in the shape of novelistic architecture. It certainly isn't well planned. It has no conclusion but just dribbles off, in much the same way it begins. This is life. My memoir is not a confession and it is not fiction to make money; it is simply . . . I am not sure what it is. Until I write it all out I won't even know what I think about it.

Look at my hands tremble! I am not well. I weigh two hundred and fifty pounds and I am not well, and if I told you how old I am you would turn away with a look of revulsion. How old am I? Did I stop growing on that day when "it" happened, note the shrewd passivity of that phrase, as if I hadn't made "it" happen myself, or did I maybe freeze into what I was, and outside of that shell layers and layers of fat began to form? Writing this is such hard work that I have to stop and wipe myself with a large handkerchief. I sweat all over. And those children outside my window! I think they are unkillable anyway. Life keeps on, getting noisier and noisier as I get quieter and quieter, and all these normal, noisy, healthy people around me keep pressing in, mouths full of laughing teeth and biceps charmingly bulging. At the second in which the slick lining of my stomach finally bursts, some creature next door will turn her radio from Bill Sharpe's "Weather Round-Up" to Guy Prince's "Top-Ten Jamboree."

This memoir is a hatchet to slash through my own heavy flesh and through the flesh of anyone else who happens to get in the way.

One thing I want to do, my readers, is to minimize the tension between writer and reader. Yes, there is tension. You think I am trying to put something over on you, but that isn't true. It isn't true. I am honest and dogged and eventually the truth will be told; it will just take time because I want to make sure everything gets in. I realize my sentences are slack and flabby and composed of too many small words—I'll see if I can't fix that. And you are impatient because I can't seem to get started telling this story in any normal way (I don't mean to be ironic so much, irony is an unpleasant character trait), and you would like to know, whimsically enough, whether I am in a mental institution now or crazy in some less official setting, whether I am repentant (a tongueless monk, maybe), whether much gore will be splattered throughout these pages, many violent encounters between male and female, and whether after these extravaganzas I am justly punished. Just punishment after illicit extravaganzas is usually served up for the benefit of the reader, who feels better. But, you see, this is not fiction. This is life. My problem is that I don't know what I am doing.

I lived all this mess but I don't know what it is. I don't even know what I mean by "it." I have a story to tell, yes, and no one else could tell it but me, but if I tell it now and not next year it will come out one way, and if I could have forced my fat, heaving body to begin this a year ago it would have been a different story then. And it's possible that I'm lying without knowing it. Or telling the truth in some weird, symbolic way without knowing it, so only a few psychoanalytic literary critics (there are no more than three thousand) will have access to the truth, what "it" is.

So there is tension, all right, because I couldn't begin the story by stating: *One morning in January a yellow Cadillac pulled up to a curb.* And I couldn't begin the story by stating: *He was an only child.* (Both these statements are quite sensible, by the way, though I could never talk about myself in the third person.)

And I couldn't begin the story by stating: *Elwood Everett met and wed Natashya Romanov when he was thirty-two and she was nineteen.* (Those are my parents! It took me some time to type out their names.)

And I couldn't begin the story with this pathetic flourish: *The closet door opened suddenly and there he stood, naked. He stared in at me and I stared out at him.* (And that also will come to pass, though I hadn't intended to mention it so soon.)

All these devices are fine and I offer them to any amateur writer who wants them, but for me they don't work because . . . I'm not sure why. It must be because the story I have to tell is my life, synonymous with my life, and no life begins anywhere. If you have to begin your life with a sentence, better make it a brave summing up and not anything coy: *I was a child murderer.*

My readers, don't fret, don't nibble at your nails: indeed I was punished. Indeed I am being punished. My misery is proof of God's existence—yes, I'll offer that to you as a special bonus! It will do your souls good to read of my suffering. You'll want to know when my crime took place, and where. And what do I look like, this fat degenerate, dripping sweat over his manuscript, and how the hell old am I anyway, and whom did I kill, and why, and what sense does it make?

2 AN INCIDENTAL HISTORICAL NOTE

Let us cast our minds about through history and see what precedents I have. A child murderer is discussed in two oblique and strangely elusive passages in Hardyng, in the second century of our era: a child of eight who must have accomplished something monstrous but who passes by silently, nameless and damned. What a loss!

Then there is a monograph by the historian Wren, on the Nietzschean "eternal return," which judges that grave concept (justifiably?) as nonsense but goes on to speculate, with a whimsy I admire, on the repetitions, throughout eternity, of the bizarre crimes of this *Peter Lully,* a child of tender years who butchered his five brothers and sisters, including a baby in his cradle and, because it bothered him, the family's shepherd dog as well. No motive is given, of course. We children are always denied sensible motives by the adults who write up our crimes. (I say "we" though I am no longer a child. My soul is a child's soul, however.)

Then there is the well-known, rather tawdry incident reported in a letter of Flaubert to Louise Colet, in which he remarked—with a savagery absolutely unfound in other of his smooth, rather phony correspondence—of the French peasant child, also nameless, who pushed his grandfather into the fire and swatted him with a broom so that the poor man could not escape. The senseless, barbaric cruelty is what caught Flaubert's attention, but I ask, is it really senseless? Barbaric, yes, and cruel to a degree that makes me want to retch, but senseless?

In literature we have a few incidents, none of them first-rate: the allusion in a lesser Chaucerian tale of a child warrior (though that's beyond my interest), the allusion in *Macbeth* to Lady Macbeth, as a child, wantonly doing away with a "blessèd babe," no doubt a sibling, and Stendhal's exasperating references to a certain irrevocable crime of Julien's, committed when he was four—that precocious hypocrite! But I think you'll agree there isn't much. A photostat of a lithograph by a seventeenth-century Spaniard is on its way to me—with the promise of flagrant, fragrant hints of corruption that could be nurtured only in a warm, masculine climate—but all this is beside the point, mere fluff, mere airy, bubbly frosting of the kind that evaporates on cake overnight and disappoints children in the morning.

In modern times these incidents have become more popular: I have compiled an alphabetical list of child criminals, beginning with Ajax, Arnold, and proceeding through Mossman, Billie, and ending with Watt, Samuel, all of them decently enough treated by society despite their obvious depravities. Oh, yes, I should mention Lilloburo, Anjette, the only girl on my list: she put insecticide in the grape drink she was selling on the sidewalk before her parents' modest frame house, a child of only seven but already corrupt and damned; two of her little friends died. I have purposefully omitted mention of Bobbie Hutter, who burned up four classmates in a tree house in West Bend, Indiana, so don't bother sending me this information. That child was mentally retarded and hadn't much idea what he was doing and—don't you see?—I have no patience with accidents. I don't want whimsy or lies, blunders, trivia. I want the real thing. The real thing: a crime of murder committed with all premeditation by a child in full possession of his own wits, with a certain minimal level of intelligence. Yes, we child murderers are snobs.

3

One morning in January a yellow Cadillac pulled up to a curb. And let's freeze that scene so I can sketch it all in. You see the Cadillac? Good. See if you can smell its new leathery odor. Yellow is a funny color for so dignified a car, you're thinking? Yes, but yellow was my mother's favorite color, or she liked to say or pretend that it was, for reasons of her own. So the car was yellow because my mother demanded yellow, and yellow it had to be, though my father wanted black. His own car was yellow too, and her car was yellow. They could never decide which of the cars belonged to which one of them—this Cadillac or the other car, the Lincoln. (They had friends in more than one automobile company.) The yellow Cadillac pulled up to a curb. It's January, you notice, and the street is a little icy, and the sidewalks, though constantly cleaned, have a cold, hard, bare look that they have only in winter. The grass is partly covered with snow and partly bare, old dried-up brown tufts you wouldn't waste a second glance at, and in the car are four interesting people:

The driver, a sharp-featured, pale man with a look of restraint, as if he finds it difficult to hold back his smiles of enthusiasm and good cheer. (He is the real-estate salesman.)

The woman sitting beside him, with a dark mink collar lifting up about her throat, her skin pale and glowing with the winter light and her lips pursed after a morning of disappointments and her eyes (those lovely eyes!) hidden at this moment by sunglasses. (This is my mother, Natashya Romanov Everett. She is thirty but looks twenty-five, twenty, eighteen! Any age!)

The man sitting behind her, leaning forward, smoking a cigar thoughtfully. He has a broad, round face, tanned from a recent and excellent Bermuda holiday, and there are bulges of flesh under his eyes that look at if he or someone else has been tugging down at them, and he has a nose with veins too close to the surface (tough luck, you people who have this trouble!), and yet he is an attractive man. No one could say why, but he is considered an "attractive" man. He is wearing a new winter overcoat—handsome and expensive in the store but rumpled and bargain-basement once he has it on—and it is unbuttoned even in winter because he sweats a lot, this man, this noisy, blustering, pathetic, attractive man, my father. He says, "Uh-huh, not bad. How does it look to you, Tashya?"

And next to him a child, not interesting as misleadingly

promised, but runty and worried, an old man already, with his mother's thin, hawkish, sniffing nose and his father's drooping eyes, shivering in the blast of heat that radiates from the front heater (will nothing ever get him warm, that doomed, damned child?). Of course, that is I. I am ten.

Now, on the far side of the street (I am considering your point of view) is a handsome old house, set back from the sidewalk, English Tudor of an Americanized sort, with great hunks of plate glass and standard evergreen shrubs, etc. You've seen thousands of such houses. And now, if you'll turn—notice how cautious I am, wanting you to see and feel everything without confusion —if you'll turn you will see what those four people are staring at. Another house. A house, that's all. A bastardized French-American affair, brick painted white, with balconies of wrought iron fastened somehow beneath the four big second-floor windows, and a big double door with gold, or gold-plated, brass knobs. The house has been built atop a hill, and all eyes are drawn to it. Banks and clumps of expensive evergreens run down in a friendly riot along the edge of the "circle" driveway to the street.

What else do you need to know? An ordinary day, partly cloudy. But Nada,* my mother, will wear sunglasses if the sky is totally overcast; she is that kind of woman. Anything else? Automobiles passing by? Just a few, and they are either nondescript cars driven by Negro maids on their way to the Continental Market Basket or the post office or the Fernwood Dry Cleaners or to the

---

* My mother had wanted me to call her "Nadia" but, as a small child, I must have been able to manage only the infantile "Nada." Hence Nada —strange name!

movie houses, with a few children, all white, bundled in the back seat; or large cars driven by suburban matrons of any age driving to or from luncheons, to or from bridge games, receptions, showers, round-table discussions, sculpting class, painting class, ballet class, "Psychology for the Home" class, "Great Books of the 60's" class . . .

Everything is sketched in. Now let us bring the scene to life.

The Cadillac pulled up to the curb. My father, leaning forward, spoke around his cigar with the public deference one uses in Fernwood toward wives. "What do you think of this one, Tashya?"

My mother was staring up at the house. The salesman, whose name was Howie Hansom, kept looking at the house himself though I could see that his face was getting strained. I could see his profile and the off-white of his eye. He and I were comrades in all this, but he did not know it or would not let on. If he happened to glance at me it was with the look you address to a squirrel: a pest supposed to be cute.

"Well, Tashya, what say we try it?" Father said heartily. He stirred himself and gave the impression that everyone was moving, everything had come to life; that was Father's style. "I know you're exhausted, Tashya, but we're out here now and Mr. Hansom would be disappointed if we didn't go in. Wouldn't you, Mr. Hansom?"

Mr. Hansom's profile tightened and he looked over at my parents, smiling. His smile was like a small, muted shriek, but they would never have noticed—something was in the air between them, some private, tugging tension. Mr. Hansom said, "I'd like very much to show you through this lovely house. I have the key here, of course . . ."

"Tashya?"

They waited. She drew in at last a long, exasperated breath, as if she'd been dragged all the way out here by these men and had no choice but to go through with their foolishness. Without answering, she opened the door and flung it out (a door that weighed a ton, built like a fortress), and we had a glimpse of her reddening, impatient ear, just the tip of it through her dark hair.

"Ah, here we are. Fine, fine," Father said cheerfully, rubbing his hands.

We all got out and trudged up to the house.

"Now, first of all, I'd like to know the price of this house," Father said.

"You'll notice that the house has three stories, and there is of course a swimming pool and a bathhouse, an automatic sprinkler system—"

"The price?" Father said politely.

"Eighty thousand five hundred," Mr. Hansom said rapidly and went on in a louder, flatter voice, "and a tax you won't believe, and a neighborhood absolutely unparalleled . . ."

I caught up to Nada and we walked ahead of the two men. I could see what they couldn't, that her cheeks were a little flushed and her nose looked as if it were sniffing at something forbidden. I knew that look. She glanced down at me and said, "Be sure to wipe your feet," and it was just nothing, not even an insult, just words for her to say to show that she remembered me and that she had power over me. And she reached out to rub my head, once, hard, to let me know that everything would turn out well. Behind us Father was striding up like a hunter, and Howie Hansom was puffing from the hill.

Mr. Hansom unlocked the front door and we stepped into a brick-lined area, and he opened another double door, French doors, and we were in an entrance foyer, quite large, oval. Need I describe this? You know the usual black-and-white tile, the French Provincial mirror with its pressed fake gold frame that gives you a face sooner than you might want it, and a staircase rearing up to a phantom second floor, and a crystal chandelier descending from heaven itself. Very nice.

"Hm, uh-hmmm," Father said, clapping his hands as if he'd discovered something suspicious. My father made brief, explosive, meaningless noises all the time. Or were they meaningless? Every grunt of Father's made Howie Hansom lick his pale lips and Nada's eyes swing around to a new object. "Well, might as well see it through. Interesting. Very clean, at least," Father said impassively.

We were shown through the house. It was empty and echoed our footsteps, Father's blustering words, and Mr. Hansom's enthusiastic, pale words. I felt my eyes begin to close: this was all so familiar to me. God, so familiar! We had seen ten, eleven, fourteen houses in the last two days. Nada hadn't liked any of them. Now we trudged through this house, which was neither more nor less impressive than the others, and Father shook his cigar ashes on the shining, maid-cleaned floor. I noticed how he glanced at Nada, at her expressionless face and those black-rimmed sunglasses of hers, which must have annoyed Father as much as they annoyed me. I wanted to snatch them off and break them in two and say, "Now will you look at me?" Then a crumbled, coy, shrewd look came over my father's face and he said tentatively to Mr. Hansom, "Would you, uh, say that this price is inflated?"

"Inflated?" Mr. Hansom said, meek and overly surprised. "Why, indeed not. Inflated? *This* marvelous property?"

Father never talked about money matters in such an abrupt, surreptitious way, and my mother turned in alarm. She stared at him. She could become pale as wax, her lips pursed in that fake-prudish look; any mention of money embarrassed and outraged her. She took off her sunglasses and held them in her gloved hands, waiting.

"Inflated, Mr. Everett? Certainly not," Mr. Hansom was saying with more assurance now, as if he'd groped and found the right trail again. "The house on Windsor Crescent, which we just saw, for seventy thousand cannot begin to compare with this, cannot *begin* to compare . . ."

"Ah—ah-ah," Father said. "What is that smell? That musty odor?"

"What musty odor?"

"Mr. Hansom," Nada said, "my husband is not serious. He's testing you."

"Honey, eighty thousand dollars is a lot of money," Father said. He was using his flat, serious, husband-to-wife voice, which always unnerved Nada. "There are matters I haven't discussed with you, matters of a personal nature concerning my promotion, and . . . of course . . . these things are precarious in today's economy." And he winked at me past Nada's stiffened shoulder. I turned away, embarrassed for both of them and humiliated by that wink, which he had meant to be just good fun.

Nada turned away. She went to the doorway of a room and stood there, outraged. Or she believed she should be outraged and was waiting for her rage to come. Her shoulders beneath the fine black cloth of that coat, weighed down by the filmy collar of mink, grew straight and youthful with anger.

"The economy is devious," Father was lecturing Mr. Hansom, with a florid, overdone camaraderie. "Things go up and down and waver. The price of everything is floating. Here today and gone tomorrow, eh? Right, Dickie? They teach my kid here things like that in school. Howdya like that, kids studying economics, finance? He studies French too. He can speak French like a native, wouldya believe it?"

"Elwood," Nada said softly.

"Honey, yes? Did you say something?"

She was blinking rapidly. Maybe she was crying— what would pass for tears between them. Who knows? I hated Father for embarrassing her and herding her around like this. She was like an animal being driven into a pen, cut off on one side and then on another, bumped and bruised and pushed back relentlessly into a trap, but like any animal she might lunge out and gift us all with a swift bite.

"Shut up, you stupid son-of-a-bitch! Oh, you loud-mouthed, vulgar son-of-a-bitch," she whispered.

"Tashya, in front of everybody?" Father cried. The pockets beneath his eyes drooped sadly. His cigar slanted down. His mouth was a fat thick line, just a line, but it too showed how dismayed he felt though—and this is the paradox—this was just what he had wanted.

Mr. Hansom, unprepared, drew in his breath sharply and had no more sense than to stare at Nada, and I smirked a little and tried to catch his eye so he'd know this was nothing unusual, don't be upset, oh, nothing unusual! Common, daily! Please understand, Mr. Hansom! But with Nada around they never looked at me, the men and women both, whole crowds and hordes of them who never looked much at Father either, the two of us males off to one side and watching Nada run through her routine like a rag doll inspired by clockwork, ticking and clicking through tears and anger and exhaustion.

"Oh, you humiliate me! You know nothing, you're ignorant, you're vulgar—you and your goddam promotion! Who the hell wanted to come here anyway? Why do we have to move?"

"I don't understand you, attacking me for my prudence —yes, my prudence," Father said, blustering around his cigar. "Mr. Hansom here is a man of the world. He understands the precariousness of promotions, business—"

"Look, I want this house. This house," Nada said.

"And this city is an excellent one. My uncle Edmund lived here all his life—he took part in the cultural renaissance of the city and helped build the library here in Fernwood. Ah yes, Natashya, whether you will grant anyone in my family such powers! Ah yes, Natashya! Vulgar? Stupid? Am I a son-of-a-bitch? And if I am, why does that upset you after all these years? It doesn't upset anyone else, so why you? Why you?" He looked around at me, sought me out and dismissed me. "Does it upset my son, our son? No. Our friends? No, no! My parents, my friends, my child, my associates? The people who pay me money? No! They love me for what I am, and I am a stupid son-of-a-bitch, yes, perhaps eighteen houses we've looked at in two days, and I'm a stupid, vulgar son-of-a-bitch, yes, but you, Natashya, what are you? Let me tell you, Mr. Hansom. My wife is an intellectual. A writer. Ah yes, yes! A famous writer—"

"Jesus Christ," Nada snorted.

"—a minor but famous writer, you know the kind. Only if they're minor are they any good. The ones we've heard of, Mr. Hansom, you and I, if we've heard of them they're already lousy, finished, just crap to the intellectuals! Crap! Everything we know about or read —and we went to college too, didn't we, Mr. Hansom? —everything we know is crap just because we know it, right? Only the minor, secret people are gifted. They are minor and famous and my wife is prominent among them—"

"Shut up! I said I want this house."

"Her vocabulary indicates—"

"Indicates, shit. I said I want this house," Nada cried. "You, take out the papers, whatever the hell you have, and write it down! We offer them seventy-eight thousand, because I want this house, goddam it, and he can talk all night and we still want it. Not enough money, eh! He can live in the bathhouse and babble to himself, who else is listening?"

Mr. Hansom smiled shakily from one to the other.

"Natashya, you forget yourself," Father said, wagging a finger.

"Don't wag your obscene . . . finger at me," Nada whispered.

"This will be our new neighborhood, Dickie's new environment. He must fit in here and be happy with his friends—"

"His name is Richard. Richard, not Dickie. Richard," Nada said. She stared at me. "Richard, go into the other room. What is that room?"

"A library. No, a sunroom," Mr. Hansom said, startled. "Which one do you mean?"

"Go in there, get out of the way. You're not interested in this," Nada told me.

So that was how we bought the house and Father got his way. He was a clever, stupid son-of-a-bitch, Father was.

4

And so we came to Fernwood, a far-flung suburb of a famous American city, and moved into a house that was too large for us but never mind, we had to live somewhere. Our furniture and belongings were loaded up for us back in our other house (in Brookfield, a suburb of another famous city), and by the time they reached us over the hundreds of miles of winter highways I had already discovered surreptitiously, and Nada announced to us one morning, angrily, that there was a family from Brookfield over on the other street, who had apparently moved at the same time we had; and not one mile away was the same house we had lived in for the last three years in Brookfield, present here in Fernwood like a miracle; and the Hunt Club was the same Hunt Club as Brookfield's, except that it had "Valley" prefixed to its name and had evidently sold its lands, bridle paths and all, to a housing contractor; and worst of all, only two houses away from us was Edward Griggs or someone who looked just like Edward Griggs, a man who had been something of a social catch back in Brookfield. He dealt in expensive antiques and had in his living room Emerson's tin bathtub (so narrow it made you wonder about Emerson's physique) and two Regency tables that had been in the collection of the Duchess of Kent, worth $19,000 and $23,000 dollars.

But Father said slowly, "That can't be Griggs, honey. How could he have moved here so fast?"

"It's Griggs," Nada said.

"I doubt it," said Father.

We all went for a stroll one evening after dinner. These first few weeks in a new home (we were always moving) drew us close together, Nada, Father, and I, a happy family even though we had the look of being three strangers who have met by accident on a walk and are waiting for the first chance to get away from one another. (A clever, bratty classmate of mine back in Brookfield, observing the Everett family on a stroll, had told me we looked like that.) Sometimes on these walks Nada's gloved hand would fall on my shoulder or touch my hair, and Father might pat my back as if urging me on, the two of them perhaps using me to show that they had something in common after all. But they loved me, of course. I think they loved me. Would it be too pathetic for me to write that I pushed this doubt back and forth through my brain until my brain was like a sieve? Like a sieve? Is that pathetic or ludicrous—how does that strike a normal reader? Anyway we strolled by the house Griggs supposedly lived in. It was a baronial Georgian thing, even better than his other house, monstrously large even for this street. It had the blank, dignified, mad look of private homes secretly used as hospitals.

"Do you think he brought his wife so soon?" Nada said.

"Honey, what would Griggs be doing in Fernwood?"

"And his cook, that ugly cook? No, she must have

been left behind." Nada had a tense, white, pained look, as if she were staring into a nightmare but could not make out its terrors. "Why do these people keep following us around, Elwood?"

"I'm sure no one has followed us, dear. The man probably looks like Griggs, that's all." And Father clapped me on the back. "What do you think, buster? Eh? Pretty farfetched, isn't it?"

We walked on and they argued without interest for a while, then the talk dissipated with a fresh blast of cold wind and the sight of a new neighbor's Rolls-Royce, a silvery vehicle driven too fast by an old man who did not glance at us. Father admired the Rolls-Royce, with the liberal abandonment of an American businessman who does not flinch at seeing a foreign industry patronized. Nada wasn't sure—perhaps a Rolls-Royce was pretentious? "They are good, solid, stable cars," Father said.

I was shaken with the cold but did not want to let on. Father was always healthy—a big bear of a man, with nerves buried far beneath fat and muscle, safe. Nada complained of headaches and faintness, but she too was healthy as a horse and certainly had the appetite of a horse though you dared not tell her that, even jokingly. (She liked to frighten us with vague tales of her Russian grandmother, who had dropped dead in perfect health at the age of forty.) Father slid his arm around Nada's shoulders to keep her warm, while my teeth chattered and I walked a little ahead of them, the way a normal child probably would. Or would a normal child say he was freezing and ask to be taken home? I suffered so much, not wanting to disappoint them.

"Ah, this fine winter air!" Nada sighed.

"Good for the lungs," declared Father.

At such times, uncomfortable as I was, I liked to think that I possessed my parents. I had them. I seemed to be leading them as if on a leash, though when they wanted to go back Father would just reach out and poke me. But I had the dreamy illusion that they belonged to me at these times, Nada and Father, and under my guidance they belonged to each other, they were in love. I did so much spying on them, you know. I'll tell you about it: years of anguished, guilty spying. I had to spy—how else could I have known what life was, or who they were, my parents, what they were? So I spied and I learned and I tabulated, calculated, speculated. But at these special times when we were together I thought that I had somehow, magically, captured a man and a woman from another land, foreign and exotic and not quite speaking my language, who were tamed by my power and love and who walked obediently after me, robust and comely and healthy as horses. Such fine horses! These were my true parents. The others—the dissatisfied Natashya Romanov, minor writer, and the blubbering breast-beating executive Elwood Everett—were nothing but cruel step-parents.

Yes, I loved them. I loved her especially. It was awful.

5

And who were their people? Well, Nada's people were a mystery. She spoke of them vaguely and with some embarrassment: emigrés, obviously, but shadowy and remotely threatening. They had had a minimum of power in their new life, Nada told people. Everyone was puzzled by her choice of that word "power," and I was puzzled too. But you couldn't get much out of her. Because she was a writer she presumably chose her words with care, but still "power" didn't make much sense. Her parents were exiled nobility, perhaps, dying broken-hearted in a vulgar, foreign land. I recall something about a hotel in New York City where other Russians were, shadowy intrigue, futility. She hinted that her father was not quite admirable, perhaps unbalanced, that her mother was wrecked by the great journey, and that she, Natashya, only child, was born in squalor and had tasted it. So, she threatened Father, she could leave him and return to it at any time.

And Father's people? You could almost guess. They were wealthy. Yes, you could guess that from Father's fluctuation between superb and bestial manners, his inches of exposed hairy skin when he crossed his legs, the way he sampled and rejected chocolate candies, roasted peanuts, hors d'oeuvres both hot and cold, spoke of friends with an anxious condescension ("He's only a doctor, but . . ." "He's only with KRH, but . . ."), the way he bossed us even when we weren't listening, the way he tipped waiters and waitresses, doormen and door-women, countermen, counterwomen, bellboys, bellmen, everyone in uniform, with a happy, hopeful smile, like a dog anxious to be petted. Ah, Father! As I write this he is still alive and he will certainly lead a long, success-ful life. Good! Wonderful! And he loved me, yes. He loved Nada and me, and that was what did us all in, his extravagant, stupid love for Nada.

But I was speaking of his family. Philadelphians. His

father had been killed at the age of fifty-two while flying a light plane, drunk, reportedly buzzing a friend's pasture of riding horses. The plane crashed at the climax of a daring swoop and the horses fled in all directions, shuddering with terror. I can imagine those horses, their foaming mouths and heaving sides, but I can't imagine the burning plane and the man locked inside it. My mind flinches at such an idea. But that was my grandfather and that was it. My grandmother was a gentle, deaf lady who never seemed to know who I was. One Christmas we flew to Chestnut Hill and were just in time for a dinner party. I had to endure a long, long meal, and at the end Grandmother begged Father to take her out ice skating, it was such a nice night. Father laughed and blustered and joked with her, making excuses while everyone smiled helpfully, and the old woman finally declared to the table, "He always was such a pansy, this Edmund." And who had been most shocked of all?—after me, of course, since I'd never thought of Father as a flower of any kind—Nada, naturally.

Father had two brothers and, like him, they had left Philadelphia and rarely returned. I had an uncle in Italy, whose business was connected with a medical supply company and was always on the verge of being raided by the police; and another uncle who, just like Father, was always being promoted and shoulder-tapped by other corporations, transferred and stolen and relocated back and forth across the country as if he were a precious jewel. The two brothers rarely met, though once they bumped into each other in a men's lounge at Midway Airport. One was on his way to a board meeting in Boston, another on his way to Los Angeles. I forget which was which. And I think they met one other time, when Father was searching for Nada and turned up at various relatives' homes, unwelcome and always drunk, demanding information; but maybe the brother hadn't been home when Father arrived.

Father hadn't graduated from college but had skipped out after his sophomore year (never to open another book unless it was a paperback left on an airline seat) and joined the Army, did well, was discharged and taken into a small Rhode Island concern that manufactured plastic Christmas tree ornaments, and did so well with sales that he was snapped up by a business that dealt with blotters, paper tubes, and corrugated cardboard. His star rose so rapidly that he hopped about from bolts manufacturers to underwear manufacturers to a brief spell with a top-security concern that made, overtly, children's toy bombers; from there to vice-presidencies in seat-belt companies, wastebasket companies, certain curtain companies, certain steel companies, and so on to the present. It exhausts me to think of all this. I never had a job in my life and never will, unless you want to call this memoir my life's work, but Father has had innumerable jobs. Perhaps he's had so many, did so much, because he could sense that his only child would accomplish nothing. But Father didn't really sense anything. He didn't bother figuring out emotions or intangibles. His I.Q., you'll be interested to know, was only 120. What accounts for his success, then? (At this writing he is president of Crescent Steel.) Good stomach juices, I think, and an acute apparatus for balance in his inner ear. One of Nada's annoying friends, a psychiatrist named Melin, declared in my hearing (I was behind a sofa) that Father's business successes were due to a gland no more than an inch long at the base of his spinal cord, but he might have been joking. That bastard Melin was a big joker.

What else would you like to know about Father? I want to draw him in here so that when you see him, in the following pages, you'll know who he is even if he behaves strangely. Most novels, which are fiction and therefore limited, have to build up characters slowly and don't dare allow them to be eccentric or surprising unless this is planned; but my memoir, dealing with real people, who are already alive and quite ordinarily living but who may then do things that seem out of "character": a gentleman who is also a son-of-a-bitch, a dope who is also shrewd, etc. Father's waist sagged despite his golf and steambaths, and he was too vain to wear glasses, so he had to hold his newspaper slightly off to one side when he read (though he didn't read much), and he was fond of wrestling matches on television, and he liked steaks with mushroom sauce, steaks with garlic, steaks on boards, and steaks pierced through their bloody hearts on silver sticks, only one kind of potato (mashed) and lots of cheap doughy bread, and sweet, ghastly sweet, little pickles—baby midget gherkins he'd eat by the handful, chomping and chopping his way with his big teeth. And Scotch. Too much Scotch. His clothes were expensive because he had no idea there were cheaper clothes available, but on him they looked as if he'd worn them on an overnight plane ride from Calcutta or Tokyo. With his cheerful, sad brown eyes, always a little puffed, he looked like a bloated elf, like a man who has been awake all night, lying in his rumpled street clothes. I have a photograph taken of him in Tokyo, incidentally. He is standing with his arms folded in imitation of a great statue of Buddha that is in the distance behind him; both he and the Buddha look drunk, though the Buddha does not look as rumpled as Father. The back of the photograph is scrawled over with Japanese, and the "secret" of the message has long been lost to Father. (I have a drawer full of photographs and other sentimental trash I've brought along from my life as a child, my living life. I'll go through them in a later chapter and remark upon them, especially Nada's. But how strange these people have already begun to look, especially myself!)

The oddest thing of all was that while I loved Father I did not really believe he was my father. All my life I had visions of another man, my true father, and while he might appear in the body of the father I had been stuck with, his voice, his personality, and his soul were entirely different. For instance, my father was always happy. What can you do with a father who is always—nearly always—happy? He was happy putting up with Nada's boorish intellectual friends, he was happy with me when I failed him as a son (when I tried out for sixth-grade baseball at Wells Lorraine Boys' School my glasses were broken in the first fifteen minutes), he was happy when around him everyone was miserable, in bad weather, in stock-market declines, national emergencies. Listen to him come into a room, carrying his drink, and declare in a loud nostalgic voice:

"What good does it do, eh? What good does it ever do? You give your best and you drop dead like Arnold did. My God, what a shame. What a shame. He was what? Only forty-five? When I think of what he had to offer! What that man had to give! Right? You know . . . well, I mean . . . I mean all the po*ten*tial that man had to give, it's a goddam shame." And he would shake his large head slowly and stare at the tip of his shoe and after a philosophical moment in which he let his ice clink he would start to nod his head, as if making his way up from the bottom of a dreary sea of sorrow. And his shoulders would make an attempt at straightening, one maybe a little higher than the other, and by the time he raised his glass to his mouth he would have "come out of it." "But you know life's got to go on and nobody realized that more than Arnold. If anybody knew that, he knew it. I think . . . I think maybe I'm crazy, but I think that we owe it to him to keep going, keep his memory going, you know, and keep thinking about him while we go on living. He would have wanted it that way. Wouldn't he? Yes, that man would have *insist*ed we be happy right now no matter how miserable we felt because life has to go on and nobody knew it more than Arnold . . ."

(I used to spy on their cocktail parties all the time.)

But just the same, though I knew him so well, I somehow didn't think he was my real father. I thought that another father might be waiting somewhere off in the wings and that at the next cocktail party, if I listened hard and crept as close to the living room as I dared, I might hear the strong, hard, even brutal voice of my true father.

6

On our way back from that walk, heading into the wind, we were just passing the house Nada believed Edward Griggs lived in when the man himself turned into his driveway. He was driving a car I didn't recognize.

Nada seized Father's wrist in that urgent, melodramatic way she had and said, "What did I tell you? Look!" We were blocking his driveway, and the gentleman in the car nodded at us and smiled uncertainly. Father, a little confused, nodded energetically and smiled back. But he neglected to move out of the way, so the man in the car —should I call him Griggs?—sat for a moment without moving. His smile gradually faded.

Finally he did the only right thing: he lowered his window and leaned head and shoulder out. Father approached with a step bouncier than usual. Nada did not budge.

"I believe you're our new neighbors. Just moved in, haven't you?" the man said.

"Yes, just moved in!" Father cried cheerfully.

This was the moment for them to admit knowing each other or to puzzle out identities, but, for some strange reason, they did no more than stare worriedly at each other.

"Nice house down there," the man said.

"Nice, very nice! Nice neighborhood also," Father said. "Nice town!"

"It is nice, yes," the man said slowly. He was looking at Father in a reluctant, perplexed way. "I have always thought so, in the short time I've lived here in Fernwood."

"Is this Fernwood?" Father said. But he recovered at once, laughed, reddened, and launched off on another enthusiastic speech. "We've just moved in too, but of course you know that, haha! You just mentioned that, or did I mention it? No, you mentioned that *you* have been here only a short time. We've been here a week now. How long have you been here?"

"About a week."

The man who might have been Griggs was trying not to look at Nada, who was staring gloomily at him. A few awkward seconds passed. I stamped on the sidewalk, letting my weight fall on one foot, then the other. Nada put her arms around me and kissed my ear. "Poor little boy, freezing out here while that idiot in the car pretends not to recognize us. How stupid! And that bigger idiot pretends not to recognize *him*."

"We'll have to get together sometime," Father said.

"That's an excellent idea," the man said. He smiled shakily at Father, as if Father represented something terrifying he did not want to concede. Or perhaps he could not believe that Father really stood there, Elwood Everett himself. I thought it was strange that they did not introduce themselves and shake hands, the way adults always do, as if they'd at last met the one person in the world they had been aching to meet. Father and this man did not behave in the usual way and being so rude made them uneasy. Father chattered nervously about the good healthy air, about the state of the economy, about skiing conditions somewhere, until Nada told me to go get him. So I went and tugged at his arm. The man in the car—even I was not sure any longer if he was Griggs or not—had to look at me and his eyes moved upon me reluctantly. I thought I saw a look of muted, uneasy recognition, but it faded at once.

"My son Dickie," Father said.

"Yes, Dickie. Richard."

"You know him?" Father cried.

The two adults looked at each other with reddening faces. There was a moment when they might have asked whether they'd known each other in another life, just a week past, but the moment went by and they were left stubborn and miserable in silence. They could think of nothing to say.

Finally Nada said, "Elwood, are you coming? We must go home."

"Wife's calling," Father said with a fast small grin.

The man raised his eyebrows in a fake perfunctory look of surprise and saw Nada, who was standing a few yards away, as if he had truly not noticed her before. He made a slight bowing motion with his head which Nada did not acknowledge.

She and I were halfway back to our house by the time Father caught up to us.

"So?" Father said.

"Was it him or not?" I asked.

"Was it?" said Father.

Nada said nothing.

"So? What did that prove? Did he know me? Did I know him?" Father said.

"I think that was him," I said.

"How would you know?" Father cried with a hearty fake laugh. "You don't know Griggs. You'd be the last person to recognize him."

"I think it was him."

"But he didn't know me."

"Yes, he did."

"No, he didn't."

"Yes, he did."

Nada made a snorting sound. "The bastard was just as terrified at seeing us as we were at seeing him. None of us can ever escape."

"No, I don't think it was him," Father said.

"Think it was *he*," said Nada.

7

Fernwood was an expensive, innocent town, but it was there that all my troubles began. It was in Fernwood that I began to disintegrate as a child. You people who have survived childhood don't remember any longer what it was like. You think children are whole, uncomplicated creatures, and if you split them in two with a handy ax there would be all one substance inside, hard candy. But it isn't hard candy so much as a hopeless seething lava of all kinds of things, a turmoil, a mess. And once the child starts thinking about this mess he begins to disintegrate as a child and turns into something else—an adult, an animal. Do I sound too earnest and knowing? Too intense? Indeed I am intense, yes. Earnest also, because who else would stay laboring over this miserable typewriter (if only I could afford an electric typewriter!), dripping lardy sweat onto the keys, for no reward? And knowing, yes indeed. Knowing. In another chapter I'll tell you about my IQ so your faith in me will be strengthened.

So it was in Fernwood that it began. It accelerated. Any reader could tell, however, that the seeds had been sown much earlier. For instance:

I am a small child, perhaps an infant. I am a creature warm and cozy in a soft woolen outfit, wrapped in a blanket. I am sitting in a rocking chair just my size and Nada (she taught me to call her "Na-da" before any other word) is reading to me. I do not know what she is reading. I do not understand the words, but they are wonderful, like music. The cover of her book is shiny and the light from the table by the bed strikes it, making the cover glow so that I can't see what picture is on it—maybe that picture of the rabbit in dungarees. Nada is reading in a fast, excited voice. I am happy here with her because I haven't seen her for a while, this warm, soft person with the dark hair lying loose on her shoulders; when Nada is gone off somewhere a woman with dark, dark skin and a white outfit takes care of me, pushing me out for endless walks in the sun or letting me sit wretchedly in the sun while she chatters shrilly with other dark-skinned women in white, yellow, or light blue outfits.

But now Nada is back and I can see that she loves me. She is reading me a story. As she reads her eyes keep jumping up and behind me, as if she is waiting for something. She is wearing a pink nightgown just like mine, the same color, with a silky ribbon tied at her throat. Over this she has a flowered robe. She is so pretty, this Nada, with her loose hair and her shiny, smooth face and suddenly there is a noise outside. On the stairs. Her eyes glow up from the book and catch the light the way the book cover does, and her words stop at once, and outside there is the thud of running feet and a sudden louder thud and the sound of wood splintering, and Nada and I both look up to see a strange man crashing through the door, the door flying back and slamming into the wall, and a blinding exploding flash of light, and then everything is still again and there, behind him, stands Father.

The strange man has a black instrument with a light bulb on it. He pauses and stares at us. Father, entering the room slowly through the smashed door, stares at us. Father wears a soiled coat and he is wet. The strange man is wet too. That is because it is raining out. The man checks something on his instrument and turns and hurries out, bumping into Father. Father seizes him in a kind of embrace and lifts him aside, without looking at him, and the man leaves. Father is still staring at us. He is staring at Nada. I cannot hear what they are saying to each other in this silence, but the room is filled with their screams and their cries of hatred and rage and triumph. The room is filled with it, and I could drown in its very silence.*

* As I read this over, this rendition of infant impressions strikes me as very bad, but let it stand. The experience is there, the reality is there, but how to get at it? Everything I type out turns into a lie simply because it is not the truth.

9

One detail about someone in Nada's family, an uncle or bizarre distant cousin: he committed suicide by overeating. He decided to kill himself by forcing food down his throat and into his bursting stomach, eating his way through a roomful of food. Admirable man! I can almost see him, can't you? Some dismal, philosophical-faced, hawk-nosed, masculine version of Nada, lost in the gloom she too sometimes fell into, and, unable to rise out of it again, deciding on this only half-serious method of committing suicide. The word "committing" necessitates a certain amount of judicious consideration, and it has always seemed to me idiotic that a madman can "commit" murder or indeed anything. He does it, that's all. Or rather it gets done somehow, with or without his volition. But when you set forth to "commit" a crime you do it with your heels springing off the ground with glee, your brain cells whirling and popping with energy, and, I think, a certain air of magnanimity toward the world. After all, you are leaving it. Whether you kill yourself or someone else you are leaving the world, and if any of my readers succumb to the enchanting music that so cruelly deafened me, they will know just what I mean. The rest of you are in no position to judge.

So this man committed suicide by eating. I had overheard Nada tell this grisly anecdote more than once, but never when Father was around. She told it once to a good friend of hers, a man with a skimpy, sandy beard who kept staring down at the floor and breathing harshly and sympathetically through his beard. He kept saying, "Yes, yes," while she told the story of this uncle or cousin (I forget which) who locked himself up in his room and ate until the lining of his stomach burst. Did he die in agony? I don't like to think of that. I like to think of that supreme moment when he broke through the slippery, stubborn wall of his own stomach and entered eternity at once—I don't like to think of lesser details. He did it, Nada said, to rob his family of dignity and to make fun of the way they gorged themselves. They were such gluttons—she laughed—and they had to move away from that city out of shame, though they did not stop being gluttons as far as she knew. Behind all her mysterious, melodramatic contempt she was proud of that family of hers.

The anecdote always inspired in those who heard it, and in me, a strange jealousy along with our natural admiration. I suspect we are all very suspicious and jealous of those who commit suicide, anxious to prove that it was "cowardly" or "painless," we could do better, indeed we will do better, wait and see.

10

And so we came to Fernwood, the town of my disintegration. There I bade farewell to myself as a child. Should I bother to describe Fernwood, or can you imagine it? Fernwood and Brookfield and Cedar Grove and Charlotte Pointe are always the suburbs farthest out, but don't confuse yourself by thinking they are the newest. No, they are the oldest. They are the "country," where the country houses of the past had been built for the wealthy of the city many horse-drawn miles away. Now, of course, in between these suburbs and the city are those absurd new towns and villages, row after row of clean, respectable houses and maze after maze of buff-brick housing developments, all overpriced and treeless, the slums of tomorrow. The hell with them. The "country" was where Father always took us, sure in his instincts and surer still in his bank account, for nothing more was demanded of one than money in this world. There was a jolly camaraderie because of this fact. Fine. Great. Fernwood had been the site of these old country estates, and enormous estates they had been too; it would make your heart swell to the danger point to see one of them. A few were left, but most of the land had been divided up into, say, three-acre plots for other houses, and in the more citified part of the village plots as small as two acres. Our Fernwood house, on a winding street called Burning Bush Way, was one of these lesser homes, of course.

Imagine Fernwood like this: an odor of grass, leaves, a domesticated river (with ducks, geese, and swans provided by the village, and giant goldfish swimming gracefully), blue skies, thousands of acres of faultless green grass, not Merion Blue but the low creeping type used on golf courses, and an avalanche of trees everywhere! —and enormous stone houses, brick houses, fake Scandinavian houses, English, French, Southwest, Northeast houses, a sprinkling of "modern" architecture that never manages to look more than nervously aggressive in this conservative environment. And mixed in with the odor of lawns being sprinkled automatically on warm spring mornings is the odor of money, cash. Fresh, crisp cash. Bills you could stuff in your mouth and chew away at. My mouth is watering at the thought of that tart, fine blue-green ink, the mellow aroma of the paper!

Should I digress and tell you a strange little incomplete tale about cash? Bills? Raw money? One morning back in Brookfield, my eight-year-old self was dawdling on the way to school when I happened to see one of Nada's friends drive up. I could tell by the way she braked her car and slid into one of our evergreens that she was distracted, and when she jumped out of the car she left the door swinging ponderously. So I followed her quietly back to our house. She burst in the back door without knocking, into the kitchen, and cried, "Natashya! Natashya!" I peeked in through a window, inclining my ear to the screen. The gauzy kitchen curtain hid me perfectly. Nada came in, and the woman said, before my mother had a chance to show surprise, "You'll never guess what I have in this!" A moment of silence, then Nada's hesitant murmur, which I couldn't hear. Then the woman cried out with a horrible, ugly triumph I can still remember, "Look at this! I found where that bastard has been hiding it all!"

And I took every chance and looked up. Yes, entranced by her frenzy, I raised my head to peer through the window, to see the woman holding open a brown leather ice container stuffed with bills.

"Thousands! Thousands! A million maybe!" she said, panting.

Some of the bills spilled onto the floor. I could see the woman's saliva in the bright morning sunshine, and the sight so unnerved me I lost my balance and fell a yard or two to the ground.

So you see? Cash like that. And other forms too, in tiny books and stamped on pieces of paper. Oh, it was wonderful, wonderful, and in a way I wish I still had access to it. If I wanted to stuff myself with money and die in that unique way I couldn't; I don't have enough cash. But I want to tell the story of Fernwood, and cash is only part of it. It is the foundation of it, yes, but we like to rise above our foundations, our muddy beginnings. We like to rise without looking back because that is perhaps declassé, and when there are no true classes, what greater horror than becoming declassé, unfit for even the classless society?

11

My school was a private school by the name of Johns Behemoth Boys' School, not affiliated with any religion, pure and Anglophile, like all these schools, with an unmarked bus to take care of the few "town boys" who did not board at the school. The school was one of the old estates (I promised that your heart would swell to see one), and surely no mortal human beings had ever lived in that big main house. No, I like to think that giants had lived there, archangels or monsters. And up behind it, terraced into a hill, was a garden of exquisite beauty tended by a deaf-mute, whose only justification in life was to keep the blown petals swept up off the grass, the roses trimmed, the rhododendron spiced with acid, the rich soil tilled, the insects at bay. Any monstrous hero would have cultivated this beauty as a delicious contrast to his own degradations.

The buildings were covered with ivy, very staunch and brittle. A bit ugly, like all these schools. The architecture was solid and masculine, squat, unimaginative, English and prisonlike in an easy combination. Graveled walks for the boys to bicycle upon, and a series of waterfalls set up for visitors and parents and magazine photographers. (The water was *verboten* to us boys.) Rather narrow, cheerless dormitory rooms, but built solidly, with good solid imitation antique furniture. Country English. Down in the classrooms the floors were smooth and polished as if by a hundred years of feet, caressed by boys impatient for learning. Small classrooms; a table and chair for the teacher instead of a desk; desks were —shall I guess?—declassé because the public schools had them. We boys wore ties every day of our anguished little lives, and blazers, and we worked hard, very hard. I am not joking. The school started with seventh grade and took in all of the high-school grades, but Fernwood's conservative parents had been blocking and graphing out their boys' careers for over a decade before they entered Johns Behemoth. Public-school students matured before we did in every way except intellectually; the typical Johns Behemoth boy was undersized, lank, intense, nervous, and given to sarcasm and superb, automatic manners. In the presence of girls he regressed to early childhood. I believe about thirty per cent of my classmates were in analysis, a good many of them to the same man, Dr. Hugg, who specialized in disturbed adolescent boys. I never advanced that far because I was kicked out of the school in a few months.

Of all the ugly things I have to tell, stored up ripe and rotting in my memory, being expelled from that school is in a way the most shameful.

A man can admit with a cheerful shrug of his shoulders to larceny, wife-beating, treason, even murder (as I am to do shortly), but trivialities concerning his honor arouse the most shame. This is because the ego's threads of radiation never quite stop, even in the most depraved of us, and we must always think, "Yes, but my essential honor wasn't touched. Yes, but my dignity wasn't touched. Yes, but . . . But . . ."

But . . .

It was January when we moved to Fernwood, and Nada found out at once about the schools. The public school was out, she decided, because my nervous little mind needed more stimulation. She had had an interest in the Catholic Church for a while, a fluctuating interest like all her interests, but people told her emphatically that the local Catholic school wasn't good enough for her son. (She talked in a rapid low voice about her "son," who was me, a prodigious child never understood by his father or his teachers.) So she drove me over to Johns Behemoth one frosty morning.

Let me describe Nada on such a morning. She was dressed in her suburban style (she had two general styles, as you will see) and most fiercely and proudly was she adorned, in her simply cut dark wool suit, and two dots of silver that were earrings, and white leather gloves that looked like baby's skin, bleached, and a purse to match, and the jeweled wristwatch that Father had given her for no particular reason—no reason that I had been able to snoop out—a month before. Her shoes were made of leather, her legs were smooth and scintillating in the vivid light, covered with invisible nylon, and she wore over her suit her sporty fur coat, which was something to wear "in the country," alternating bands of white and caramel fur, and from all this arose a faint halo of warm perfume that might have been Nada's magic radiance. A child, I did not let on that I noticed the interested gaze of men we drove past, mere gas-station attendants or sometimes village executives strolling to work or down to the train depot. I did not even let on that I noticed the looks Father gave her sometimes, sad and yearning and vulnerable, when she would hurry into a room Father was in, looking for something she would never find in that room—or in any room he and I were in, drooping, happy Father and I, her prodigy. Much of my child's life consisted of averting my eyes and turning away from things I was not supposed to see.

She took the Cadillac that morning. Father was at work. He had driven off that morning at seven and he was at work, in an office all his own some distance away. I will take you there eventually, but Nada is always more interesting, and this is the story (or is everything in my life only an anecdote?) of how she brought me to Johns Behemoth, saw what the challenge was, and conquered it. In the lovely yellow car she wheeled around the un-paved lanes of Fernwood Heights, which was adjacent to plain Fernwood and much more expensive. We passed stone walls and brick walls and walls of evergreens that must have hidden extraordinary homes, twisting and turning in a kind of perpetual pine forest, until we came to the wrought-iron gate and the sign

"We're going to get you into this school, Richard," Nada said grimly. She looked at everything and took in everything. I could feel the jolt of this place on her body, my poor mother, who was so simple in her way that all things ostentatious and expensive seemed emanations of a higher existence, which she never questioned the way Father might. She attributed this to his vulgarity.

Quietly watching them both, which was my life's work, I could see that Nada's superior mind disqualified her entirely for judgments concerning anyone who didn't compete with her on the intellectual level. She criticized scornfully and recklessly those writers she loved best, Tolstoi and Mann, embarrassed by occasional lapses of taste or power in their writing, but any society matron or business executive with the smell of money about them rendered her helpless. It was a good thing she never made it into high society! What could she do? She was as much a child as I was, now that I think of it. She had married Father the way a girl goes on a date with a man she does not at all like, or even know, simply because he will take her to a special event where the very lights and the very sweetness of the flowers set everywhere make up a world—no people are really needed.* Father knew nothing, but where his imagination should have been, in that emptiness, where his sensitivity and taste should have been, in that larger emptiness, there was a

* Let me question all that convincing crap and say—bravely, blurtingly!—that she might possibly have married him because she loved him. What then?

[43

crude common sense as reliable as a dime-store bottle-top opener.

JOHNS BEHEMOTH
FOUNDED 1880

That was impressive to both of us, and the cobbled streets that wound through Faculty Row (a quaint long building of one-storey houses joined amid a surplus of evergreens and pines), and the large snow-dappled open-ing that promised a park or a green in warmer months, where bemused bright boys might read Latin verse, and the many elms (some of them dead, but in the winter no one could tell), and the enormous library, and a building with its own modern steel sculpture out front: an angular, emaciated human being, perhaps a man, holding erect a globe that has become skeletonized but evidently no less heavy. A symbol of Science, and that was the Science Building. The Humanities Building was the big one, with a surly, encrusted look, its windows like multiple eyes with thick, leafless vines over them like eyebrows. Nada and I liked this building best. Here there were no de-ceptions about the torment knowledge promised, the way there was in public schools where knowledge was shuffled in with dances and basketball games and camera clubs.

"We'll get you in here, Richard, the two of us," Nada said. The exquisite, muted ostentation of this place had unnerved her a little, but her voice simply lowered itself and went on, grimly and confidentially. "When we go in for the interview, please remember to sit straight. But don't look rigid. And don't for God's sake, look like your father, as if you're ready to fly out of the chair and slap someone on the back. Look reserved and a little

44]

abstracted. Look intelligent. How do you look today anyway?" And she turned to stare at me.

It was the first time that day she had bothered to look at me, and I felt the anxiety of her solemn dark eyes though she tried to show nothing. Nada had fine clear skin, rather pale. Suburban style dictated her hair, which was "done" once and sometimes twice a week so that from behind or at a distance she looked like an ordinary resident of Fernwood, a housewife who had no housewifely chores but wasn't "society" either and was terrified of seeming pretentious—short hair, set to rise above her elegant head in feathery sections that fascinated me, everything smooth and disciplined and rather familiar. Nada's hair was very dark, almost black. Suburban style dictated her entire face, actually, because she wore nothing on her eyes—no messy black goo, no blue or green eyeshadow of the kind up in her bedroom awaiting the minute she would tire of this life—and her mouth was a handsome, wholesome, unsurprising red. Her manner this morning was suburban and wholesomely nervous, American as the flag that rose above the frigid evergreens in the park at the center of enormous Johns Behemoth.

She said, "What's that on your face? Nothing? Fix your hair, push it back. Darling, you look fine. You look" —and she cast her mind about for the best word—"you look like a little scholar."

We parked the car in an area designated for visitors. Walking up the cobbled path to what had once been the Behemoth mansion, we drew in the fresh air as if we expected strength from it. I had to hurry to keep up with her. If Nada and Father had nothing else in common, they both walked fast. They were always striding and rushing as if trying to break through crowds or anxious to see what was attracting a crowd up ahead.

"Remember, look intelligent. Don't fail me," Nada whispered.

Like all mothers, she tended to whisper one last piece of advice that is given too late, too close to the zone all children know should be dignified by silence. We were inside the building when she told me this, and at once a middle-aged woman appeared in a doorway and cast upon us a bemused look. She glanced at me in a kindly way as if to assure me that I did look intelligent.

"Mrs. Everett?" she said. "Dean Nash will be with you in a minute."

We were led into a curiously modern room, like a doctor's office where everything has been ordered from a catalogue, even the abstract paintings and the fake ferns, and there we both reached for the same copy of the *Scientific American,* scorning the *Reader's Digest.* "Come, sit by me, we can read it together," Nada said. She might have thought the magazines were set out as part of a test. I ignored her, my face still hot from the encounter with the kindly woman.

That woman returned to her desk and began typing something, paying no attention to us. She had the look of a hospital matron who had seen many mothers and sons come and go, wistful and rejected. As she rolled yellow forms of varying sizes into her electric typewriter, skillfully and with a long-fingered grace that reminded me of Nada, she raised her eyebrows and inquired of us politely, "Are you new to Fernwood?"

Yes, we were new, Nada said. We lived on Burning Bush Way. (She wanted to let the woman know we weren't wealthy but at least respectable.)

"Very nice," said the woman. "And Richard is . . . twelve?" She peered at me as if she thought this rather incredible.

"No," Nada said carefully, "he is almost eleven. But he's been attending seventh-grade back in Brookfiield."

"Oh, I see. That's very interesting," the woman said, her eyes turning a little watery as if she were in the presence of a crippled boy. "You know, Mrs. Everett, this is such a fine school, and so many fine boys want to attend it, but, of course as in everything else, there is so much pressure and only a limited number of openings."

"I understand," Nada said.

When we went into the Dean of Admission's office Nada poked her finger into the small of my back to indicate that I should stand straighter. I was already walking with my spine stretched so tight I thought I might faint with exhaustion. Was it my fault I was only ten, and small for ten? But never mind, on with my miserable story. I won't blame Nada for my inadequate height or for whatever else has come to pass.

Dean Nash was an interesting man: about fifty, stylish and dandyish, as if he'd just stepped out of a Hollywood movie filmed on the set of a prep school. He was someone's idea of an Anglicized American headmaster. He smiled a dazzling dentured smile at Nada and said, "We're very happy to hear of your interest in Johns Behemoth, Mrs. Everett. Our institution represents something of an experiment, as you may know if you read the literature I sent to you—yes? fine, Mrs. Everett— an experiment set up by the executor of the Johns Behemoth estate some years ago, with the specific recommendation that this school start its program in the early grades. We did experiment with younger children, but this aspect of the venture was gradually phased out so that we could concentrate more intensely on individual, private work in the higher grades. I believe you know, Mrs. Everett, that Johns Behemoth provides one instructor for each five boys in certain classes, and for a senior desiring intensive study an adviser who will devote upward of six hours weekly to this student, and a faculty of several people constantly available to him. We have work-study clubs, foreign-language clubs and tables in the dining room, and a quite successful Overseas Year for our juniors."

Nada glanced over at me, warmly and kindly, as if I had already been granted a year in Greece.

"Our record for scholarships, Mrs. Everett, is quite frankly the highest in the country with the exception of one school in New England, rather more heavily endowed than Johns Behemoth," the good dean said. He was sitting on the edge of his glass-topped desk and smiling down into Nada's excited face. With a silver pen he tapped his knee and said, "I haven't yet had time to glance through Richard's application forms, and is his health report in? —it is?—and his recommendations are in, yes, one is right here on my desk I see. Fine, fine. Now today he will be taking the entrance examination, you know. You are all prepared, Richard, for our little tests?"

He squinted at me as if, after Nada's brilliance, I was a kind of dark, dim light.

"Yes, sir."

"Have you brought pen, pencil, and eraser?"

"Yes, sir, and paper."

"We provide the paper," he said a little softly, as if I had said something foolish. "Mrs. Everett, I do sincerely wish you and your son the very best luck, but I must remind you that our openings are extremely limited, and it is rare, rare indeed, that we accept a boy in the middle of the year."

"I understand perfectly, Dean Nash."

"I thought you would, yes, yes," he said, smiling vaguely.

Nada sat with her white-and-caramel coat open about her and her legs crossed, and for once I was glad of her being so beautiful; maybe it would help.

"Our examinations are in five parts, Mrs. Everett, each consisting of an hour section, and so . . . Should I explain the examination to you, Mrs. Everett, while Richard begins it?"

I felt a sharp pang of disappointment. I wanted to hear about the exam myself.

"Yes, that's an excellent idea," Nada said. "Richard is very anxious to begin, Dean Nash. He's a perfectionist —I mean, he's very happy when he's doing exams, writing papers, reading. He's a very dedicated child . . . boy."

"I assume that you and your husband have provided him with the proper kind of cultural background, in that case," Dean Nash said happily.

"I hope so."

"You would be surprised, my dear Mrs. Everett, astonished at the irregularity of the cultural backgrounds of some of the boys who take our entrance exams! Boys from, need I say, homes in this immediate vicinity." He stared at Nada for a moment in silence to let the profundity of this remark sink in. "But I must say, without keeping it back any longer, that I am not quite unfamiliar with you, Mrs. Everett, and . . . and here, so you see," he said and reached around to pick off his cluttered desk Nada's first book, a novel published three years before.

The blank white cover with its fluted red lettering startled me, as if it were a private, personal part of her suddenly given out to a stranger's hand.

"Oh," Nada said, leaning forward in surprise, letting her coat fall farther open about her. She touched her mouth with one gloved hand in a neat and exquisite and not at all spontaneous gesture I had seen her make many times before. "But how did you know—I mean, I write under my maiden name—"

"I have always been interested in literature, passionately interested," Dean Nash said with a grin. He called attention to his appearance by involuntarily glancing down at himself—impeccable heavy tweed suit, dark tie, polished dark shoes, everything perfect. For a big man he looked light on his feet. He smelled faintly of shaving cologne, as Nada did of perfume. "I've made a few attempts at writing myself, but above all I am interested in contemporary American writers. I subscribe to four of the 'little' magazines, including *The Transamerican Review,* in which you've just had a story, right? And may I say I have quite a collection of our fellow contemporaries? A sizable collection you might be interested in seeing. I have your two books on the side of my library devoted to living authors." And he laughed with an embarrassment that seemed to be feigned. "Of course you are still alive, Mrs. Everett. I would like to show you my library and get your opinion, and I would hope that, if I'm not being too aggressive, I might have you autograph your books."

I could see that they had forgotten about me, so I got to my feet. This brought Dean Nash's eyes reluctantly around to me. "I'm ready to begin the examination now," I said. It didn't come out with any sound of authority or confidence, but Nada smiled to show me I had done right. Dean Nash rose from the edge of the desk, all six feet three inches of him, lean and knobbly wristed and handsome in a caricatured Englishy way. He drew in his breath slowly and thoughtfully, like an athlete, making an interesting facial expression—pursing his lips and pulling them down, as if to make room for the air to soar up into his nostrils. He contemplated me as if he did not quite remember who I was.

I took the examination in a classroom in the Humanities Building. Dean Nash and Nada took me over, herding me delicately before them. I heard Nada's vivacious, betraying laughter behind me as Dean Nash pointed out something droll or quaint or joked about me. Who knows what he was doing? Oh, that bastard, that lecherous son-of-a-bitch! My heart pounded with hatred and a strange, wistful admiration for him, and I wondered how I could ever be equal to those two demanding people, giant and giantess, who were striding so healthily behind me. If I failed the exam I would lose them forever.

"Farrel will glance in every now and then," the good dean told me as I settled shakily into a desk.

Farrel was an instructor who wore a suit like the dean's, though smaller. His face was younger and less handsome, and Nada did not bother to glance at him. I don't think she really "saw" short men. Nada had taken off her lovely white gloves, and on one finger her diamond ring glittered enough to break my heart and on another finger an emerald glittered in such a way that stretched every bone in my body to the breaking point. At such moments of panic and disbelief I stared at her and wondered if she was my mother, if *she* was my mother, and how had it come to pass? How was it possible she made me undergo such torture and had nothing to offer me as consolation but the glitter of Father's jewels?

Farrel shook some papers out of a soiled manila envelope, quite a few papers, and began slapping things down on my desk. My pen and pencil rattled on the shallow groove in the desk, or perhaps my trembling fingers made them rattle. While Farrel talked into my face I tried to hear what they were saying by the door. Something about lunch? Lunch together? What?

"It is ten o'clock now, Mr. Everett," Farrel said, checking a big watch on his wrist. "You will begin the first section now, and you will have it finished at eleven. I'll be right down the hall in the lounge, and I'll look in at you occasionally. Are you ready?"

I looked around and they were gone. An empty doorway, and outside an ordinary empty hall, the barest glimpse of the corner of a bulletin board at the left—and nothing else.

"I'm ready," I said in a croaking voice.

With a professional flourish, like a magician performing a trick, he turned the papers over. My eyes leaped to the heading, but for a few seconds my sight was blotched, I couldn't see.

"Please read the instructions before you begin," Farrel said. He walked backward to the door, his hands in his tweedy pockets. It was clear that he thought little of me.

And now I could make out the first question: "The word closest in meaning to *syzygy* is . . ."

Off and on, as I sweated my way though the exam, I glanced out the window in the hopes of seeing that white-and-caramel coat waiting for me bravely in the snow. But I saw only the figures of a few boys walking fast across the campus. It was the midterm break now, January 20, and they had a week or so off before the spring semester began. Seeing those boys, who looked older but not much healthier than I, gave me a shock because until now I hadn't really thought of this place as a school—that is, a place where children would be found. It had seemed to me an elegant nightmare concoction made by adults for adults, to further the aims and fantasies of adults, and what have children to do with such things?

I plowed through the first section testing "verbal skills" and leaped into "reasoning skills," and, famished, ravaged with thirst but afraid to ask Farrel for permission to get a drink of water, I plunged into the thick "achievement" pamphlet, and my eyes bulged at the diagrams, tiny drawings, and graphs that awaited my strained brain. It was one o'clock by now and my body was pounding with hunger, with thirst, and a kind of slow, seeping terror, but I would no more have indicated my discomfort when Farrel peeped in to say in a bored voice, "Any questions? Problems?" than Nada would have talked of Thomas Mann to the village ladies she meant to befriend and win.

And where was Nada? I paged though the pamphlet desperately, trying to find a question I could answer, and at the back of my brain was the thought of Nada, my mother, and where she might be, and what might be happening, for it was often because of me, somehow, that those things happened. (My dentist in Wateredge, who kept calling me back in order to check my cavities, my gums, who knows what, and to discuss me in detail with Nada, in his private office; a handsome hairy artist had sketched my face in charcoal one Sunday, in a public park in Chicago; and others, many others, had looped their snaky necks around me to see past me and ogle my mother.) I stared for two minutes at a diagram of a cylinder with its various dimensions indicated and gradually a sensation of disgust and horror rose in me, mysteriously, until my trembling hand moved over the thing to hide it.

When Farrel came in at two to collect the test he seemed to have split slightly—two Farrels, a confusion of eyes and arms. I rubbed my own eyes and breathed hoarsely through my mouth, making a sound like the one I had made when I had bronchitis. Did I mention that I had thrown up my breakfast that morning? Yes, Nada had made a lovely mother's breakfast for her son, who was going to please her so that day: pancakes, orange juice, milk, tiny sausages. My stomach had cringed wisely at the smell, but eat everything I did while my mother watched over me, a little prisoner gorging himself on a final meal. As soon as she disappeared I dashed to the back bathroom and relieved myself of it, a big, hot, steaming mass of slop that had no resemblance to anything my mother could have prepared with her delicate hands. Then I trotted back into the kitchen, every nerve in my body ringing as if in sympathy with a ringing telephone in the other room, and sat panting and sweating at the table until Nada should return. So now at two o'clock I was starved. I watched the two Farrels—not quite two, just one and a half—sort out the many papers I had smudged and sweated upon, slap down another pamphlet, and turn to go. He had no idea of my misery. It would have surprised him to think that I was a human creature with a soul.

I think this experience was the beginning.

Shall I be so blunt? The obvious beginning, yes. Nada brought me there, Dean Nash led me to it, but for some reason it was Farrel, that small and indeed insignificant man, who made me realize a dizzying truth about human beings: they don't care.

No, they don't care, and it means something irreparable to know that. Not just to be told it casually, or to be shouted down by a playmate, "Drop dead, will you?" No, I mean *knowing* it, feeling it, tasting it with all your insides.

So I wrote on, dazed and swaying in my rock-hard little desk, in the midst of the "Attitudinal Testing" and such questions as:

"Which would you rather do? 1) Hit your mother 2) Hit your father 3) Burn down your house 4) Eat a worm"

And: "If you came upon two cows mating, which would you do? 1) Hide your eyes 2) Take a picture 3) Call your friends to look 4) Chase the cows away"

Ah, old familiar questions! I'd taken this part of the exam before, many times, and though I never knew what the answers might be there was a kind of comfort in recognizing the questions. And while I did this (as I was to learn) Nada was treated to an excellent luncheon by Dean Nash and his wife, a tall, husky, athletic person, the well-preserved golfer type who always came, in various forms, to my parents' social events. And innocently treated by the dean, yes. My fears turned out to be crazy. Nada was to declare to Father that evening, "They're both such wonderful people!" with the special glittering look that meant They had money and charm and taste and education, They (whoever they were) were to be added to the catch if it killed Nada, and Father had better help her if he wanted peace.

But that was to take place at dinner, and I knew

[55

nothing of her happy, joyful, innocent luncheon, in an English Tudor home with pegged floors and two grand pianos and two Turkish rugs, having the usual flattering, mutually assuaging, affirmative conversation such people have. I was still taking my examination and I felt as if I were trying to fly with wings soaked in sweat, feathers torn and ragged, falling out, and on my shoulders Nada rode with triumphant, impatient enthusiasm, her high heels spurs in my ribs—me, the child, the shabby angel pumping his wings furiously and weeping with shame; Nada, the mother, digging in her heels and cursing me on. I kept struggling up into the sky, my eyes bloodshot and my heart just ordinarily shot, waiting for the end . . .

I threw up what remained of that breakfast between question nine and question ten of "Conceptional Coordination Skills Testing" but kept on bravely, trying to grind the mess away to nothing beneath my feet before Farrel noticed. The smell was bad but I was writing too fast, reading and gasping too fast, to move to another desk. Onward, onward! My blood vessels were singing in a chorus, like aged radiator pipes. I ground my heels into the floor in a kind of rhythm: in comes a breath, in comes a question, and around in a counterclockwise motion go my anxious feet; out goes a ragged breath, down goes a fast-scrawled answer, and back in a clockwise motion go my feet. In a while the vomit was gone, worn away or just plain evaporated, though there was an oval stain down there that keen-eyed Farrel might notice, and on I went to the last three pages, the last two pages, finally the last page, until I came upon a question dealing with the speculative coordination of conceptions: "X is related by blood to C, but C' is a relative by law. The relationship of X to the social unit MDJ is approximately that of the relationship of C to C', though the MDJ unit is a temporary crystallization. If X . . ." My mind bulged and nearly burst at this, seized control of itself again and read the question over, and over, until nothing at all was coming through and I began to weep, miserable failure that I was. I lowered my head to the desk and wept. My tears burst out onto the pamphlet, and everything would have been lost, drowned and smudged away by my incontinence, if Farrel hadn't come in. He walked softly, on ripple-soled shoes, and I could sense the awful embarrassment in the air before I even knew he was staring at me.

"Are you finished?" he asked.

12

And did I get into Johns Behemoth? Yes indeed, as you already know. And did I get kicked out again? Yes, sad to tell. But my expulsion belongs to the merry month of May and my memoir is still, more or less, on January 20. I want to preserve a phony but convincing chronology, so that there is the impression of development—wrong word: degeneration—in the child-hero. So let's arbitrarily fix the date as January 20, 1960, when I began to disintegrate.

c

13

So I began life as a student at Johns Behemoth, and life back at Burning Bush Way moved a little out of focus. Nada joined the Village Women's Club, under the sponsorship of Hattie Nash ("Such a wonderful person," Nada said), and Father and Nada joined the Vastvalley Country Club under the sponsorship of a business associate of Father's, so they were happy. Nada began going out to lunch every day, and at dinner she would tell us about the Gorgen clan's plans for an Oriental trip, what Thelma Griggs wanted to do with her living room (her husband was in the antique business, what a surprise!), and what she, Nada, had planned by way of a dinner party two Saturdays away—nothing big, just eight couples, and Ginger would help. (Ginger was our maid, who had orange hair with black roots.) Father, chewing candied midget gherkins cheerfully, grunted agreement to all this.

"And I heard the strangest story about that big house up on Epping Way," Nada said, slitting her eyes. "They say those people have no furniture, not even beds, just mattresses. The rooms are practically all bare, but they belong to the Fernwood Heights Country Club, can you imagine? They . . . they're trying desperately to . . ." She paused.

Father, chewing, let his jaws grind on for a moment or two before he caught on to the silence. He said, "Yes, dear? Eh?"

"Nothing," Nada said.

"What were you saying, Tash?"

"Nothing."

"That big house, the big one? Eh?"

Nada sat dazed and pale, and only after a moment did she recover. She put a cigarette between her lips and Father lit it for her. Father stared at her but she did not seem to meet his gaze.

"Does it upset you, Tash?" Father said. "Don't believe everything you hear, after all. In Chestnut Hill—"

"I'm all right," Nada said shortly.

After a moment the uneasy burden between them shifted and rolled down the table toward me. They looked at me and asked about school. What grades today, Richard? Oh, 90, 95. That was good. And how was math? All right. What did Mr. Melon say (history teacher). He said . . . And Mr. Gorden? Enthusiastic (this about my research project on drumlins in the Midwest). Did I ever happen to see Dean Nash, dear Arnold? Not often. (One of my classmates said scornfully that Nash was a fairy, and I told the group of them in a sad, solemn, unarguable voice, no, indeed he wasn't. They believed me.) French class? *Formidable, mais bien,* I guessed. (Monsieur Frame, our *professeur,* gave us vocabulary tests daily and wandered out in the hall, smoking, while we wrote. Everyone cheated. On the first day I had shakily begun the test only to notice that the rest of the kids were sliding out their notebooks and opening them skillfully on their knees. Aghast, I waited with pounding heart for Monsieur to rush into the room waving his arms and denouncing us, but though the good *professeur* wandered by the doorway and might or might not have seen us, nothing happened. So I said to the kid beside me, a red-haired, demonic, demented-looking child, "Lend me your notes," and everyone turned to stare at my effrontery. I managed to carry it off. With dark circles beneath my eyes, two years younger than some of them, physically uninteresting and unpromising, I think it was my simple, bold daring that did it. The boy hurriedly finished his test and slipped the notebook over to me and, though I'd studied for hours the night before and did not need to cheat, cheat I did.)

"Mais, qu'est-ce que c'est le grade?" Nada said.

Thank God, I was able to tell her 95.

14

I don't know if I mentioned that Father traveled a great deal. He was in and out of Fernwood, in and out of the house, with a fast chuckle and a fast rumple of my hair. "Off to San Francisco, buster. It's a hard life!" He'd be rushing into the kitchen for a last doughnut, which he'd stuff in his overcoat pocket so that the white sugar fell everywhere, and if Nada was sitting in the breakfast nook she would very daintily—and I think unconsciously—draw her feet away so that he couldn't step on them. She wore lovely feathery bedroom slippers. Father would loom down over her for a fast kiss, and if I came up to him I'd get another of his wet enthusiastic kisses spiced with doughnut sugar, and off he'd go.

"Your father is an enormously busy man," Nada said,

and she drew me to her, unhappy, puzzled Nada, and kissed my face. I wanted to throw my arms around her neck and say, "Please be happy! Please stay home this time!"

"Let me tell you a story, Richard. Once I went ice skating. It was at night, out in the country, everything was dark and lonely. I went skating by myself, though that was forbidden. Look, none of this story is true, you must know that, but . . . On one side of that pond the ice had melted a little that day, in the sun, and when I skated over there the ice cracked and I fell through. Not very far, it wasn't deep, but the ice was cracked and the edges were sharp. Can you imagine that, or don't you have any memories of ice? Ponds? Ponds out in the country? No, I don't either, but imagine what it would be like to be a child skating all alone, and you hear the ice groan and crack, and you feel the water that's warm at first . . . you would know how alone you were then, wouldn't you? So, Richard, let me be sententious and tell you this: it isn't a question of skating or not skating, but only a question of how safely you're going to skate. You don't want to fall through the ice and drown, do you?"

I didn't know what she was saying. She often talked like this, you see, when Father was gone. She talked to me in a low, fast voice, and like a cat she would stir restlessly under the teasing of her own words. Words to Nada must have been different from everything else in the world—weapons but not just weapons, candies, spices, jabs of pleasure and pain—and it made no difference whether they were about anything "true" or not. I think my own problems about life, about what is real

[61

and what is fiction in my own life, in this memoir, might come from her, though I don't want to blame her for anything.

She went on, apparently talking about the same thing. "Today I'm going out to lunch with Bébé Hofstadter and what's-her-name, Minnie Hodge. I'll meet them at twelve-thirty and we have reservations at The Peacock's Tail. I want to steal one of their menus sometime. I want to preserve it somehow, in a short story, somewhere, because that menu has vast meanings. You're too young to understand, but . . ."

Yes, she had left us before. She had run away from us before, leaving Father and me miserable, shabby bachelors. She had left us twice, once when I was six (and Father declared, drunkenly, that she had died) and again when I was nine. Now I was almost eleven and I could feel her getting restless again, even when she was praising Father and Fernwood and The Peacock's Tail. So I went to school and cheated and worked like all the other boys, but my mind pondered upon Nada, and I tried to imagine her at lunch, at bridge, leaning forward prettily to hear what Bébé Hofstadter had to say (she was a small doll-like woman with a trumpet blast of a voice, whose son Gustave was in my classes) and squinting with a pretty helplessness at the bridge hand she'd just been dealt, pleased to be losing.

Sometimes I called home between classes, but Ginger answered, so I hung up. I tried desperately to hear if there was some sound of Nada in the background—drumming fitfully at the piano, clattering around in her high heels—but there was never anything and I didn't dare ask for her. When I was home and the telephone rang I always got to it before Ginger did and said no,

Mrs. Everett was not home, but who, who was calling? Always women. I pumped them innocently, assuming a younger child's voice. "Oh, who is it? Who? Do you live near us?" Once a man called, and when I told him Nada wasn't in there was a curious silence. Then he said, "Where is she?" and this shocked me because in Fernwood no one talks that way. Out to lunch, I said. Bridge. I began to sweat, listening to him think and not knowing what he was thinking, and finally he hung up without giving his name.

And one afternoon just as I came into the house the telephone was ringing and I rushed to it, outdistancing Ginger, and that man said again, "I want to speak to Mrs. Everett." I slammed the phone down. Ginger adjusted the telephone receiver and said slowly, "He say somethin' bad? One of them like that's always at my mother . . ."

By now they were entertaining all the time, and often Father flew in, was brought to our door in a limousine from the airport, showered and shaved while guests were arriving, and then he'd thump happily downstairs, smoothing his hair back from his temples, quite the gay, welcoming host—nothing was too much for him! At such times Nada would be really beautiful, as if every pore and every nerve in her body had been bred for this sort of thing, her hair burnished and burning with excitement, her eyes like jewels, everything lean, smooth, lovely, and what anguish I felt, seeing one man after another arrive with wife in tow and not knowing whether there was *one* of them at whom she looked in a certain way. I would be lying flat upstairs on the landing, afraid to look over the edge. What I heard was just babble. "Isn't it a lovely . . ." "Isn't it . . ." "I'm so happy that

. . ." If a woman arrived whom Nada had known from some other year and some other suburb, they would exchange chaste ceremonial kisses, like birds pecking delicately at each other.

Sometimes Nada let me meet her guests if they arrived fairly early, and sometimes I could pass hors d'oeuvres around, wearing a little gentleman's outfit of dark, sharply creased trousers and white blazer with the Johns Behemoth shield on the breast pocket. God, I must have been cute! They didn't look at my thin, harassed face but only at my outfit, and I was said to be darling. They breathed their liquory, perfumy breaths in my face and exclaimed over Nada's eyes in mine, the men glancing up to Nada who stood behind me, as if they couldn't possibly bother with me if they had her to look at. "Say something in French, Richard," Nada would say casually, having her cigarette lighted by some gentleman with silvery gray hair, and I would perform shyly and briefly. "*Il me l'a donné*," Nada would say, exhaling cigarette smoke and indicating the most recent trifle I had bought her—one time a little fake ivory elephant from a carving exhibit at the Art Museum. Everyone thought I was precocious and sweet.

Our house at these times had a certain soft, magic, misty air to it, not just because of the candlelight and Nada's newest dress but because of something else, some sense of languorous adventure. If this were a story of Nada's I would mention the odd, sinister air I sometimes noticed too, but it was so intangible—perhaps it didn't exist except in my imagination. But there was the sense of adventure. Do you think people like those people are adventuresome? No, they are not. My readers, my far-flung readers, I eavesdropped for eleven years of my pathetic life, hiding behind doors, in closets, on landings, listening over telephone extensions, sneaking, skulking, holding my breath and wondering if the next second would expose everything, and I can tell you that the good people of Fernwood (and Brookfield and Water-edge and Charlotte Pointe and the rest) are not ad-venturesome. They do not swear. They do not drink beyond a certain point, because beyond that point they might come loose. They do not spill drinks, upset trays, burn holes in tables or rugs, because by doing such things they would come loose and these people never come loose. Watch them. Listen. They would never give you a sly sideways wink, they'd never tap your chaste foot with their own. True, you hear about them being divorced and being remarried, and occasionally someone dies and is never heard of again, but it is done in an orderly way. So where did our sense of adventure come from? Only from Nada. She was intoxicated with it. She was intox-icated with our house—with her new expensive furniture, her marble-topped table and her exquisite bookshelf, given to her by Father's great-aunt and worth—oh, let me tell you!—quite a bit. She was intoxicated with expensive tidbits Ginger had unfrozen not half an hour before, and she was intoxicated with her white, white dress and her emerald necklace, and the tinkling made by ice in drinks, and by the mystical sense of her being at last in power, in control, a part of the secret, invisible world that owns and controls everything.

Because Fernwood does control everything, like it or not.

If these people ever mentioned her writing she would raise one lovely shoulder and smile and change the subject at once. She wanted nothing so much as to

c*

grovel and annihilate herself before these people, the only people in the world she admired because they were the only people she could not imitate. She could never compete with them, never. The most ignorant, most self-complacent, ugliest dowager of them all bowled Nada over simply because—guess why!—she had never read Thomas Mann, had never heard the name, and gave not the slightest indication of regretting her loss. My poor mother . . . Perverse and selfish as she was, I never for an instant doubted that she was my mother. It was my father I doubted. I kept waiting for another man to appear, not bounding into the room with that bulky, boyish, wet grin my father had but walking quite sedately and confidently in, taking over. Did that man, that phantom father, that real father ever appear? I'll deal with that in a later chapter.

So they started giving parties and going to parties. It began suddenly, in one week. They "caught on" the way they had always caught on, in other towns. Father had the kind of easygoing swagger that made him welcome anywhere, as a lesser guest. He was the man hostesses thought of after they listed their main guests. Nada must have been a mystery to them; they were interested in her for her "mind," though she never demonstrated much intelligence in their presence. She refused to discuss her writing, not understanding that Fernwood was a hundred years beyond the bourgeoisie that scorned the intellectual: today's Fernwood wanted to hug intellectuals and "artistes" to its matronly bosom until something of their mysterious dark charm smeared off. At the age of ten I could tell they were proud of Nada for being a "writer," but she never caught on. Even after the women chatted energetically about their ballet classes, sculpting classes, theater groups, Great Books Round Tables, Creative Writing Clinics, she never caught on; she had a certain opaqueness, a failure of vision common to people who see only minute things well.

There was this woman, a giant huntress type with a hairdo that looked like a fan, or like a Tudor get-up out of a history pageant; she lived in Fernwood Dells, a semi-good section, better than ours but not as good as Fernwood Heights. She was a widow, but very healthily and robustly a widow, as Fernwood widows are; she played tennis and golf, swam, paddled canoes, went "hiking." She wore chiffon dresses that looked odd on her hefty frame, but I overheard Bébé Hofstadter say once, "No one dresses as well as Tia." This woman's name was Tia Bell. She tried sweetly and insistently to draw Nada out, asking her about her writing. What were her themes? When did she find time to write? She invited Nada to the Fernwood Heights Episcopal Church, there to hear John Ciardi speak of the mystic force of Dante, and another time she took Nada to a popular and quite affluent synagogue in another suburb, famous for its intellectual life, where they heard Norman Mailer give a perfectly coherent, surprisingly pedantic talk on "The Great American Novel: When Is It Due?"

And Bébé Hofstadter herself came over one afternoon, bringing her laconic son Gustave and a copy of my mother's second novel for her to autograph. Nada flushed with pleasure and confusion and suggested that Gustave and I adjourn to the library. This "library" was just a pleasant room facing the south and hence sunny, with a fireplace in which no fire had been lit in my memory, and comfortable furniture that had no pretensions to the elegance and discomfort of the rest of the house. So Gustave and I wandered in awkwardly and tried to think of something to talk about.

"Nice house y'got here," he said. I could tell by the booming, husky voice of his mother, coupled with her strand of pearls, that he lived in a house just like this, or better. We sat heavily in leather chairs facing the empty fireplace, both of us pretending weariness since this was a kind of convention with Johns Behemoth boys.

"Y'do the math yet?" he said.

"No, you?"

"No."

Another convention Johns Behemoth boys observed briefly when together was a certain sluggish colloquialism, an attempt at toughness that fooled no one. We sat moodily in silence.

In the living room our mothers were chatting happily. "Just let me fix you one, just one," Nada said. Gustave lifted his head as if listening. His mother's deep voice vibrated out to us, and one corner of his pale, thin mouth turned up.

"What d'ya think of—" I began, but he interrupted me by making a silencing gesture. He was listening to his mother. As far as I could make out she was chatting about another woman, or a family, or a horse, nothing much, and I resented Gustave's manner. He was in a few of my classes but we did not know each other. Like me, he sat alone at lunchtime in the brick-entombed cafeteria, and like all Johns Behemoth boys who sat alone, he had the look of being very content. I knew very little about him except that he had an extraordinary method for cheating in math, an invention of his own that he sold to other boys for five dollars apiece. The price was said to be reasonable. Night after night I prepared my homework, night after night I studied for tests until my brain rattled, but when the time came for a test I usually cheated. I knew all the answers, yes, but it wasn't enough to know the answers. Most Johns Behemoth boys knew most answers. But that wasn't enough: you had to be steady enough to take the test, and the only way to be steady was to allow no room for error. Even a mild blood clot on the brain would not be enough to keep us from scoring 90 on an exam, with our ingenious cheating devices.

"I want to hear what she's having. A little Scotch evidently," Gustave said. He folded his arms, a twelve-year-old blond replica of myself, both of us with the same kind of glasses—clear, pinkish rims and lenses sadly thick for prepubescents. He glanced at me. "Your mother is a very beautiful woman," he said. "What do you think of her writing?"

"I don't have any opinion."

"Haven't you read it?"

"No."

"Why not?"

Nada forbade me to look at anything of hers, of course, just as she forbade Father; neither of us could even enter her study. I made an impatient gesture as if Gustave were too stupid for me to bother answering.

"Well, I think I understand," Gustave said sympathetically. "It's too personal—she's your mother of course. But, Richard, you should understand that it's always an awkward situation. Having a mother, I mean." Here he hushed suddenly, listening again to his mother. She was complaining about her maid. I heard her expression, "that little colored chit," several times. Gustave crossed and uncrossed his legs restlessly. He said, "You're very fortunate. Your mother is young and beautiful, and you must know that most of our mothers, the mothers of kids at school, are sort of getting along. My mother is at that age now, you know, where I have to watch out for her."

"How?"

"Oh, tag along like this, eavesdrop, make sure she doesn't lose something or burst into tears," Gustave said casually. As if to demonstrate, he got up and went to the doorway, pretending to check a book on a shelf near the door.

In the other room our mothers were sitting on the sofa, chatting. Nada's black hair was growing out; she had missed one of her appointments, and the salon owner, a Monsieur Freytag, refused to take her back. Bébé Hofstadter had silvery hair that was very stylishly done. She wore an expensive yellow wool suit and a few too many bracelets on one wrist.

"My mother is inclined to hysteria," Gustave explained. "It's the change of life, you know. You can't be too careful with them at that time."

"What's wrong with her?"

He stared at me coldly. "It is a biological condition," he said.

Biological conditions of mothers always frightened me, so I said nothing.

"It began a few months ago, and I knew at once what it was. I had had sense enough to be reading ahead. Father doesn't have the slightest idea what's going on —he wouldn't want to admit his own age—and I can't possibly tell him. How could you tell your father anything so personal? I've left a copy of the *Reader's Digest* around with a lead article on the subject, but . . . My mother gets upset all the time, she cries if the toast is cold for Father, she's always picking on our maid Hortense, and she's always on the telephone, it's embarrassing, and yesterday her parakeet Fifi died and she spent all day crying, then accused Hortense and me of not giving a damn about the parakeet. So she took the corpse into the kitchen and put it in the garbage disposal, and before I could stop her she had turned it on. She was hysterical about that. This is a difficult time of life for both of us," Gustave said vaguely.

"It's nice you . . . you're caring for her," I said. I wanted to tell him that I too took care of my mother; but everything I did was a failure. I admired Gustave's strength. You got the impression that when the time came he would get up and go get his mother and lead her home, safely.

After about thirty minutes of our leafing through old *Business Week*s, Gustave craned his head around. "Uh-uh," he said grimly. He did indeed get up and stride into the living room. He was a small, skinny kid, nothing much, but he knew what he was doing. "Mrs. Everett, thank you so much for an enjoyable hour," he said to Nada, bowing his head slightly, "but Mother has to leave now. I think she's forgotten her hair appointment."

"My hair appointment is Thursday," Bébé said.

"Mother, it's today at five-thirty. You always do forget," Gustave said.

"It isn't. It's tomorrow," said his mother. "I can't have a moment to myself. He's always . . . he—"

"Mother won't have time for that drink," Gustave said. "I'd better be getting our coats."

And he went to get the coats and, still chatting away while his mother whimpered, he helped her into her mink coat and stooped to pick up one of the gloves that had fallen from a pocket to the floor, doing everything smoothly and confidently, simply raising his voice to drown out his mother's complaints.

"Very nice to have met you, Gustave," Mother said.

"*Enchanté*," Gustave murmured at the door.

We could hear his mother whimpering as they walked down our bone-dry walk. "Isn't that strange," Nada said, closing the door slowly.

That was one of her "friends," Bébé Hofstadter. In a novel you would get to know such a woman better, but in real life you never do—women like her are perennially about to age but never quite do, they're always at a distance no matter how close, etc. Though Mrs. Hofstadter will return again in this memoir she will never develop, never get any clearer. And we saw a little of her husband, Gregory, but not much; he was always traveling. And there were many other interesting people. Let me see—Charles Spoon, who designed automobiles and was always six years ahead of the current season, consequently irritated and distracted by the present, a balding, intense loud-laughing man with a considerable fortune, most of it made in the last decade, and a lank, quiet wife from the Upper Class, one of the season's choicest debutantes many seasons ago. And Mavis Grisell, one of the area's few active divorcées, a dark-blond woman with exotic eyes and an interesting Aztec profile, given to Egyptian and Indian jewelry and the exclaiming of monosyllabic words from unintelligible foreign tongues. She had traveled a great deal since her divorce from a rather odd man who, for some reason, had cleared their large home of all its furniture and objects of art one day when Mavis was visiting her sister in Cedar Grove (you'll become acquainted with Cedar Grove in good time), leaving her nothing but her clothes and a mattress in what had been their bedroom. It was a sensational Fernwood scandal, and the divorce settlement, for Mavis, had been generous. Nada didn't like her but Father though she was a "good sport."

"In our society it's impossible for a woman without a man," Father said gallantly. Or maybe he was warning Nada. "We should do all we can for poor Mavis, who's been through so much."

And there were the Nashes (Dean Nash and his good wife Hattie), and the Griggses from down the block, and Harrison Vemeer, whom Nada admired extravagantly without knowing, as I did, that he was considered *no one* by our other guests. Mr. Vemeer was a successful contractor whose rise to fortune was legendary in Fernwood. He operated out of gulleys, swamps, small woods, hopeless eroded land, erecting identical colonial houses—you've seen his trademark, a red-brick colonial with navy blue shutters and navy blue windowboxes and a white wrought iron kitty-kat crawling up the chimney, all for only $39,900?—which often tilted, or sank, or cracked in twos and threes after the new owner moved in. Mr. Vemeer sometimes was prudent enough to change the name of his company, and continued to build "Distinctive Modern Colonials," sometimes across the street from the outraged homeowners. I say "street" but I mean rutted muddy lane. His most amazing coup was the draining of a swamp so that he could erect fifteen more "distinctive Colonials," resulting in a nearby lake ("Picture Lake," in the center of another housing subdivision) filling slowly and mysteriously with black mud. It oozed out through a twenty-four-inch pipe. The outraged homeowners took Mr. Vemeer to court but somehow he escaped. There were suits and countersuits. But perhaps his really masterful venture was the flood-plain episode. Mr. Vemeer owned land everywhere, being by now enormously wealthy and having a zest for adventure, and so he moved truckload after truckload of dirt from a flood plain which he "owned" to another lower, sunken area near a road which he also owned, in order to build houses on this site. When the spring rains came a creek overflowed and houses near the original flood plain were flooded, exactly as anyone could have foreseen, and Mr. Vemeer was again taken to court but declared innocent by dint of an obscure, helpful particle of the law which says that one may improve his own property.

In our home Mr. Vemeer was fond of exclaiming, as if he were a parody of a provincial French miser out of literature, "Buy a good lawyer and buy him first. That's it. I've been sued now twenty-seven times and no one has collected once, not once, and the secret is to buy the best lawyer and buy him first."

Everyone knew this (Fernwood despised lawyers) but no one said it so bluntly; hence Mr. Vemeer was considered crude, ungracious *nouveau riche,* and his Catholicism did not help. I overheard many a guest of ours complaining about him, a rapid, whispered "Isn't he awful!" from the throaty depths of Mrs. Hofstadter, a muttered exotic syllable from Mavis Grisell. Tia Bell, her headdress of stacked, banked red-tinted hair quivering, her giantess's frame barely restrained, must have liked Harrison Vemeer in spite of everything because she often giggled, behind a large suntanned hand, "Goodness!" when he launched into one of his anecdotes. He scandalized her. But the gloomy frowns of Dean Nash and his good wife were obvious, and I wanted to tell Nada not to invite Mr. Vemeer back again. Did she want to endanger her standing? Nada was enchanted with Mr. Vemeer because she had the idea he was an ideal businessman and that her guests must certainly admire him and be grateful to her for bringing them all together. Mr. Vemeer's wife never went out; she remained at home with their eight children.

Anxious to help Nada out, I wrote her a note in big block letters and mailed it from the corner. It said:

YOU WOULD BE WISE TO DROP VEMEER. HE IS A CROOK.

When Nada opened this letter she stared at it, puzzled. Then a haughty flush brightened her cheeks and she crumpled the note in her fist.

I said, "What's that, Nada?"

"The work of a depraved mind," she said.

So I wrote her another note. This said:

HARRISON VEMEER IS ABOUT TO BE FOUND GUILTY OF FRAUD. YOU WOULD BE WISE TO DROP HIM.

Nada received this on the morning of the day she and Father were invited to the Vemeers' for a cocktail party, and she did indeed read the note with concern. She said nothing to me. The cocktail party was a failure because no one came except Father and Nada and poor Bébé Hofstadter, desperate for an audience to whom she could tell about the deceit of her maid Hortense, who had invited in a colored gentleman friend of hers and slept in Bébé's bed and then cleared out, not even leaving a note. "Oh, my dears! My dears! I don't think I can face reality again," Bébé kept moaning. "You should have seen what they did . . ."

But what finally decided Nada against Mr. Vemeer was a simple touch of genius on my part. With beautiful innocence I said one day that Farley Weatherun, the grandson of the internationally known Weatheruns, had told me in French class, *"Ce Monsieur Vemeer, il est laid,"* and why had he said that? "I always thought Mr. Vemeer was kind of nice," I told Nada. "Why would Farley Weatherun say anything so mean?"

"He must have had his reasons," Nada said slowly.

After a moment she put her hands to her eyes and sat there in silence. What was she thinking? She might have been overcome with the chaos of trivia and garbage that had overturned upon her. I could almost read her mind. I stared up at her pale, nervous hands and thought: If she would just look at me and talk to me I could save her. But she sat like that for a while, alone and shivering. Then her hands dropped away suddenly and she lit a cigarette. She was smoking too much these days, and I hunted up news articles in the paper to show her, about the dangers of smoking.

"Nada, you okay?"

"Of course, honey."

"You look kind of pale."

"I'm really quite all right," she said, smiling to show me she was all right. "Tell me, are you very good friends with that Weatherun boy?"

But her facial muscles tightened as she spoke, as if something inside her hated the very sound of those words. It made me feel sick to see how she looked at me as if I were no better than anything else in this world. A chill ran up my body and I wondered if I was really going to be sick, again, and maybe that would be good because she couldn't leave home if I was sick. She couldn't leave me if I was sick.

Yes, I loved her, and do you know how I remember her most? Not dazzling and lovely, greeting her guests, and not pale with despair as she was sometimes, turned away from Father, from a few fast-spat words that had passed between them, but off, off on her own: strolling down the front walk to the street with a letter to mail, her hair loose, girlish and quite alone, with the look of a person absolutely free and meaning no harm, no harm.

15

One morning at breakfast Nada said to me, "Can I interrupt you?"

I was jotting down cheat-notes for a history quiz to be given in an hour, but I looked up politely.

"Richard, I was talking to Mr. Nash about something that means a great deal to me. I don't want to upset you or worry you, but, frankly, Mr. Nash was kind enough to tell me the results of your entrance examination. That's something he usually refuses to do, because some mothers take these things too seriously. Anyway, he did tell me, and I'm afraid I was a little disappointed with your IQ score."

"What was it?"

"I can't tell you. But I was a little disappointed."

My heart hung large and heavy in my chest. I watched Nada's fine white teeth bite off a piece of toast and chew on it, the way she was chewing on me, and I tried to make my haggard face look pleasant. "Yeah, well, I'm real sorry. What was the score?"

"I said I can't tell you," Nada said patiently. "But it was lower than my own. That's ridiculous, I don't accept it. You know, Richard, I don't want you to be less than I am. I want you to be better than I am. I can't bear the thought of some kind of degenerative process setting in. I see myself as less than my father was, and now you . . . Do you understand?"

"I guess it isn't anything we can help much," I said feebly.

"Im not so sure about that. I've made arrangements with Mr. Nash for you to take the test again."

"What?"

"I've made arrangements for you to take the test again."

"The test again?"

"The test again?"

"Just part of it. Half of it, I think."

"But, Mother," I said, my stomach beginning to tremble where no one could see, and even laughing to show her how calm I was, "Mother, if my IQ is a certain IQ, it won't matter how many tests I take, will it?"

"Please don't call me that," she said.

"But it won't matter, will it? I mean, will it? The test is just a measure. It . . . isn't—"

"I want you to take it again, Richard."

"Take it again? That test?"

"Yes, Richard."

We stared sadly at each other. I did not know and I do not know today how much she hated herself for all these things. Every word of hers, every gesture, was phony as hell, and as time passed in Fernwood this phoniness grew upon her steadily, like the layers of fat I have encircling my body. But who was going to rescue her? Once or twice I caught her, sitting alone, staring out into our unused backyard and screwing her face around in a mannerism not her own: drawing her lips down, tightly pursed, and seeming to lift her nose slightly as if straining for purer air. But no, Dean Nash wouldn't help. I never found out how close they were, Nash and Nada. But though they would have been a fine couple— he was no more than Father's age though he looked younger—I don't think she got much strength from him. He was just a son-of-a-bitch anyway, as you'll see.

16

And was I good friends with that Weatherun boy?

I got to know him through Gustave Hofstadter, who had become my best, indeed, my only, friend. Gustave and I were fond of playing chess, which we played seriously and silently, like two little old men in a terminal ward of a hospital. If we played at his house (a baronial estate with a house that was gabled, ornamented, towered, as cute as a gingerbread house in a Mother Goose story), Bébé ran in and out of the room, looking for things she could never find, and shot at us muttered remarks: "Still playing that game! Still at it! I don't understand children . . . Such a sunny day . . ." If we played at my house we had the sweet, serene quiet of the library, bathed with winter sunlight, the feel of a house empty and silent everywhere except for Ginger's vacuum cleaner roaring away upstairs, while Ginger probably rifled through Nada's bureau drawers (I had caught her at it once). We loved and respected the game of chess, both of us. Gustave was going into math and I had no idea where I was going—indeed I couldn't have predicted exactly where I would end up!—but I joined him in his admiration for this precise and beautiful game, which leaves nothing to chance, unlike that hideous game, Bridge, which Nada pretended to like, or that still more hideous game of life. (You can trust a degenerate to turn philosophical.)

Another chess-lover was Farley Weatherun, who was a freshman at Johns Behemoth. Farley was a slow, gentle, distracted boy who had the best room in the dormitory with the exception of a couple of rooms in the seniors' wing. His family was famous and indeed is still famous. You will find one Weatherun or another mentioned constantly in gossip columns or in *Time* magazine ("Aqualung Enthusiast Si Weatherun Announces His . . ."; "Socialite-Flutist Virginia Weatherun Announces Her . . ."; "Admiral-Playboy 'Taffy' Weatherun Announces His . . ."). But fame counted for little at Johns Behemoth, where it was vulgar to speak of anyone's family, especially your own, since you were supposed to be an individual and nothing more. Nothing less. The president of the school, a waspy, wispy man named Sikes, told us repeatedly that we were on our own, each of us was a young man, an individual working his way through life. And, indeed, we did work.

Farley, with his amiable slowness, had a difficult time. He spent hours copying other boys' homework (at that time it cost you fifty cents to copy homework from a good student; the rates have probably risen), and even copying seemed hard for him. He'd leave out whole sentences or, in mathematics, ledges of numerals, decimal points, or digits that rendered everything invalid. Gustave and I liked him, but playing chess with him was frustrating because he took so long to make his moves. He had a pale, freckled face, a milky skin beneath the freckles that was rather like Nada's skin, hands that were just as freckled as his face, and gnawed knuckles. It seemed to me that he was as sickly as I, because he was always taking medicine and pills of one kind or another.

He'd stare at the move I had just made, look up at me keenly, gnaw at a knuckle, and say, " 'Cuse just a minnit." He would go to his closet, inside which was a small refrigerator, and take out a bottle and drink from it. The bottle had an angular, medicinal appearance. If Gustave was with us, curled up on the bed and studying French, I would notice how Gustave glanced up at Farley's back and how, if I caught his eye, he would ignore me. If I was alone I speculated about cheating, moving a strategic piece while his back was turned; but I never quite dared to do this. And anyway I always won. Gustave usually beat me, and I usually beat Farley, and Farley would laugh and say, "Shit. Lost again," in the kind of happy, self-pitying voice Father sometimes used.

One afternoon he kept going to the refrigerator after every move of mine and finally he brought the mysterious little bottle back to the table with him. "Lemme fix y'up some Coke," he said. He sounded sleepily pleased. He dropped some ice cubes in two scummy glasses, poured in Coke for us, and said, raising his reddish eyebrows in exactly the same way Father raised his when making a drink, "Y'want some of this?" holding up the bottle for me to see.

It said "Log Cabin Maple Syrup."

"But what's that?" I said.

His glance slurred by me as if I were beyond hope, and he poured what remained of the dark liquid into his own glass. "Now, son," he said, "stand back 'cause I'm gonna make my move."

He was the first alcoholic I had ever met, and he was only thirteen. It was a surprise to me at that time, though very shortly I was to encounter Blazes Jones, a dazed, moony child of twelve who not only drank secretly but went around humming and muttering under his breath and making pawing motions in the air. Rumored a genius, Blazes was the center of a special clique in which I was never quite allowed—or, to be truthful, I was never allowed in it at all, they didn't want me. So much for him. He has since died.

And I was shortly to meet Francis Bean, Jr., who took pills of various kinds to keep awake and to keep going merrily; he was sporty and wild, affecting boxlike jackets of olive wool and fur-lined, cream-colored gloves. His sister Greta, a lovely child of fourteen, took these mysterious pills also, and in the last month of my hopeless stay at Fernwood she was reported to "juvenile authorities" for having offered a marijuana cigarette to Suzie, a worker at the Pandora's Box Beauty Salon, in lieu of a dollar tip. All this got around; it was a mild scandal, soon forgotten.

Farley was my friend. I desperately needed a friend that wretched; he gave me hope in the midst of my hopelessness. I recall him lurching down the corridor to the lavatory, smiling a sick, tilted smile, and, as the snows abated and a false spring came to us in March, plodding around out in the colorless park (called our "green"), kicking last year's leaves around. He wore bedraggled and outgrown clothes, poor pleasant Farley, socks that did not match, underwear with holes in it. His family sent him money in spasms, forgetting him for long periods, and he used what spending money he received for liquor. His sweaters were always worn thin at the elbows, and he forgot to wear a white shirt under them, *de rigueur* at Johns Behemoth, so his necktie was no more than a bowtie on a black elastic band that fastened around his neck. Sometimes I saw him late in the morning, just rushing out of his dormitory with his bowtie crooked around his bony, doomed neck and his red hair rising in ghastly dry tufts above his face—stumbling and staggering, his eyes no more than slits against the light. He bought his liquor from someone in the village, a restaurant owner who had once said hello to Admiral-Playboy Weatherun and was inordinately proud of this fact. Farley was rumored to get a very reasonable price.

17

"There is this boy at school, from Boston, who's so miserable and mean," I told Nada. There was a galaxy, a menagerie of odd misfits in the fake Johns Behemoth I had constructed for her, all extensions of myself, with problem parents that were extensions of my parents; I made everything up, out of a peculiar distrust of the truth. It would never have occurred to me to tell my parents the truth about anything. "His mother is an alcoholic and he loves her a lot, I guess. He worries about her."

"That sounds terrible," Nada said.

She fixed her eyes upon me, not to see if I was lying —why would I lie?—but to see how far my childish mind had assessed the gravity of the situation. I made a habit, in those days, of saying things I couldn't possibly have understood, in my innocence.

"Are there many unhappy boys in your school, Richard?"

"I don't know. Maybe."

"Do the boys miss their parents?"

"Sure."

"I hope you're friends with them. Don't ignore them."

She had the sunny, myopic belief, like all mothers, that her son was popular and had the power to "make friends" with anyone. I always fooled her, and maybe that was my mistake, because if my poor health wasn't enough to keep her at home, maybe my failure as a social organism would have done the trick. But I had too much pride. And anyway I liked to please her. There was nothing so nice as Nada pleased, smiling a real smile, an unfake smile, and showing her lovely teeth. On the day I agreed to take the examination over, she showed her teeth in a breathtaking smile and hugged me, and after I took it she dragged me around to the expensive and pretentious village "shoppes" and bought me a tennis racket, what she thought to be a handsome shirt, two dozen pairs of identical dark blue socks, a book in a series of novels about a boy detective which I had stopped reading years before, and other presents. I remember that day well—it's coming back to me. Yes, I remember it well though I haven't thought about it for years. Let me see: sharp, tangy wood smoke in the air, perhaps an advertising gimmick, and a fine late winter sun, and Mother jauntily beautiful and suburban, leading me around, her precious son, her darling prodigy who was to carry the genes of genius into the future, brought all the way to America from sad, dark Russia.

We went into a teen-agers' hangout, luckily deserted at this time on Saturday, and had luxurious ice-cream sundaes for lunch. Have I ever mentioned how Nada ate? She ate as if she expected a disembodied hand suddenly to pull her plate away from her, and if it had she would have continued eating, leaning over the table until she could no longer reach the plate. She was a hungry, greedy woman. She loved food, and when she ate I must admit she let her shoulders slouch a little toward the table, her long-fingered hands delicate and a little bony with the intensity of her eating. Spoons and forks were manipulated in Nada's fingers impatiently; they got in the way, they often clicked and clanked against plates. I believe she ate more than Father did, though she never gained any weight.

And what a fine day that was! Nada was to be informed the following week that I had done extremely well on the examination, raising my IQ score by a healthy margin, and Nada was to hug me for this, and talk feverishly of my "career." I somehow think she wanted me to be a great writer, like Mann and Tolstoi and herself, though she never mentioned this to me. She probably thought it was in my blood and that it would emerge by itself. But even though I didn't yet know I had done so well, I felt that I had at least improved the score that had so disappointed her and that I would carry the Russian genes on to the next generation without damaging them. I was burdened with boxes and bags, all the presents that I greeted with the same smile of gratitude and humility, saying, "Nada, you really don't have to . . ."

"Of course I don't," she said in her parody of Bébé Hofstadter, lowering her voice until it seemed to scrape the back of her throat.

She surprised me by driving down to the zoo, which was inside the city limits. We rarely descended into the "city," though Father worked downtown. There was a tradition, stemming from Wateredge, when I had been recovering from rheumatic fever for many months, that I loved the zoo and that Nada and I, and not Father, visited the zoo whenever we could. This was all phony, because Nada hadn't taken me for several years, and I really did not care that much for the animals; abstract, ambiguous puzzles like the chess board now interested me, and the enigmatic conversations I overheard on the upstairs phone while Nada downstairs talked to some man in New York. I did not know it at the time but I was beginning the second stage of my disintegration, marked, as most degenerative processes are, by a false cheerfulness. Yes, I was cheerful!

And, on that day, what else did we encounter? A gigantic silver balloon in the sky, like a remnant of some lost ahistoric age, a monster descending to gobble up my lovely mother and myself and keep us locked forever in his warm, dark belly. Just the two of us. But the balloon turned slowly in the blue sky and exhibited a most disappointing tail: *Buy Baxters Buicks*. I remember that the omission of the apostrophe annoyed me very much. There were the usual kids riding bicycles along the edge of the highway, real kids in blue jeans, canvas jackets, legs pumping with the kind of energy I was never to know. I remember touching my eyes and making my vision go slightly out of focus, so that the cyclists became cloudy and vague and no longer seemed children like myself, competitors. And the cloudiness did not go away but remained with me like magic, as if protecting and soothing me; it must have been the kind of mistiness Nada inhaled at her dinner parties here and in our other homes. If only Nada and I could have shared the same magical dream . . .

Near the zoo we noticed a small crowd milling around a drive-in bank, and Nada, always adventuresome, turned into the asphalt drive. "What's going on here, Richard?" she said. She had a polite, gallant habit of asking any man in her presence what was happening, though she could see for herself. This time it wasn't so clear what we were seeing though. Four teen-aged girls in slacks and boots and windbreakers stood in unnatural silence, staring at the front of the little bank (there's one near you: colonial brick with wide white shutters, very nice, a place just like home to store your $10,000), and a woman in a dazzling pink sports car was also staring. At the door of the bank were several men in trench coats, and it passed through my mind that the air was still too cold for coats like that. One man was carrying a small suitcase in an unnatural way, balanced up against his hip.

Nada pressed a button and her window slid down jerkily. "Do you think something strange is happening here, Richard?" Her nose seemed to lengthen. The teen-aged girls looked around, puzzled. One of them was trying to talk the others into walking away. Nada leaned out the window, letting one gloved hand pat against the car door. "Good God!" she exclaimed. She jerked back and seized the steering wheel but drove nowhere.

Out of the bank's wide white doors rushed three men, and the men standing outside in trench coats opened fire on them. I saw a blaze of fire from the barrel of a big hip-hugging gun. Two of the three men fell, and the door, which was slowly and automatically closing, was pushed open again; a woman in a white skirt and lavender sweater stood there with her hand to her mouth in an exaggerated gesture of awe. One of the men who had fallen jumped up and brushed off his clothes. He began to argue with the trench-coated men, and another man joined them from somewhere to the side.

"Oh, Christ," Nada said faintly, "it's a television show or something. A rehearsal."

I was trembling as much as she was but I didn't let on. "Oh, Nada, what did you think it was?" I said.

When we got to the zoo we saw the disappointing sign, WILL OPEN MAY 10. "I should have known better," Nada said. She glanced at me to see how badly I was taking this, but I was her darling, her good genius, and of course I didn't care about the zoo but only about her, and I was still upset from the fake bank robbery. I had never seen anyone killed in front of me, even if it did turn out to be make-believe.

"We'll come by again on May tenth, honey. I promise," Nada said.

But the wonderful day had not yet come to an end. We swung around and drove back home, seeing for ourselves how handsomely Fernwood emerged out of the anonymous miles of suburban wasteland that lay between it and the city. First you passed by a jumble of motels, gas stations, bowling alleys, discount stores, drive-in restaurants, overpasses, underpasses, viaducts, garished by giant signs of plump-cheeked boys holding hotdogs aloft, and one sign that caught my attention: a very American-looking man holding aloft a can of beer, with a puzzled expression, the caption being, *Read a beer can tonight*. Do you think I could have made up something so marvelous myself? Never, never! America outdoes all its writers, even its amateur writers!

Then you made your way through the first suburb, proletarian and proudly white Oak Woods, a dinky, arrogant neighborhood with a preponderance of American flags waving in the wind, and many used-car lots along the "Miracle Motor Mile." Then came the slightly better suburb of Pleasure Dells, as bereft of dells as Oak Woods was bereft of oaks, but decked out perhaps with pleasure and equipped with three vast, sprawling magnamarkets that sold not just food, apparently, but lawn chairs, cheap clothing, and all the drugs you might want to kill a vacant hour or so; an oceanic tide of automobiles was parked around these buildings.

We sped up a bit for the next suburb, where the highway's shoulders fell back and buildings were built farther from the road. This was Bornwell Pass, inferior to Fernwood but acceptable for certain kinds of shopping. One shopping plaza here with its parking lot must have covered several acres. The stores were not "shoppes" like those in Fernwood but just plain stores. "Isn't that vulgar?" Nada said.

Then we nearly broke through to the country, but it was an illusion—just a housing subdivision called Country Club Manor. As Nada raced by I glanced through the

D

gate (not a real gate but just two pillars of red brick to match the red-brick colonials inside), and Nada said, "That awful Vemeer built this slum." Her attitude cheered me.

On the other side of the highway, which had branched out now to a magnanimous eight lanes with snow-encrusted grass in the center, were more subdivisions, one after another: Fox Ridge, Lakeside Groves, Chevy Chase Heights, Bunker Hill Towne, Waterloo Acres, Arcadia Pass . . . Real-estate salesmen with no taste had driven us under the red-brick archways of some of these settlements, and Father had had to explain apologetically, "I'm afraid that . . . this sort of thing just won't *do*." Our English teacher up at Johns Behemoth, catering to the prejudices of his well-bred young pupils, kept referring to the "Fox Ridge mentality," which we were to understand was a conformity of deadly intensity, a mediocrity which stopped precisely at the clean white-and-black sign that proclaimed: FERNWOOD VILLAGE LIMITS SPEED LIMIT 45.

We sped past at sixty, and Nada said, more or less to me, "This is a lovely place to live." Slowing reluctantly for a traffic light, she said again, "It's lovely here," and after a few minutes muttered sideways to me, "Are you happy in Fernwood, Richard?"

"Some of my classmates aren't happy," I said, deliberately choosing the word "classmates" because it sounded so natural. "That boy whose mother drinks—"

"But are you happy?"

"Some of the kids who worry about their parents, you know, their parents fighting and maybe getting a divorce . . . well, they're pretty miserable, but not me."

"That's good," Nada said vaguely.

She swung off and into a parking lot, the one shared by the courthouse, the police station, and the library. All three buildings were constructed of the same red brick, with white shutters and trim and handsome broad chimneys.

"I want to check something," Nada said.

We went into the library, which looked just like a pleasant, homey home, with windows divided into many small white-rimmed squares and the words FERNWOOD PUBLIC LIBRARY in fancy wrought-iron letters, painted white. Coming out the door was Mavis Grisell, who smiled her fake exotic but perfectly friendly smile, showed an expanse of gums, and said, "Why, hello, Nada and Richard! Isn't it a lovely day?" Nada managed to get away from her, sending me a sideways glance that thrilled my poor nervous, fluttering heart. When she looked at me that way, inviting me to share a secret with her, I could not believe that she would ever run away from me again.

She sent me off vaguely in the direction of the children's bookshelf, me with an IQ high enough to impress the jaded Johns Behemoth, but I was agreeable and stood leafing through a book of big print and smudged illustrations, dealing with flying saucers. My nose had begun to run and I hadn't any tissue but I was cheerful just the same. Weren't the two of us together? I peeked around and saw Nada browsing through the *Recent & Readable* section, and then over to *Literature & Classics,* then twisting back around and surprising me, coming up to the *Leafing Shelf* where a few Fernwood ladies stood leafing through magazines and whispering together. Nada hunted around and found a magazine and opened it eagerly. I fixed the colors of the cover in my mind, so that I could look it up another time and see what had drawn her to it.*

The library had a kind of front lounge area, with comfortable leather sofas and chairs. For Smokers, a sign said agreeably. Everything in Fernwood was agreeable! The area was clearly modeled after an outdoor café or a cocktail lounge, and perhaps this accounted for the slightly confused, disoriented faces of the women and the two or three men who were sitting there, browsing and smoking. When I saw Nada head for the lounge I joined her there. She opened a magazine and let it lie on her lap. "Isn't this library nice?" she said. She spoke with a fierce whisper that was like a threat, a test: did she really hate it and wondered what I would say? What did she mean? On a sofa near the wall sat a man leafing idly through a magazine. I saw Nada's eyes move toward him several times, then she opened her purse and searched through it. "Richard, ask that man for a match," she said.

"Maybe I can find them in there," I said, reaching for her purse.

But she drew it onto her lap and let her gloved hands lie primly on it.

I approached the man shyly and whispered, "May my mother borrow a match?" The man did not glance up. I edged a little closer and said, "Mister"— and my voice gave a sudden croak so that the man jerked his head up and stared at me—"may my mother borrow a match?"

He looked past my insignificant head and took in Nada

* It turned out to contain an article on "The State of American Fiction," two-thirds of it concerned with the deaths of Faulkner and Hemingway, "which left a vacuum in our culture," and one brief paragraph near the end busying itself with twenty-one new, young, promising writers, one of them being Natasha [sic] Romanov.

and said, "Sure." His hair was close-cropped, blond maybe, shading into gray, but he wasn't very old. He had startling blue eyes. The matchbook he gave me was from the Whispering Dunes Motel, in Pleasure Dells of another state. I came dutifully back to Nada with this prize, and she lit her cigarette, and after a minute or so the man came, long-legged and casual, over to join us.

"Is that *Fortune* there?" he said, indicating something on a table.

"I don't know," Nada said.

He sat down anyway and leafed through some discarded magazines. "Huh," he said flatly, coming across a headline on the yellow banner of the *Reader's Digest* that struck him, "not that again." With one tobacco-stained finger he moved the magazine so that Nada could see the title, and she showed her fine teeth in a smile of pleasant sarcasm, and the two strangers exchanged sideways looks rather like the one Nada had given me over Mavis Grisell. My nose began to run alarmingly.

18

"There is this boy at school, whose parents live in Boston, who's so miserable and mean," I told Father the next time he appeared at home. "His mother's an alcoholic and she fights a lot with his father, and he worries about them—"

"Look, you ask that kid over for dinner," Father said sternly. "You hear? The poor little bastard!"

And he hurried upstairs, his scuffed shoes thumping heel-first on the carpeted stairs. He was in a rush: he'd just flown back from Ecuador and had to dress for a wedding reception out at the Vastvalley.

19

I'm sorry that the Vastvalley Country Club doesn't figure much in my memoir, because some people are interested in country clubs. Actually, my parents took me out there only once, for an expensive dinner in the presence of Mavis Grisell, the Spoons, a quiet, mousy, fawning couple named Hodge who had a fat boy my age, and an extremely charming man with a tiny mustache who later scandalized all of Fernwood by publishing, in the *Post,* an inside story on the fortune he had made by bugging (wiring) homes for jealous husbands/wives, and the pseudonyms he used to disguise his rich clients were impudently transparent.

Vastvalley is not the oldest or quite the best country club, if I am to believe the kids at Johns Behemoth and not Nada, who was much too defensive about the whole matter. I think she felt that she had leaped too quickly at the Vastvalley, and might well have held off for the Fernwood Heights. But anyway the Vastvalley was expensive enough to be reasonable, and rather hideously constructed. Imagine a very long building tugged in at each end to form a kind of semicircle, everything built of aged red brick and trimmed with black wrought iron in Englishy style. Imagine many gas lamps, and uniformed Negroes in quiet, efficient attendance, and the Ladies Lounge (again no apostrophe!) so thick with scarlet carpet that I could see, from outside, how Nada's high heels made a track in it, crossing and crisscrossing the tracks of other fair ladies. Imagine a pointlessly long hall, not quite straight (remember the construction of the building), and raw-looking but really quite finished wooden benches, redolent of English manors and primitive hunting halls now vanished from the earth, and wrought-iron lanterns dangling from the walls on spear-like devices. An odor of cleanser, perfume, and tobacco. In the lounge a pleasant odor of alcohol. Voices muffled by the thick rugs everywhere, and from distant rooms the sounds of billiard balls clicking, ice cubes clicking, cards being thrown on invisible tables with a clicking noise.

It was a dizzying trip for me, following all the adults and the one waddling fat boy along corridors, up and down short meaningless flights of steps, until we emerged into a great gold-ceilinged dining room that was not very crowded, out of which white-coated waiters moved hesitantly toward us like ghosts welcoming us to a graveyard. It was all very velvety, very nineteenth century, overdone with chandeliers and too many dusty plants in the corners, not quite far enough away for one to believe they were real. This was my dinner at the Vastvalley, on one lucky Sunday of my miserable life. It was just as bad for the fat boy, who had been promised (as I had) a "new friend" but who (like myself) was too shy or too stubborn to make the first gestures of friendship. After dessert he broke out into hives. While the adults had coffee and smoked luxuriously around the big table the fat boy reverently fingered his blotches and I sat waiting to leave, distracted from Nada's animated face by a furtive movement back in a corner—a shy cockroach trying to ascend the gold-papered wall.

20

When we got home Father said to me, eyebrows raised, as one man to another, "Buster, you certainly didn't contribute much to the conversation."

Nada said at once, "This child is ten years old!"

"Almost eleven."

"He's ten years old and extremely sensitive. What on earth do you mean by attacking him like that?"

"Tashya, I didn't attack him. I only said—"

"He hardly had his muffler off and you attacked him. Why should a child of ten, as intelligent as our son, bother with the drivel that went on around that table today? God! And that pimply-faced fat boy—"

"I only said . . ."

I took off my muffler miserably and hung it in the closet. Behind my back they were probably making signals to each other, to delay the argument for my "sake," and when I turned, Nada was brushing her angry hair back from her face and Father was smiling the way he smiled when guests were pouring in our front door.

"Guess I'll go up and do my math," I said.

I went upstairs, and Nada said gently, "Richard, you

should stand straighter." I was no sooner out of sight when I heard Father say, "That's the fourth time today you've told him that! Do you want him to . . ."

Upstairs I made my feet trudge along the familiar path to my room, and once I reasoned that they had moved to another room I kicked off my shoes and went back into the hall. I hope you won't think I was one of those round-foreheaded, pipsqueak, smart-aleck little brats if I tell you that I was certainly a genius—the devices I had for spying! And none of them suspicious, none of them likely to call attention to itself. In the kitchen, which was my parents' favorite refuge for serious talks, I had long ago known enough to leave the laundry-chute door slightly ajar. The door was painted green, like the wall, so it was very subtly camouflaged, my spying—standing up in the hall, with my head stuck inside the laundry chute, I could hear everything they said . . .

The fight over a stained silk cushion on a Queen Anne chair, on our first day in the house.

The fight over Father's Negro jokes at a party.

The fight over Father's "baggy trousers."

The fight over Father's shirts, which were all dirty.

The fight over Nada's correction of Father's pronunciation of "incognito."

The fight over Nada's naïve admiration for the local and internationally famous H—— F——, whom Father renounced with middle-class gusto, along with his wife.

The fight following from this, when Father called Nada a *parvenu.*

The shrieking fight over the mildew in the front lawn, which was gray-blue and deadly.

The hysterical fight over my eyeglasses. ("Whose eyes did he inherit, whose? He'll have glasses like the bottoms of Coke bottles . . .")

The fight over the canned goods in the basement storeroom, whose labels had all peeled off mysteriously.

The fight over the warped piano key—I believe it was G two octaves above middle C.

The fight over . . .

And, a week ago, another fight over—I believe it was over Jean-Paul Sartre, whom Father rejected as a "Communist writer."

And . . .

And all the other fights that were about nothing.

They always began like comic-strip fights, Father and Nada talking wildly and accusing each other of anything that came to mind. "Well, you looked at me as if I were dirt," Nada would cry, and Father would say, panting, "Well, you turned your back on me!" And I could almost smile with the familiarity of it all though I was sick of the game they were playing. Would it strain your patience if I were to suggest that they weren't really this stupid? My mother wasn't stupid but for some reason I will never know she acted stupid most of the time. She was deliberately, spitefully, stubbornly, passionately stupid. Father bellowed and blustered and stammered, but really, he had made a marvelous career in business, somehow, don't ask me how. He wasn't stupid either. He was stupider than she, but when they fought their famous fights it was almost a draw. The accusations, the stuttered insults, the invisible blows of abuse and torment that rose up the laundry chute to my tingling, jangling ear!

"Oh, you stupid man, you revolting vulgar bastard!" Nada cried. "How much longer can I take this? What are you doing to me? Why did you marry me if you hate me so much?"

"Me? What? Jesus Christ, you always switch things around—"

"You aren't even material for a good novel, you and those ignorant fools! It's just caricature, it's slop, I can't take it seriously and I'm losing my mind here—"

"*You're* losing your mind? What about me? You're starting the same tricks you used before—"

"Don't use that word *tricks*!"

"The same fucking tricks," Father boomed, "that you used two years ago, and this time if you pull out you can go right to hell and I'll bring up the poor kid my own way so he'll be safe from his nut of a mother—"

"You dirty bastard," Nada whispered, "you dirty filthy lying bastard!"

"Yessir, his *nut* of a mother! It's well known that you're neurotic as hell, and I wouldn't be surprised if all our friends knew it, I wouldn't be surprised if they all sat around and talked about it . . ."

When all their stage props were ripped away, they always showed that they needed no fresh reasons to hate. They simply hated.

21

I was too sick to go to school the following day, so Nada waited on me, brought my breakfast upstairs, pampered me. I noticed that her hair was long, brushed straight back from her forehead; it looked as if it hadn't been washed for a while. She brought me some magazines to read, anxious and apologetic, as if she knew I had overheard everything, and I leafed through the new *Time* and glanced at photographs, until my nausea rose suddenly at a picture of a mutilated Communist riot victim (the caption read, "After the dance, the piper to be paid") so that I leaned back trembling against my pillow.

Nada was looking out the window, distracted.

Have I ever mentioned Nada's total lack of interest in politics, in events, in reality? She never read the newspaper, never listened to the radio. Never. She might have believed that only vulgar people kept track of history, I don't know. "For me, history is what is in this room, nothing more," she had declared pompously to someone, sometime, within my hearing. She might have believed her brain too finely developed to be overloaded with the trivia of daily reality, daily suffering. Her brain was instead stuffed with books. What was "only real" couldn't be very important, and I have to confess to feeling this way myself. I have caught her solipsism from her, the way I used to catch colds and flu from her. A contagious woman!

It was a quiet day. I read, she read. But this quiet meant nothing because it was not a peaceful quiet. It was a heart-throbbing, pulse-quivering quiet, more terrible than screams and crashes. I wanted to crawl out of bed and press my aching eyes against Nada's ankles, kiss her feet, her shoes, her stockings, and beg her not to leave. Oh, don't leave! Not again! When she ran away from us the first time Father had told me sadly that my mother had died; I wasn't quite old enough to understand this. The second time she ran away I overheard his conversation (via an upstairs extension) with the private detective who was on her trail; but this time—no, I didn't think I could survive another time. I was too old now. I knew too much. I knew what those certain looks meant, the casual, friendly, erotic glance between strangers in a library browsing lounge, and my heart leaped at mysterious phrases spoken in German over the phone, with that sinister voice from New York. I had journeyed too far, I was Nada's son, I couldn't let her leave me. I would rather see her die than lose her. I would rather see her dead, wax-white, her smiles and sneers vanished, drained of blood and energy and appetite . . .

22

In the days of Nero (forgive my mentioning that beast's name, but he is appropriate) there was an odd fellow who had found out an exquisite way to make glass as hammerproof as gold: shall I say that the like experiment he made upon glass I tried to make upon myself? A metamorphosis? Shall I bother to add that I failed? My friends, I never shattered in any obvious way. I never exploded into pieces. And, seeing my bulk as it is today, you would smile to hear me talk thusly. Such a poor fat pimply boy, and only eighteen . . .

But yes, I am glass, transparent and breakable as glass, but—and this is the tragedy—we who are made of glass may crack into millions of jigsaw-puzzle pieces but we do not fall apart. We never fall apart. Instead we keep lumbering around and talking. We want nothing more than to fall apart, to disintegrate, to be released into a shower of slivers and have done with it all, but the moment is hard to come by, as you can see.

23 HOW TO WRITE A MEMOIR LIKE THIS

Since my forlorn days as a child, so minutely investigated here, I've done some reading in an attempt to acquire the language needed for me to write this memoir. You ordinary people who read and do not write, who "like to read" and know nothing of the sufferings of writers, how fortunate you are! You are truly blessed! My very brain ached with the agony of taking on Western Culture, and I fear very little of it got to me; if I were to dedicate this novel to anyone it would be to *that other unfortunate traveler* from whom I have stolen so much. It's no noble gesture for the dead to be honest. I acknowledge my master.

But I discovered something else, a depressing fact. Literature, art, like civilization itself, are only accidents. They are not planned. You gentle readers who opted to take Humanities courses now and then in college, who set upon a course in Shakespeare with a hearty stoicism and a big notebook, little did you or your professor understand that the whole thing is an accident, the art product an accident, like the products of violent seizures of nausea that overtake many of us after an arduous dinner. The work could have come out in any form, but it happened to come out in one form, and that form has crystallized and seems now, hundreds of years later, somehow planned.

But no, my friends, and no again, because once I thought as you do, once I assumed a majestic order and symmetry in art, thinking that, dear God, order and symmetry must exist somewhere. They must. But you don't find them in "art," because of all human endeavors "art" is the most pulsating, rippling, seething, improbable, and unpredictable of all the creations of man, like those babies born after expectant mothers' exposure to certain drugs and diseases—if you'll excuse that only halfway accurate metaphor. (I am very conscious of metaphors.) No, I'm afraid that you start out writing a memoir that seems simple enough, wanting only to get the truth down and forget about it, or, if you're lazier, you try to write a novel, something capricious, but somewhere in the process everything breaks down, won't work, is just an illusion. I sought a language for my memoir and turned desperately to the works of our "culture" but found there the same kind of seething, tortured products as the one I am turning out. There is a surface order and beauty, yes, but don't let that fool you. It's all as Tennyson remarked wisely, "We poets are vessels to produce poetry and other excrement."

I don't know what area of study I would have pursued had I not disintegrated; like Gustave, I might have "gone into" math or something similarly solipsistic and unhurried. But thinking it my duty to stretch the flayed skin of my childhood on some sort of skeleton of convention (I am anticipating alert readers for these metaphors!), I began to burrow and mutter through volumes of such works as are famous in our "culture." Therefore the technical devices I, as a writer, use, I readily admit them. I want to admit them, and everything. Maybe there are a few of you who want to write also, who have a lesser tale to tell—lesser, I should hastily qualify, in terms of moral cess-matter. Maybe there are some of you who have, in your homes, dog-eared copies of *The Writer* with earnest articles that will see you through crises of mental blocks, third-person narration, limerick verse. If so, I should call your attention to these short, cheerfully blocked-out, and fast-moving chapters. Or aren't they fast-moving? No matter. I have based some of them on an article concerned with "building suspense" and—you see how honest I am—even dull stretches can be used to build suspense if there is the promise of some violence to come. I do indeed promise violence, yes. VIOLENCE . . . VIOLENCE (this is for people standing at *Browse & Leaf* shelves in clean surburban libraries). I offer to them also ECSTASY . . . MORAL ROT . . . ANGST . . . KIERKEGAARD . . . and other frauds that bring a sardonic smile to your lips and mine, my university-educated readers, but that will snare lesser folk. FLAGEL-LATION interests some, those who know what it means, those who suspect what it means, and the great nation of those who want to look it up in order to use it three times and make it "theirs."

(All this is taken from an article called "Just What Is Reader Interest?")

Now you are wondering, what good did it do me to read a great deal? Ancient, Medieval, Renaissance, Neo-Classic, Romantic, Victorian, Modern, Avant-Garde—everything, what good did it do? Not much. My fever-ish mind, sievelike and pulsating constantly, loses most of what it takes in just as my stomach once lost most of its intake. I am a mess and messes don't take well to culture; they somehow distort it to look like themselves. But I learned enough to take the following steps for my memoir:

1. I know my characters. (Christ, I should know them!)
2. I know "where my story is going." (How could I not know?)
3. I am addressing a certain audience that shares with me a disdain for or outright rejection of murder, committed by a child or by just anyone at all. (If murder becomes acceptable again my memoir will be tossed upstairs in attics to molder quietly with *Penrod Jasper, Uncle Tom's Cabin, U.S.A.*, and other forgotten works.)
4. I provide some possibility—don't I? for "reader identification." (My theory is that we have all been children, each of us. I hope this common experience is enough.)
5. I provide a moral stance. (Indeed I do, and this stance I am taking with poor, blistered, sweating, swollen feet flat on the earth is that crime does not pay. It is not very original, I know.)
6. I write in a clear story line, with specific illustrations and description limited to "what's really necessary." (See January 1967, *Amateur Penman*, "Just What Is Really Necessary in Your Writing?")
7. I am wringing for all it's worth the "device of emotional preparation," that is, letting the readers come to know the characters. Will they give a damn about some poor bastard who is killed

on page one? They will not. They are hard-hearted and cynical. But move that poor bastard's death to page 300, build a story around him, and they will care if you've done your job and they have any tears left to be wrung out of their skulls, those selfish bastards.

8. I hide my hostility toward you, my readers, though I know beforehand that you are glancing through this book as you sit in the bathroom attuned to other activities, or as you wait in someone's downstairs den for that someone to announce he's ready, or as you wiggle and waggle around the library *Browsing & Drowsing* shelf, thinking *Expensive People* must be a social guidebook to Philadelphia highlife.

9. I observe just as much parallelism of paragraphing and sentence structure as I dare. (Note that each of these remarks begins with "I." Or did you already notice it, you clever son-of-a-bitch?)

10. I hide my hostility toward my readers. Desiring change, counterpoint, contrast, or whatever it is called, I sometimes vary paragraphs, sentences, and even chapters, that is, one chapter carries forward the story line but another retards it spitefully, building up "background" and human interest, if there are any humans to interest.

Other devices—for instance, my elaborate scheme of symbolism—I will leave unexplored, for my friends in the academic world to sniff out. But one influence I will admit is Melville, since I want to invest my story with as much significance as possible, taking two steps back for each single step forward, and therefore . . .

Therefore you will allow me certain rhetorical flourishes and tricks, and the pathetic Melvillian device of enormous build-ups for flabby walk-ons—opening paragraphs and even entire chapters that pave the way concretely enough while frisking about on a kind of ethereal abstract level in order to relate my confession to things sublime and infinite. I wouldn't mind a hesitant essay called "Rousseau and Everett: Liars or Saints?", or "Stendhal and Everett: Incest and Inscape," for instance. Since I plan on committing suicide immediately after this memoir is finished I won't be around to throw a damp blanket into the cogs of any critical/scholarly machinery and ruin anyone's theories. You can trust me! (Did I mention the suicide plan yet? I don't think so. More of that soon.)

And my style too, bogged down with adjectives and adverbs and a wistful reluctance for verbs and nouns —this is my "grand style." I have another, "colloquial style" or "just-a-good-kid style." This is self-explanatory. The grand style, though, may well get on your nerves (my stomach quivers when I embark on one of my Ciceronian tightropes), but it's necessary, and I'll explain why. I should have liked to write this memoir in epic form, in melodic and oratorical verse preceded by the strumming of a lute, but unfortunate the time is past for such epics just as they all say the time is past for tragedy, and "Just How Dead Is the Novel?" * So the best I can do to summon up the beauties of a past age is to juggle my syntax as well as I can, feeble though it turns out, at times closing my eyes and giving my fingers license to probe out what they will on the typewriter,

* Chapter from *Let's Write a Novel!* by Agnes Sturm. See also the much more chic *Waiting for the End* by Leslie Fiedler.

splattering out loose spines of sentences with as much frantic desperation as one steers a soap-box cart down a sharply inclined plane, hoping for the best but not expecting it, with a pale bravado of a grimace, a grin, for the spectators standing uneasily on the sidewalk: yet conscious of the many times the splatter falls short, dribbles, vomited out with the sort of asthmatic gasp that emits rusty water from antique faucets or rusty blood from panting fat-encrusted hearts.

This chapter must at one time or another throw up its hands in defeat ("throw up" is a deliberate pun, part of a pattern of puns, my dear squeamish readers!), and as good now as later; indeed, it can have no natural ending because it has no beginning, being just an off-the-keys aside to aspiring writers who have never "taken the plunge." I can't think of any final sentence for it. If I had it to do all over again—and I don't—I would omit this chapter altogether. Yes, I think I would omit it, but I don't want to mess up my page numbering. Ideally, I would go on at once from that pleasant little paragraph of a chapter, Chapter XX, to the following:

24

So Nada stayed around the house and nursed me. She was the kind of woman who looks at you only when something has gone wrong—eye blackened, a length of stark white bone piercing your skin. But maybe I'm being too hard on her. She was like any mother, I think, if this hypothetical mother had a prodigious intelligence, a romantic restlessness, and confused memories of a childhood that was, so I gathered, soured with tales of Russia, a dark planet all to itself. And if this mother was beautiful too, that's important. Don't crab about beautiful women and their immoral lives if you're too ugly to have had the opportunity for immorality; psychology, homegrown and professional, has exposed all *that*. So she was intelligent and imaginative and beautiful, and let's blame a few hyperfunctioning glands and nodes as well. I think she was what most American women would like to be. Don't sneer, don't hiss. I am an amateur at life, and would it surprise you to know that I am only eighteen years old? Eighteen, yes, but precocious. And I think that most American women would like to be Nada, just as Nada thought she would like to be Nada —that is, the image, the dream self that was Nada, not the real, unhappy, selfish, miserable, and rather banal person.

You women, wouldn't you like to be Nada as she appeared to outsiders? I hope you noted the coats, the clothes, the yellow cars, the house, furniture, parties, country club, etc. And she was also a writer! "Why, I think that's just wonderful!" "How do you find time?" "What does it feel like to be so talented?" "And what does your husband think?"

And you men, you would all like a Nada of your own. If your income is above a certain level you'd need her to show it off, wouldn't you? That pleasant, sandy-faced woman you married would fade into a living room's beige walls if Nada walked into the room, not just because she was beautiful but because she had . . . whatever it was certain women have, I don't pretend to know. Your wife supposes herself chic, and salesladies flatter her, but Nada didn't need anyone's flattery. You'd rather have Nada, bitch that she was, and notice other men's envious stares. The reality would be hell, but then reality is always hell.

Nada, Nada, Nada . . .

If this sounds delirious it is because I was a little delirious. There was something so vicious and final about their argument the night before that I knew she was leaving. I think I knew it before she did. All that day she wandered in and out of my room, she sat on the edge of my bed and laid her cool, remote hand on my feverish brow, glancing at me with the dim, mild surprise of a person noticing life in a store dummy or in a corpse. I never meant anything to her, never! I was perhaps some outlandish protoplasmic joke Father had wished upon her one night late after a cocktail party. I was flesh and bone and blood and brain tagged Richard, and "Richard" must have evoked in her mind mechanical thoughts of guilt and responsibility and love. She loved me when she was happy. She loved me when she happened to notice me. She loved me if I was good, if Father was good, if she'd been invited out both nights of a weekend, if the world was going well, if the humidity was low and the barometer agreeable: whereas I loved her always, when she was a bitch or when she was saintly, lovely or ugly, with short shining hair or long greasy hair . . . I loved her and what good did it do either of us?

"There are certain times in a person's life," Nada began, trying to smooth out the wrinkles in my sheet with her hand, "when one simply has to shake himself free. You remember how your little puppy Spark used to shake water off himself? Wasn't that cute? Well," she said, her eyes vague with the impropriety of this metaphor, "well, everyone must free himself of impossible presures, of restraints and burdens that suffocate him."

"If you leave this time, don't bother coming back," I said.

"There is nothing personal, never anything personal in freedom," Nada went on, maybe not hearing me or not caring, "freedom is just a condition one has to achieve. It isn't a new place or a new way of living. It's just a condition like the air that surrounds the earth. We can't breathe without it but—"

"I know all about the air!" I shouted. "So forget it! Shut up!"

"Richard, what?"

"Forget it! Forget everything! Shut up and get out of here!"

And she stood, quiet and serious, looking at me the way she looked at Father or women with their hair in rollers out on the street or the messes neighborly dogs made on our lawn. Her face was magnificent and pale, her eyes dark, a little demented, as if tiny curving pieces of glass had been fitted over them for some weird theatrical purpose. Oh, I don't know! I don't know what she looked like! I watched and watched her for years. I stared at her and loved her. I have photographs of her in my desk drawer that I finger and caress and still I don't know what she looked like; she passed over from being another person into being part of myself. It was as if Nada, my mother, had become a kind of embryonic creature stuck in my body, not in a womb maybe but a part of my brain. How can you describe a creature that is lodged forever in your brain? It's all impossible, a mess . . .

25

For instance, let me revert to an earlier memory. I am eight years old and asthmatic. Nada nurses me, fusses over me, dresses me in Junior Collegiate Togs: resentful of my sickness for eleven solid sulky days, on the twelfth day she suddenly blossoms with love. Yes, good. All this is familiar enough. Nada—"Call me Nadia, Nadia," she pouts prettily—Nada blooms and swells with love for me, her son. It's a mystery what is behind it—who knows? An argument with Father? An overheard remark at someone's party questioning Mrs. Everett's *motherliness*? An accidental glance at my red-and-white blotched, mealy face? An article in a doctor's waiting room titled "Do You Harbor Unconscious Hostilities toward Your Child?"?

Most things remain mysteries.

Nada bundles me up and piles me in the car, not today will she leave me, not for a moment, absolutely not! She and I are "good friends." We will "stick together" and "tell each other everything." When I was eight I had little idea of the vast world beyond our village, and so I could not yet imagine the fabulous attraction every other part of the world might have for Nada. I was ignorant then and safe. She takes me to the Village Gourmet Shop on that day, to buy specialties of Chinese and Malayan and Viennese cooking, wrapped up in trim white packages and never showing a bit of that streaky, watery blood that shows through packages bought at the plebeian supermarkets Nada detested. No blood, nothing. Cleanliness. She takes me along to the library (another library, an innocent library, with a gaudy bulletin board in honor of Halloween, perhaps, announcing on orange posters the "Village Literary Society Will Meet Nov. 5 —Discussion: How to Relate to Beatnik Poetry"). A lovely library—how I love libraries, any and all libraries, those sanctuaries for the maimed and undanceable, the lowly, pimply, neurotic, overweight, underweight, myopic, asthmatic . . . Few are the flirtations in a library, I insist, though Nada never had to search far for an adventure. Few are the assaults, physical or verbal. Libraries exist for people like me.

And beautiful, heartbreaking, are the chance encounters in a library—that reverent hushed tone, that respectful, resigned seriousness even the most flighty of ladies cannot help—all these are beautiful. For, in front of that very bulletin board a lady in a powder-velvet lavender hat stopped to chat with my Nada, a handsome, ageless woman of forty or so, gloved, nicely shod, friendly. "We would be so very, very honored if you would come to our little meetings sometime," the lady whispered. She indicated the orange poster. "Of course we're just amateurs but we absolutely love to read. We're just wild about literature. Especially the very latest things. And the oldest things too, I mean the classical things that will never die out. Do you think you might ever come talk to us about your own creative writing? Please think it over, we'd be so grateful! Next month is my turn to present a talk. I'm in charge of the Italian Renaissance and it's such a responsibility. I get so frightened standing in front of a group, but the minute I begin I forget all my nervousness . . ."

And Nada takes me merrily along with her to the florist's, where she orders some expensive flowers for a party or something soon due at our house, and the foppish young man behind the counter stares at her with that awed reserve, that grudging admiration, that the effeminate male must acknowledge in the presence of a beautiful woman. I see all this, and more. Such memories come back to me in my sick states, snares of the past, what sorry past I have. And she whisks me off to the next stop, the El Dorado Beauty Salon, where few children are brought and those who are brought spend their sullen time running aimlessly up and down the aisles. Not I, not Richard, good asthmatic Richard, content to sit in a harmless unpadded chair, staring. How lovely the El Dorado Beauty Salon is! (I wonder if it still stands.) Imagine a panoramic confusion of plush pink and fragile gold, of slick plastic evergreens perched high atop plastic pillars. Imagine the sweet, lisping strains of music that seem to be engendered out of the very air itself. Imagine the many ladies moving about, smoking cigarettes, their hair bunched up in dozens of pink rollers, like bobbins. Imagine the forbidden archways, done in gold, with baroque signs above them: *Tinting Room. Pedicure Room. Wig Room. Electrolysis Room.* A glimpse of more beauty inside, ornate mirrors, black porcelain sinks, stools, couches, big gold ashtrays. Ah, this is the other side of suburbia's public heaven!—the wings, the backstage, the private dressing rooms of the beautiful.

Richard sits still, alone and hard of breath. A harmless child. No one sees him, no one can guess what violence lies leaden in that tube of a body, that wheezing reed. Eight years old and looking more like six, behind his thick glasses he sits dutifully and awaits his mother.

Back and forth before him stroll ladies of monstrous appearance—some of them dressed in very sheer, flimsy outfits of blue with El Dorado stitched on the collars, the outfits worn for special rinses, tintings, bleachings, and who knows what other rare chemical changes. Atop their heads are masses of plastic cones and cylinders, some of them enormous as tin cans, others small as my little finger, which is fairly small. They stroll about, smoking, chatting, quite content.

Other ladies, grounded, sit beneath great blowing hairdryers and smoke and leaf through fashion magazines. A Negro woman of feline suppleness sits before one of the ladies, doing her nails. A cart on two big wheels, like a flower cart, and indeed it is an imitation flower cart, is set before the lady and on it are dozens of jars of fingernail polish and many other items, vaguely surgical in appearance. The Negro woman chatters happily as she does her customer's nails. Pink seems to be the only acceptable color; red is out. Pink nails. Pink toenails. Pink lips. Some ladies wear, wrapped over their profusion of bobbins, a netlike thing of pink, which is tied loosely in back and which gives them the dreamy, exotic look of having been pulled up from the sea, a perfumy sea that is their true element.

My Nadia is for the moment behind a screen of slick plastic ferns, in the hands of a Negro woman who washes hair. Three Negro women wash hair behind the ferns. Forever and ever, day after day, they wash hair behind those ferns. Nada is made to sit back, her chair is partially collapsed and her hair drawn down into a black porcelain sink; so strangely passive is she, so wondrously obedient, that it is possible for me to think she is not so unusual a woman: she could be any woman. A blasphemy!

Not Nada, but any other woman? Could any other woman have made me what I am? Now the washing is over, Nada's chair is brought back up and she is sitting, making a face, and the good handy Negro woman wraps a white towel around her head. End of the first step.

I pick up a copy of *Vogue* with a ripped cover so that Nada will not see me watching her. She stands, she leaves the vale of ferns and crosses to a larger area, all mirrors and gold and waxy fake flowers in big black vases. Women everywhere! Nada passes through them, to a certain chair, a certain man. He is Mr. Stanevicus, a very popular hair stylist, very expensive. Mr. Stanevicus eyes Nada with cool indifference. I have to inch my chair out a little so that I can see everything, though it might break my heart. With *Vogue* on my meager lap I look up to watch Nada, jealous of Mr. Stanevicus and resentful of his indifference, his flippant razor and his stiff, high-brushed blond hair; she sits, he drapes a white cloth around her, he stands with all his weight on one foot while he questions her about something, then his razor begins, his hands move deftly about her wet humble head, and the danger she is in suddenly terrifies me. Is it possible that Nada might die? Some day die? That her lovely blood might be spilled?

I open *Vogue* hastily and find myself staring down upon a photograph of Mrs. Stanislav Proctor, a beautiful woman with hair snipped shorter than mine, slicked back, smoothed to the skull, her eyes fixed up elaborately with thin rims of rhinestones on the eyelids, and eyelashes thick as fern or ivy in a sumptuous garden—heavy, heavy eyelashes, sooty tangles. She stares at me from under these lashes. Decked out in a pilot's outfit of gold and silver, she wears boots that dazzle the eye so that one cannot tell if they are gold or silver or another precious substance; her gloves are nets of silver through which her enormous spiked golden fingernails protrude; in the careless crook of her left arm she carries her pilot's helmet, a large helmet decorated with sequins. Careless also is the unzipped front of her cockpit suit, which shows an alarming dip down into the pale privacy of her bosom. My eight-year-old's eyes sting, lured down into such depths. A caption tells me that she and her cousin, the famous diplomat Hendrick Hundt, have been flying private planes since their childhood and that they hold world records.

I turn the page and here is another beautiful woman, with shoulder-length wild hair and large sunglasses over her eyes. She is the Duchessa of Vilesia, wife of Silas Hobbit the movie-maker, and she is modeling her custom-made ermine hunting outfit in preparation for an expedition to the Arctic. The lovely Duchessa of Vilesia! Even her knee-length boots are of soft ermine, and her pale, pale skin has the downy look of some magic texture, hardly ordinary skin. Careless in the crook of her arm is a rifle with a powerful scope. Behind her on a wall, slightly out of focus, is an enormous moose's head, stuffed, upon whose nose someone has jauntily stuck a pair of sunglasses that are the exact copy of the Duchessa's— how truly conquered is that beast!

I look up. A few yards away appears a handsome lady of about fifty. She takes off her fur-trimmed coat and gives it to an attendant, she approaches one of the chairs and is welcomed into it by another male stylist, much like Mr. Stanevicus; a solid lady with thick, shining blond hair and platinum fingernails. But, alas, at once the wig comes off in the young man's hands: out come pins, fixtures, and the wig is rigorously brushed while the lady herself sits pallid and suddenly ugly in her chair, with her own flat, skimpy brown hair reflected back to her in the mirror. She is given the wig and brushes it herself, fondly and vigorously, while her stylist begins to brush her hair, her own hair, and the two of them perform exactly the same motions, their arms moving in exactly the same rhythm, one brushing a wig and the other brushing a head.

I turn the pages of my magazine. It is all I have, all I've been given. Time passes. An hour passes. Another hour passes, very slowly. My eyes are puffed up from the hairspray in the air, or the smoke, or the perfume, or the swampy female heat that is everywhere about me. At last Nada appears, a new Nada, with her dark hair cut short and shaved on her neck but teased up to a peculiar height and looped down upon her pale forehead in snaky ringlets. My Medusa! I am leaden but her appearance wakes me; I manage to get out of the chair by myself, but I look so feeble that Nada stoops and says, "Are you having an attack?" The finest moments of my life have been those when I was able to tell my mother truthfully that I was not having an attack.

When we get to the car Nada notices with alarm the packages of food—forgotten all these hours!—and marred now with watery, sticky streaks of blood. In disgust she throws them out. She throws all three packages in a barrel marked FILL ME UP.

. . . And so she did exist outside me, I can see her or half-see her, she did exist, she was a quite independent being. Two Nadas existed—the one who was free and who abandoned me often, and the other who has become fixed irreparably in my brain, an embryonic creature of my own making, my extravagant and deranged imagination—and I loved them both, I swear that it was both of them I craved. And so when Nada said to me on that day, "There is nothing personal, never anything personal in freedom," I understood that the free, restless Nada was asserting herself, and that I could not hold her back. *If you leave this time, don't bother to come back . . .*

26

Father had flown to South America again on a Wednesday, and when he returned on Saturday Nada was gone. On Friday afternoon I jumped down from the Johns Behemoth school bus (a station wagon without markings) and ran boyishly up our front walk, to show a possibly watching Nada that I was healthy again, and when I opened the front door the foyer smelled of her luggage, a smell I didn't know I knew so well, and there came Ginger shuffling apologetically toward me, rubbing her nose with a wretched, distracted, embarrassed air that told me everything I needed to know.

I took from her the letter Nada had left me and went with dignity up to my room. I did not cry. I lay on my bed and looked up at the ceiling of this strange house, wondering how I had come here, who I was, to whom I belonged—which harnessed set of adults—but knowing there was a hard, sharp kernel of fire in my stomach that had to be kept from bursting out into flame. And did it burst out? Did it?

Everywhere else in my body, flooding into my brain

and my poor aching eyes, there was a desire for sleep, for heavy, inert, dry-mouthed sleep of the kind drowned men sleep, tossing and turning gently on the ocean floor. So I slept and I did not dream. Ginger scratched and snuffled outside the door and finally knocked, but I told her in Nada's precise stagey voice that I was "all right, thank you," and finally she left, and the day turned into night and I slept, I slept peacefully, and the next day dawned without my noticing, and I woke to hear Father yelling into my face unintelligible nightmare words about some bitch who had run out on us for the third time.

27

Thereupon followed a strange idyllic interlude lasting ten days. If Father received any communication from Nada he did not tell me about it. We journeyed about together, he and I, two feckless, energetic bachelors, taking in movies, having dinner out at sunny, friendly restaurants in which children like myself were welcome, going to a "live" wrestling match all the way downtown where the very air about us stank of sweat and silky shorts and cigar smoke and everything fake and honest in its fakery, dreamily honest! And we took in late late movies on the television set in Father's room (he and Nada, sad to tell, had not shared a room for several years) and ate potato chips and pickles and other slop together until two in the morning, sleepy, slow, oddly pleased with each other, the way men on a slow, sinking ship must be pleased with the companions fate has doled out to them—who are they to complain, after all? And we went for odd meaningless drives in and around Fernwood Heights, Father with a cigar stuck in his teeth and his sad, pouched eyes roaming about the late-winter hillsides.

One evening, coming out of the Fernwood movie house, we encountered Tia Bell and a middle-aged woman who looked like an aunt, and Tia strode over to us and seized Father's hand. "Elwood, is it true?" she said. Father withdrew his hand with dignity—the most dignity I had seen in him—and said he had no idea what she was talking about. But hadn't Natashya . . . hadn't she . . .? Father explained that his wife had gone east to visit relatives, that was all. He stared into Tia's widened, sympathetic eyes and lied with no skill, so abrupt and reckless that Tia must have admired him for it. No doubt she went home and called all of his and Nada's "friends" to praise Father for his stoicism.

Father took me down to work with him. He had his own office, and there was a hallway of smaller offices that were "under him." He had his own pert, cute little clipped-haired secretary, so much more pleasant than Nada that it was painful to see. He was a vice-president of some kind, I have yet to explain. I don't know what he did though he explained it to me several times that day. He showed me his company's product, a strand of very thin, nearly invisible wire that glowed in the light from the window behind him. (This company was GKS, I think. Before this he worked for OOP, and afterward for BWK.) Oh, he was a fine giant of a man still, with his hair grown a little thin on one side of his head but thick on the other, and one shoulder maybe sinking a little more than ever toward the earth, and his suit was

E

rumpled and twitching with good humor, and the tip of the white handkerchief in his breast pocket was drooping, and one of his socks was royal blue and the other navy blue; and his teeth looked stained, for when Nada left us ordinary sanitation measures were suspended, and as he held the wire up for me to see, his big thick fingers were trembling. We were grim and happy together, like two bachelors. Sometimes I caught him glancing at me as if thinking, Who is this scrawny little bastard I'm stuck with? But then he would smile like a large Boy Scout and offer me some Sweet Peach chewing gum, which he carried around all the time, to give to office girls and all the other simple, eager-to-please souls of the sort that swarmed in the part of the world he controlled.

Here he had a handsome, broad desk cluttered with things that looked important, and a buzzer system, a few telephones, many loose plastic pens, a letter opener of brass, a paperweight of heavy purplish stone, anything one might want in an office. At home he had nothing. Here the other men and the office girls smiled at him and knew who he was; at home there was no one to smile, and anyway he was nothing. But he was a brave comrade for me in those days, allowing me to skip school, as if Nada's escape were a kind of holiday, and I want to record how good he was to me up until the time he too cracked.

This happened one evening after we came home from a bowling alley. We were both lousy bowlers, and I think that might have precipitated his breakdown. Father was the sort of man who cannot bear to be outdone at anything. I had heard about him from boys at Johns Behemoth whose fathers knew him, or who had friends who knew him, and the rumor was that Elwood Everett

admired men like himself, young men, who did everything he had done at that age except for the one final
fatal step that suggested they were perhaps equal to
him—then the game was over. This was a joke among
people who knew, but Father never knew, thinking himself broad-minded and fair as any American. The fist-
striking, back-slapping, ale-drinking bowlers at the Oak
Woods bowling lanes we went to got on his nerves, not
because of their lower-class happiness, but because of
the way their pins crashed and flew and fell, rolling
helplessly at the back of the alleys, like creatures fallen
with side-splitting laughter. Ah, we both hated those
men!

And he kept ducking back into the sleazy bar off the
alleys while I bravely plodded around in my too large
and ludicrously stiff bowling shoes, carrying my too heavy
bowling ball balanced against my chest, so that on the
way home his driving was extravagant and caused people
to honk their horns at him. All this got him into the
mood, but it wasn't until he had downed a glass of some
special Irish whisky that he began to blubber.

Have you ever seen a large man blubber? Well, perhaps blubbering always indicates large men; small men
whimper, I suppose. I'm large now myself, and I blubber
every night and sometimes while I write this memoir,
when a word or two releases in me whole floods of salty
tears. Father did indeed blubber, wiping his nose on the
edge of his forefinger, but he did more than that—goddam him, excuse him, forgive him—he began to talk.

"Now, Dickie, your mother is unstable. We know
that. We are rational about that, we understand," he
began. He was looking at me man to man; nothing
terrifies a boy more. "But we are human beings too,

yes, we are human, and human beings can't always control themselves. Look, I'm not ashamed of crying. Don't be embarrassed, son. I'm not ashamed and don't you be ashamed. I'm an honest man. I have nothing to hide."

He poured himself more whisky and seemed about to offer me some, then remembered who I was. "We want to understand her sickness and forgive her and make her well, Dickie, my poor kid, but it's awful hard when she's such a . . . she's such a bitch, why hide it? Everybody knows it, why hide it?" He laughed. His laughter at such times was bearlike and wheezing. "Women in this country, Dickie, this good old America, are all trying to be like Natashya, and Natashya has succeeded, oh yes, she has succeeded, she has everything she wants and then doesn't want it, she doesn't know what she wants, she never does any work—good sweet Jesus, never, never!—even though she was living in a room with a hotplate and cockroaches when I found her, but you won't hear about that! Bébé and Mimi and Fifi and Tia and all the girls won't hear about that, and you can bet your ass that Dean what's-his-name, that fairy with the English accent, you can bet he won't hear about it, that phony son-of-a-bitch with his phony vocabulary! *Aggrandizement*, he said the other night—what the hell kind of talk is that? He pulled it out of the air! And talking about some poem to Lesbia—what the hell kind of talk is that with women present? Those intellectual bastards always get onto things like that. Their minds are filthy, and it comes out disguised as a joke. Where I come from, buster, you don't joke about serious things like that, anyway not with women around, and I'll warm your skinny little ass if I ever hear you talking smart. You understand? One of us is going to teach you some manners and it won't be your bitch of a mother, that's for goddam sure—

"Now, look. Look. Sit still. I want to tell you how things are, I want to make it all clear and aboveboard," he said, sobbing again so his nose began to run, and I sat in a agony of terror at what he might say. "One of us is going to tell the truth! Oh, not her—not her! Fancy little Natashya with one hand in my pocket and the other inside my trousers—not her, she won't tell it, but I will! I don't lie! All your life you can look back on this talk and think how your daddy told you the awful truth, no matter how it hurt him, and how your mother wouldn't give you the time of day if you were drowning in the bathtub, and you remember that—

"What's wrong, where are you going? Sit down. Sit still. It all began when she was going to have a baby, and that baby was you," he said, slowing a moment to get his bearings and bending over me with one arm out behind me along the back of the sofa and the other extended, his big fingers closed about the glass. "Yes, that baby was you! Jimmy—I mean Dickie —what the hell am I saying? Jimmy's my kid brother, he's forty now, how's that for a scream? My kid brother is forty! No, you're Dickie—Dickie—that baby was you. Now you know where babies come from, don't you? They teach it in school now or somewhere, so you know . . . Stop crying for Chrissake, I'm not going to hit you, you think I'm like your mother? Shut up that crying! It started with her pregnant, and maybe she wanted to flit around a little more and blush over the compliments she got for her ass, or her stories, or both— you know her!—and she started acting nuts right then, a lovely young girl of twenty and already cracking up, selfish like an oyster you can't pry open and the only way you can get it to recognize you is to smash it against the wall! Well, she was pregnant and stayed out late, sitting around brooding in the park and maybe picking up stray niggers that wouldn't object to a round back in the bushes, even with a nut that wouldn't wear stockings to her own wedding until I said to her, What the hell are you pulling? What the hell? Just what the hell? So she knuckled under and wore them no matter how hot it was that day, and that was that, but then when she got pregnant she went nuts again and said how she wanted to have an abortion and stayed away in some goddam hotel and had the doctor all lined up—

"What? No, sit still, the bathroom can wait. You can go to the bathroom all night long when I get through! She had the doctor all lined up, Dickie-boy, and it was a matter of money, and she called me up and started screaming over the phone and calling me every filthy name she knew that the niggers or somebody taught her, maybe those fake Russians that were crawling all over New York and trying to write poetry—they think they're so much better than the Reds but I say shit, at least the Reds stayed over on their side of the ocean and that's more than all those goddam other immigrants are doing, and I don't exclude those spics and crud coming up and landing in New York, and it's the same way in England, don't worry! Same goddam mess! And then she called me up next morning and said no, she didn't want the abortion, and she talked about it the way you talk about buying a new car, you think you should wait until fall to economize, then she changed her mind again and said she did want it, she couldn't live with me and couldn't have any kid of mine—but she could have some nigger or spic or Jew kid, I suppose, I wouldn't doubt that, she's balled more Jews, Dickie-boy, than I have black-balled in my clubs, and I kid you not. But listen," he said, his voice breaking, "listen. She's run out again and it's just us and we gotta stick together, what if she doesn't come back? What if she doesn't come back? We gotta forgive her, she can't help it if she's a bitch and her father or somebody was nuts. We gotta forgive her and understand and . . ."

And he waddled his big buttocks over across the cushion to me and lowered his face onto my shoulder, weeping. He snuffled and bellowed and the whisky glass tilted so that whisky ran onto my leg and down inside my shoe, and I didn't care, I just sat there waiting for it to be over so that I could sleep. Even the nausea in my stomach was pressed down by this paralyzing heaviness that came over me, and I thought, Thank God I'm going to die. Thank God I won't be alive after this.

28

I stayed in that languorous trance for a few days. Then, on my birthday, I had enough foresight to ask Farley Weatherun if I could visit with him overnight, since Father would take me out to a restaurant and for dessert a simpering waitress would bring a cake adorned with a giant sparkler to our table, and I wasn't up to it, not quite up to it. So Farley said sure, why not, though it was a little strange because we weren't especially good friends, and we were fooling around with a few other kids in the dormitory when a gay, floating sensation rose in me and buoyed up my heart and I told them excuse me, I'd be back in a minute, and ran down the corridor and outside without bothering with my coat.

Intoxicated, serene, and mindlessly happy, I floated across the campus, and no stares or glares caught my eye, neither from bemused after-dinner-tramping instructors nor my classmates, so accustomed to nuts. We were brilliant, we Johns Behemoth brats, but we were nuts, and why hide it? But there are nuts and nuts, just as there are mothers and mothers, and far better to be a serene nut than one who overturns tables. Oh, what did I have in mind when I ran out? Not a little was I buoyed along the walks by a pleasant thought having to do with how I could get her back, or how I could discover why she had left—what was lacking in me—how I could amend it, humbly and with slicked-down hair, a good kid, just a good kid trying to survive, prelobotomized and prepubescent!

Now I beseech the fates to visit me once more with that eerie happiness, that dazzle of nutty chaste innocence that flooded my body on that day, seven-thirty on a March Wednesday, my eleventh birthday and first deathday! I beseech the fates, the saints, Christ, and God Himself in his gold foil robes to electrify my flabby waste of a body with the glow of that fire! I swear to you, my readers, that I was at last coming alive, and I had been in a trance for many days. Do you know what it is to be sleeping and yet awake, awake and yet sleeping? How you can't shake it off, can't quite open your eyes? My God, nothing is more terrifying! I had sunk into that kind of stupor listening to them argue, through

128]

the laundry chute, and rose temporarily out of it only to ebb back again when Nada tried to smooth out my sheet with her hand and told me everything I expected, and then I had sunk heavily into it when Father wept on my shoulder and told me . . . what he had told me— I won't go into that again (words on lavatory walls are poetry compared to Father's man-to-man combat), and now I was coming out of it again because—do you see? —it seemed to me I was going to find out an answer at last.

I vaulted up the steps of the Main Building but everything was dark. Did I let that stop me? No more than temporarily! I vaulted over the side of the little brick wall and ran around the corner, on the path that said DELIVERYMEN USE THIS ENTRANCE and that was off-limits for us scholars. The backdoor was locked and darkened too, but without hesitating, in my warming, dazed excitement, I tapped at the windowpane with my gnawed knuckle and it broke like magic, shattering down upon me. I brushed everything aside, splinters, slivers, tears (was I crying?), and crawled through the window, severing a small vein in my leg but never mind, never mind. Once inside, I ran along the dark corridor and even sped past my destination, braking suddenly and skidding into a porcelain drinking fountain, but whirling about, and there it was—the Records Room, the sanctuary where so many secrets lay entombed about us Johns Behemoth boys and we powerless to know them. I got inside this room too, somehow, though the transom atop the door was rusty and cranky, and the blood that came from somewhere was slippery as hell, and once down inside the room I threw on with a triumphant flick of my wrist a whole galaxy of flickering, shivering

E*

fluorescent lights, and there it was! A wall of filing cabinets! This was heaven itself! My heart was pounding with excitement as if I were about to witness a vision. I ran, slipping and sliding, to the drawers and groped around looking for "E," unable to find it for an agonizing few seconds, until I remembered sharply that "E" was near the beginning of what was called the alphabet. I yanked out the big drawer and pawed through the manila folders, panting, gasping, and when I found "Everett" a cloud seemed to pass over my mind and I was quite mad with happiness, but only for an instant. Then I yanked it out. I slashed through the papers— papers of graphs and numbers that looked like the exam I had taken, and there was my pathetic medical report, filled out by an indifferent quack who charged Nada sixty dollars, and my five letters of recommendation from former teachers, gibbering with enthusiasm no doubt, but I hadn't any time for them, and finally I found what I wanted. It was the IQ score. There were two papers and one said 153 and the other, dated more recently, said 161. I stared from one paper to the other until it dawned upon me what those numbers meant.

Then the hot kernel of fire burst in my stomach and I began to sob. I sobbed with rage. What did she want from me then? What more could she want? I couldn't do any better. I had even pushed myself beyond what I could do, and still it wasn't enough for her—I wasn't enough for her—and what else could I do? I tore the papers in pieces. I picked the rest of the folder up from the floor and tore it, and I yanked out the drawer so that it fell and struck my leg (later a great black-and-orange bruise was to appear, big as a grapefruit, on my thigh), and suddenly there were folders everywhere, flying in the air, being torn, struck, ground underfoot, and I picked up a stool and sent it crashing into the flickering fluorescent tubing overhead with a strength I didn't know I had, and I swear to you—yes, I formally swear—that never in my life until that moment had I truly been alive! Never!

Now every cell and tube was throbbing with a joy that had no humor, was beyond humor, and my bones creaked, so much was demanded of them, and the little muscle in the center of me, my delicate, wheezing heart, swelled like any fine organ to take on this challenge and sent blood pumping to all nooks and corners of my body! It was wonderful! Wonderful! I yanked more drawers out, I skidded on the papers, I crashed sideways into someone's desk and turned my rage to it, my fingers groping in a drawer and seizing a jar of ink that crashed against the wall not a half-second later, and the splattered droplets mingled with my hot, happy tears, and by the time they came for me I had thought of something further, the best and happiest trick of all: I was vomiting over everything, summoning up from my depths the most vile streams of fluid that had ever graced any Record Room in history.

29

That was the end of Johns Behemoth for me, and it got back to me from Gustave, via his mother, via the Spoons, from the very mouth of Dean Nash himself, that he had always had reservations about the Everetts, all of them. The cultural background was spotty, irregular, Bohemian when it wasn't just plain Philistine, the emotional maturation levels of both child and parents were clearly low, and Johns Behemoth would never again lower its standards out of a desire to accommodate someone's pleas. No, never! And Gustave imitated the way our good dean must surely have pursed and stretched down his lips and tilted his nose up as if to get a whiff of fresh aristocratic air unbesmirched by the stink of vomit that seemed always about me.

part II

1

My body tingled for a few days, then I heard a high uncertain buzzing in my ears, then the tingling faded away and the buzzing disappeared as if someone had pulled out my plug.

I remember crying against Father's shirt front and feeling his big loving hands on me, patting my back. He forgave me. And now we had a new maid named Florence, who supposedly knew nothing of our troubles, and she said I was her good boy, her good, good boy, and her voice was always raspy and sincere. People came to visit—not me but Father, who needed visits—and I overheard Mavis Grisell and Tia Bell and Charles Spoon and the Griggses and Bébé and everyone tell Father to drop in for cocktails soon, and if he had to leave town they'd be glad to take in Richard (me) for a few days, and above all he shouldn't *worry*. Things would turn out in the end. After that we didn't hear from them any more.

And life without Nada was a surprise, because it was so much like life with Nada. We discovered that she hadn't been around the house that much. It was good to discover that! "What do we care, huh? What the hell," Father would say in a brave, gruff voice to me as we raided the refrigerator at midnight. We ate like pigs. Father gained weight and patted his stomach, saying to what few people stopped in around five for drinks, mostly businessmen on their way through the city, "Really putting it on, aren't I?" And he'd pat himself as if patting a dog.

With Nada went our old maid Ginger, for reasons I did not understand, and now we had a nice white, middle-aged lady with a kindly brow, and she lived in the maid's room above the kitchen, whereas Ginger had always been a nuisance: someone always had to drive her down to the bus stop, where she boarded a bus for a nine-mile ride down into the city, and out of Fernwood, Bornwell Pass, Pleasure Dells, and Oak Woods.

The first time I saw Florence a strange thing occurred. In pulling off her black, lint-specked gloves she made the same gesture that Father had made when he showed me his product, that strand of wire. Father had held the wire stretched between his hands, as if presenting something sacred to me, and Florence had pulled off one glove by tugging at the tips of the fingers, and as she said something to me—"Real cold for April, eh?"—she paused and the glove remained where it was, half on and half off, the middle finger stretched out grotesquely.

I was out of school for two weeks. It took about two weeks to arrange for a transfer to Fernwood Junior High (where, incidentally, I never ended up), and anyway Father thought it was a good idea for me to "rest."

So I lay around the big house, staring outside. The lawn was greening up. When Florence came in the room I left, not wanting to be pitied. Florence was always vacuuming and polishing and running water furiously. There was a soapy, steelwoolish, pitying odor about her, just as there had been an odor of something confused and fragrant and dark about Nada. But I really didn't think about Nada, I want you to know. I didn't think much about the way I had failed her, about being such a mess, a failure at eleven, but instead I just lay around and listened to my heart beat, wondering if it might stop someday soon and not caring much. I rested. I lost weight.

There was one room in the house we didn't "bother with," and that was Nada's. Florence did not go into it with her vacuuming apparatus and rags and polish, nor did she allude to it once Father told her not to "bother with" it. She nodded and understood, as if all houses had one special nasty room.

I remembered Nada's room from the day Mr. Hansom had taken us through. That had been the best room on the second floor, with a lovely bay window looking out onto the sunny side yard with its fringe of evergreens so that it seemed as if you were balanced atop a magic forest—that magic, sinister room where Nada made noises on her typewriter and spent her secret hours away from us. Sometimes when Father was gone I walked back and forth past the door to that room, that Room, *that* room, thinking: What would happen if I went inside?

And one day I did.

It was still a nice room but very messy, as you might expect. You knew something was odd about the person who'd lived here just by the way books were strewn around, lying flat on the rumpled bed, opened and help-less on their backs in the dust on the floor. Not very many books, just scattered messily. Her desk had been pulled over to the bay window, by Nada herself evidently, for the green carpet had four sharp streaks in it made by the desk's legs. The desk had been cleared off. The typewriter was gone. Everything was gone. A cheap aluminum desk lamp had fallen onto the floor and lay there exposing its bulb to me. I picked it up and put it back on the desk.

Nada's work had always been forbidden. I would as soon have hidden in her shower and surprised her there as read her stories and books—and she had no more told me not to do the one than she had told me not to do the other. I knew! I was sensitive and intelligent, that sort of kid. But now all that was over, and I rum-maged through her drawers—pencils were always darting out toward me, rolling noisily—and decided that I would see what the secret was. There were drawers of scrap paper and some yellowing manuscripts, but when I began to read them I felt dizzy and a little nauseated, so I put them back for another day. I had to go slowly. Sweating, absurd, I opened a notebook at random and stared at the lazily scrawled entries:

1. Look up antique shop B mentioned.
2. Inside of car cleaned—tell them about choc-olate R spilled.

Was "R" me? Was I just "R" to her? Or was that a sign of affection? I read on:

NB NB NB *Must* read Hegel sometime.

I too must read Hegel sometime; yes. And on, flipping through the sacred book with its pretty blue lines faint like veins running down the page, and one wider, prettier red one at the top, like an artery:

> Idea for a story: honeymoon couple pick up hitchhiker; ordinary talk, to the horrible, back to the ordinary again; they let him off; they drive away.

That didn't sound like much of a story to me.

> Revise "Death and the Maiden" and change title.

I wonder, did she do that? Did she revise it and did she change the title? Her simple loops and *i*'s and slash-crossed *t*'s and the agreeable slant of her writing pleased me. I could imagine her sitting up here, flooded with winter light, her hair shining and smoky and her face intent, absorbed in her writing, which took her so far beyond Father and me:

> There must be a thread of story somewhere but where? the climax will be the death of X, but one must get past. The trouble is getting there . . . and getting past. As in any first-person narrative there can be a lot of freedom. Certain central events—what the hell can they be?—leading up to the death.
>
> "comic nihilism"
>
> senseless manic behavior in some natural setting . . . woods, flower bed. mysterious meetings, parallels. . . .

Nada was coming back to me slowly. I began to feel her in the room. I could smell her cigarette smoke and hear her restlessness. My heart pounded as I read:

Idea for a short novel: the young man (like J?) leads two lives, one public and the other secret. buys a gun. frightens people, doesn't hurt them. I can stretch this out to three episodes but no more, fine . . . then the fourth, when you've been conditioned to the others, results in the murder: planned all along though maybe he didn't know it. (Too corny? Should he know it, or not?) The sniper. "The Sniper." I'll think of a theme later.

I read this over several times, bent over her desk, surreptitious and impatient in her sacred room. My heart began to pound as if it knew something already that I myself did not know.

2

Had I been a musician, I could have devised some moody thunder-haunted background for my tale, even though it would have turned out funny, there would have been a spiteful dignity to it. Had I been a painter, my patient friends, I would have devised a mural vast as my imagination, called "The Abortion that Failed," and we would see a deep, dark pool that is sleep or night or death, and Nada's long smoky hair drifting back into the darkness or drifting out from it (you may take your choice), and her face pale as it never was in life, her lips dreamy and parted upon a hesitant smile, her eyes vague, dark, lovely. Off to each side there would be the troops of well-wishers that attend every birth. Bébé, Minnie, Mimi, whatever their ludicrous names were—I am starting to forget—and men like Father and Dean Nash and Mr. Spoon, men who are never naked but even in the presence of a Birth have their ties knotted up tight against their throats. And, everywhere the lushness and tranquillity of Fernwood, approached by great expanses of highways, expressways, winding, soaring, veering roads that seem impatient with the earth, mountains of junked cars, beer cans, and broken glass. In the mist a half-formed, embryonic child's face, just the barest suggestion of a face, of a soul . . .

3

The next day the door of Nada's room was fixed with an expensive brass lock, and Father spoke to me in a modification of his man-to-man talk. This talk was comradely but shifty-eyed; I preferred it to the other talk.

"We've got to stick together, the two of us," he declared. For some reason we hadn't had dinner yet and it was getting late, past seven-thirty. He said, patting my back, "Two bachelors rambling around together, they've got to keep everything out in the open. No secrets, see? We made a deal that that *certain somebody* wasn't going to have any power in this house any more. Right?"

He was gentle enough with me, but I felt that his restless fingers might get out of control.

"Do you want her to die?" I said.

"What, Dickie? What?"

"Do you want her to die?"

He stared at me. "Now what the hell kind of talk is that, buster? Look, now. Forget it. Absolutely forget it. You never said it and I never heard it. Any kind of morbid unnatural thoughts like that." He began shaking his large head. "Look, absolutely forget it. I mean, put it out of your mind. Neither of us heard that."

"I only meant—"

"No. Forget it." He was shaking his head with his eyes closed. "It's that morbid, unnatural atmosphere of Johns Behemoth. When you start public school you'll get in with some real normal kids, and you can play football or something. Right? I think, yes, I think maybe that everything that happened happened for the good. I think maybe it did, when you look at it from a long-range view. Right, buster?"

He had to fly to New York for a few days, so I spent my free time—free time!—down at the library, trying to look up Nada's writing. I know now that none of us ever has any free time, it's all being dearly paid for. But then I didn't know it; I was exhilarated by being "free," not just from Father but from Nada, because when I was engrossed in reading her stories I was freed from her as a person. My mother. I could sit in the comfortable, sleep-inducing leather chairs ranged around the empty fireplace at the library and read the stories of this strange, delicate woman and not have to think that I had come out of her body, uninvited. Around me clip-clopped Fernwood ladies in their expensive high heels, and a dreamy halo of perfume rose from each of them. They were people in a dream no matter how thunderous the sound of their shoes! Occasionally two stopped to chat, rather loudly, and I could almost see their halos of perfume move together and overlap. They were all handsome, handsome women. I wonder what tiny lives and deaths have taken place in their bodies. Most of them were slim women, you know that. In other areas you might see fat flabby women, with upper arms that jiggle, but in Fernwood everyone is healthy, tanned from Jamaica and Bermuda, and restrained and slim, and if their upper arms do jiggle, you can be sure that their sleeves are always decorously long.

Bébé Hofstadter came in, handsomer than the others, in an expensive light green suit and alligator purse and shoes. Her hair was newly tinted; she looked as if she herself had just been set upon the street by the hands of Monsieur Janet down the block. She selected from the *Browse & Leaf* shelf a brightly jacketed book entitled *The Care and Feeding of the Middle-Aged American Male.* Then she turned, and before I could raise my book she saw me.

"Richard Everett," she whispered. She had identified me. She clip-clopped to me like a nurse, smiling. The halo of her perfume moved along with her, though jerkily, and folded me in it. She talked. Never once did she speak of Nada, as if Nada were dead, and her words flowed along with brightness and concern, mentioning the names of people I should have known, mentioning a sensational news event elaborated upon daily in the papers —"Isn't it just a shame? A shame"—and something about football. This kind, lovely woman, as nice as she could be to one so miserable, but of course her kindness meant nothing. By now you see that: all of Fernwood is kind, nice, generous, lovely, and it means nothing, nothing.

It turned out (her main point) that her husband was back from Japan, and he was going to take Gustave and a lovely girl cousin of Gustave's to a concert the next night, and would I like to join them? Her face was flushed with charity. I told her politely that, yes, yes, I would be very happy to join them. No one had been so good to me for a while, and there was an awful, shaky moment when I almost cried, but it passed. She began to talk again. Behind her, passing from the *Browse & Leaf* shelf to the more demanding *Fireplace Reading* shelf, was a woman in a silvery, shiny coat. Her back, alas, was rather broad for Fernwood, and the tug of her shoulders on the material made its shiny weave catch the overhead light. I was put suddenly in mind of the silver balloon in the sky on that day when Nada and I were headed for the zoo.

"Richard, are you all right?" Mrs. Hofstadter said.

"I'm sorry—yes."

"Are those your teeth chattering like that?"

"No. Yes, I've got a cold," I said wildly. My teeth bit at each other and settled in rigidly. They were not going to get loose and chatter again.

I walked all the way home from the library. It was chilly for April, and I thought peacefully that I would catch a real cold, catch flu, catch pneumonia. The inertia of my body was already a kind of sickness, but a pleasant one. You don't think sickness is pleasant? Try it! Lovely to lie there in sunny-smelling white sheets, legs and arms resting as if the blood in them has at last come to a stop—you don't need anyone then. Only you healthy people need friends. You're always running around, making telephone calls; you have so much energy. But we sick people have no energy at all. We are freed from it. We don't need anyone, our bodies keep us company enough, thank you. We think about dying and how pleasant that might very well be, getting rid not only of everyone once and for all but getting rid of the desire to get rid of them and the desire for any kind of desire at all. As I walked home I felt how pleasant it was to be "free," to be completely alone and to know it. Father was in New York and Nada was . . . Nada was also in New York, but of course it couldn't be the same New York. Nada and Father would never meet, not even by accident. Seeing the two of them together, you knew that they could never have met, by accident or any other way, they could never have exchanged two words, never have married. Anyone could see that!

It was a lovely long walk. These spring days in Fernwood! Everything, everything, is lovely in Fernwood! To tell you all of the sloping lawns, evergreen screens (planted at full growth), greening gardens, courtyards, oval driveways, to tell you of the luxurious pleasures of their box-shaped houses, their fishponds, the glimpses of their colored maids at windows, washing windows that are already clean—ah, to tell you of these things would be to write another *Paradiso,* and we writers are better equipped to write of the Inferno and Purgatory, as you know. Before the rare beauties of the wealth of America a writer can do nothing—his "criticisms" are just envy and everyone knows it. But what can he do? Little orchards, little cars, gray-white statues back in courtyards, half glimpsed, and gray-tweeded businessmen hopping out the side doors, faces flushed with happiness and close antiseptic electric shaves, lawn crews wheeling expensive mowers from their trucks down planks to the streets, and painters rubbing their noses happily as they examine that three-story box that will cost the owner $3000 to have painted—what can I say? What can I do besides present these things to you?

Why, you wouldn't venture into a Fernwood home without knowing beforehand that the mud rug you should not—should not!—wipe your feet on is a three-by-five $600 Aubusson, matching the living-room rug, and you wouldn't venture in without already knowing the rare fine smell of good wood and good wood polish that will greet you, and an odor of expensive roasted cashews set out in antique silver trays—just for you! And you wouldn't peek into the "music room" without knowing beforehand that the great grand piano does not mean anyone in the house "plays"; it is there because it is there, solid and polished. It is a world of property lines, surveyor's papers, title deeds, abstracts, histories, and pedigrees, and in these mansions people do—do what? Do they live? *Live*?

What does that mean, *to live*?

If God remakes Paradise it will be in the image of Fernwood, for Fernwood is Paradise constructed to answer all desires before they are even felt. Heaven and earth converge like two friendly halos of perfume, overlapping, sinuous, and the crystal chandeliers and elegant automobiles are there to please you, just to please your eye, and there is never any contrast between what is said and what is done, what is done and what is intended, what is intended and what is desired—everything runs together. And these people are not even rich, don't misunderstand me. They would blush to be called "rich" and stammer defenses. This is a story of the middle-class: you see, the men worked.

And if it occurs to you, my clever reader, that there is irony intended here—that Richard Everett, miserable slob as he is, is being cute and praising Fernwood while (beneath it all) he despises Fernwood—you are wrong. Wrong. Fernwood is an angel's breath from heaven. It is as real as any dream, more real than a nightmare, terribly real, heavily real, as real as our neighbor's lovely Borzoi dog leaping onto your chest or Nada's grand piano sliding onto your toe. Fernwood is Paradise and it is real! I will go to my death believing this, that man has done no better than Fernwood, that God Himself has done no better, that no other society, no other world, is quite equal to it. And if it turns out that there is someone leaning over my shoulder as I write this, some muse, some evil genius who is perhaps my mother—just perhaps—then you are not to assume that this evil genius is "using" me as an ingenu-narrator, no, you are not. No irony.

And what has all this to do with my pleasant feelings about sickness, and my "freedom"? You must remember that everything runs together in an autobiography. It is only in fiction that there are clear transitions between events.

When I turned up our walk, panting up our hill, a man sitting in a crème-de-menthe-colored car at the curb jumped out. "Richard Everett?" he said. He hurried up to me. Six feet two, briefcase-carrying, a rapid, competent smile, keen eyes; he shook hands with me and introduced himself. He took out a notebook. "I would appreciate it very much if you'd answer a few questions for me. Nothing extraordinary," he said. "The subject under question today is Charles Spoon, who is applying for maximum security clearance. Mr. Everett, how well do you know Mr. Spoon?"

"Mr. Spoon? I guess not at all."

He chuckled as if this reply had no meaning. "Would you say, Mr. Everett, that Mr. Spoon strikes you as a man of integrity? Or not?"

"I don't know him, I guess."

"From your necessarily limited point of view, what would you say?"

"I don't know—"

"You are uncertain?"

"I guess so."

He frowned, about to write. "Is that your final consideration? You are uncertain about him?"

"I guess so."

He wrote this down. His face cleared and he smiled again. "Has Mr. Spoon ever betrayed any weak or deviant behavior to you? Excessive drinking, boasting, telling of family or business secrets, implying political connections in high places? Boasting of physical powers, of mental agility? Have you any reason to suspect that he is being blackmailed? Has he ever—think carefully —has he ever made any proposals to you of a certain type?"

"No."

"Are you sure?"

"I only saw him a few times from the doorway—"

"What doorway?"

"In our house."

"What was he doing in the doorway?"

"No, I was in the doorway."

"What were you doing there?"

"Spying."

His cheeks reddened. He said lightly, "You have a sense of humor, Mr. Everett, well developed for one so young. According to my notes, you have been expelled from Johns Behemoth, your mother has left this house and is living in New York City with someone named Sheer—and we know all about him too!—and your father is playing off GKS against Federal Bison and BWK. So there is no point in hiding the truth, Mr. Everett."

"Who? What's Sheer?" I said. "Who is Sheer? Who's that?"

"Our subject is Spoon," he said. "Would you say, Mr. Everett, that Mr. Charles Spoon is the type of man who could be trusted with secrets pertaining to our national security? Your life, my life? Would you want to trust this man with the life and death of our civilization?"

"I wouldn't trust anybody—"

"Eh?"

"No, I wouldn't! Who's this Sheer?"

"You wouldn't trust him?"

"Who is Sheer? Where are they?"

"So you wouldn't trust Spoon—that's significant. You are the thirteenth person to suggest that you wouldn't trust Spoon with the life and death of our civilization. Mr. Everett, never mind about Sheer. I mentioned his name only so that you would understand that *I* know *you,* and there is no point in lying to me."

"I wasn't lying," I said miserably.

"When there is no longer any point in lying, no one will lie," he said gently. His eyelids were half closed; he looked for a moment as if he were in the presence of something sacred. Then he drew himself up to his full height and said in a brisk, snappy voice, "You look ·a little cold, kid. Why don't you go inside? Of course, you understand, don't tell anyone about this. You understand?"

I undersood.

This was my "freedom." *Expensive People* could be subtitled "Children of Freedom." I am too tired to go back and work in this secondary theme, about "freedom," and the many children involved in my story, and anyway this isn't fiction, it's life. "When there is no longer any point in lying, no one will lie": that would make a good epigram for a novel. But in life there are no epigrams, no reason for emphasizing one remark over another, and so I refuse to emphasize that, right? The hell with that. The hell with the government man. But it seems to me I saw him just the other day, that man or one exactly like him, bred out of the same race, standing outside the shabby "family-run" grocery store where I buy my mountains of food, and looking at me in a certain way. Does that mean they are after me at last? After so many years of freedom, of legal innocence, they've decided to believe my confession? What does it mean? What will happen? Will anything happen?

4

Gregory Hofstadter was in oil and rarely seen. He flew everywhere, dined with princes and premiers; there is a photograph of him in Gustave's room, riding in a jeep across ice-cream-smooth slopes of sand in the company of fierce white-clothed Arabs! What a father! He traveled third-class and slept with vermin, just for fun; he made a religious pilgrimage to Jerusalem, he had an audience (in a group of six) with the Pope, he snapped a picture of Khrushchev when Khrushchev was in Berlin, and Khrushchev seems to be waving at him! He went surfing out in California, in early May, and the Premier of Bongata ferried him about in a gigantic yacht one August; he was a regular guest at Saari's villa on the Italian Riviera, and I heard him talk animatedly with Father about just what electronic music was striving for: he had been in a special audience, including Queen Elizabeth, treated to the première of "Symphony for Silence" by Baxterhouse.

He took Gustave and Gustave's cousin and me all the way downtown to a concert, which was held in an expensive, modern, concrete-block auditorium at the very center of the city. Though the city was being rebuilt, no one went down there any more; just a few people who had to work there, and misguided tourists. But no women ventured into the city because why should they? Why, indeed! All you will find in the city is streets littered with papers, wrappers, dirt, grit, spit, bloody phlegm coughed up by bums, and on the blowy park benches the bums themselves looking humble and malicious in their shabby clothes. ("And each one of them a pervert," Gregory Hofstadter said in a cheerful, angry voice to us children.) No "Ladies Day" at the local theaters can lure our lovely mothers down to this squalor! Do they care if they can get in for fifty cents, or if a ripple-haired movie star will be on stage in person? They don't give a damn and they are absolutely right. Gregory

[151

Hofstadter swore at the congested traffic and blew his nose, waiting for a light to change, as if he had to get rid of his nervous energy somehow.

"I hope this trio or whatever it is is good," he said to Gustave. "We're going to a lot of trouble to get down here."

Gustave sat up front with his father, and Maureen and I sat in back. Maureen had pale, sharp-boned cheeks, a very pretty pink spring coat; she was Gustave's age, two years older than I. She played the piano and the harp, Gustave said. She attended Miss Chote's School for Girls, a most exclusive and expensive school in Fernwood Heights, whose students were the sisters and cousins of the Johns Behemoth boys.

Mr. Hofstadter was having trouble because if he got in the right lane, cars ahead of him would slow to make right turns. If he lurched over into the left lane, swearing under his breath, the car ahead of him always paused to make a very slow, creaky left turn. "Oh, those . . . oh, those bastards!" he muttered, not for us to hear. We children were talking quietly, and when Mr. Hofstadter spoke Gustave simply raised his voice to drown him out.

"Did you see that? God!" Mr. Hofstader said, wiping his forehead. "That nut turned right out in front of that other nut."

There was some difficulty at the entrance to the parking lot, since two lines of cars were preparing to squeeze into a one-lane space. We waited. Gustave said cheerfully, "We'll be inside and settled in a few minutes." His father buzzed down his window and leaned out to yell at a parking attendant. "Hey, you! Yes, you! Come over here—*you*!"

The boy limped over to us, and as he emerged out of the dark and into Mr. Hofstadter's headlights he turned into an old man with a sullen look.

Mr. Hofstadter gave him a mysterious bill, and he and we children hopped out and the old man crawled in. "How d'ya work this? Okay, I got it," the old man said sullenly. We walked away, free.

Mr. Hofstadter was a rotund, cheerful man who was always beaming down on us. When he smiled, he smiled just like his wife Bébé, but, like her, he often let his face relax and the gloriousness of his good humor drained away at once, while the smile took longer to fade. It was like looking at two people at the same time.

"Dick, I hear your father is up to some monkey business," he teased.

I didn't know what he was talking about. I was afraid it had to do with Nada, though of course I should have known no Fernwood gentleman would allude to anything that serious. So I smiled shyly and said nothing.

"Yessir!" Mr. Hofstadter said. "And did Gustave tell you about me? I'm leaving BOX and going in with Precept Oil. Did Gustave mention my new position?"

"I think so," I said.

This pleased him, and he rumpled Gustave's hair. I felt my own hair being rumpled.

The chamber-music group did unsurprising but fine pieces. Mr. Hofstadter began to cross and uncross his legs during the Andante movement, but the Allegro kept him interested. There was a moderate crowd. It occurred to me then that music was like eating, and both of them were like sleep: something to do that drew you into it, hadn't anything to do with you as a person. You could inhabit the vacuum of your freedom like a fly buzzing

F

aimlessly in a locked car, and not worry about getting out or about what you should be doing since you couldn't do anything anyway until you did get out.

At intermission, while Mr. Hofstadter went out to the foyer to smoke, Gustave said nervously, "I should apologize for Father—"

"No, no! The concert is wonderful," Maureen said.

"It's wonderful of him to bring us down," I said.

Gustave fussed with his program notes. "I'm afraid Father doesn't know much about music. But he has an instinctive appreciation of some pieces."

"It's better that way," said Maureen at once.

"I wish I had his natural instinct," I said. "It's so . . . so natural."

"It comes without any contemplation," said Maureen. "I'm ruined for anything spontaneous. I've been studying music for ten years."

"Well, Father likes things that he likes. If they appeal to him," Gustave said. He showed the slow, cautious pride one shows in hearing one's children being praised.

After all this, Mr. Hofstadter must have disappointed his son by insisting that we leave before the final work. "Want to get out of that parking lot before the crowd," he muttered. Gustave tried to argue, but his father got to his feet and started out, and we had to follow him. We stumbled over feet on our way out, but in the aisle we were joined by a dozen, two dozen people slipping on their coats, looking shrewd and relieved on their way to the parking lot. The trio had just begun its final piece.

"Too much congestion," Mr. Hofstadter said.

In the small crowd of those desiring to avoid congestion we descended into the chilly April evening. Mr. Hofstadter walked fast, as Father did. Fernwood men always walked fast. Seen from the back, they looked angry; that must have been why Maureen said to Gustave, "I hope your father isn't angry about anything." Gustave said, "Why should he be angry?" but his reply was dubious. We had all learned long ago that when adults did favors for you, their jolly good natures could change suddenly and inexplicably.

"They're all trying to kill us, it's nothing personal," I said.

"What was that?" said Gustave, cupping his ear.

But Mr. Hofstadter was waving on the three of us —obviously children who had never been childish or even especially young.

Need I mention that Mr. Hofstadter was an excellent driver? Had you seen how he swung his big Lincoln around some mediocre automobile and roared up to the exit, squeezing in ahead of several other cars, you would certainly have marveled at his skill. Fernwood men drive well, and they never have accidents or get tickets from the police. When Mr. Hofstadter got into his car he looked enthusiastic and pleased. I noticed that. Gustave climbed in beside him, with a quick, unconvincing smile that was meant to bring us all together, adult and children, but which had no effect at all.

I think that Mr. Hofstadter had already forgotten about Maureen and me in the back seat, and that he gradually forgot about Gustave, as the intricate skills of driving captured his imagination. He was a born driver. The "driver" is a man who settles himself into his "driving" the way others of us settle into a good book or a good sleep. You can tell when the "driving" sets in by the change of expression. But no, it isn't really a change, it's a solidification, an intensification. Let me explain. The first five minutes on the expressway were taken up with Mr. Hofstadter's genial chatter. I think he was chattering about a new painting he had bought, or his new position at Precept Oil, and how unfortunate it was that Gustave would have to leave Johns Behemoth —it was his fifth, or sixth, school in the last three years —or maybe he was talking about the next trip he would be taking, to Australia. Then, as the "driving" set upon him, his sentences faltered off into nothing, his shoulders straightened bulkily, I could see his neck grow thicker and stronger as if preparing for battle. In the rearview mirror I could see his eyebrows furrowed down close to his narrowed eyes. His lips were pursed together hard and a tiny film of perspiration glowed on his forehead.

Gustave talked on bravely, but Maureen and I only mumbled our replies. Mr. Hofstadter changed lanes, swerved in front of slower, moronic drivers who couldn't keep up, tapped his horn, leaned on his horn, swore out through his flawlessly clean windshield at the anonymous faces of fellow drivers who just couldn't keep up. "Accidents caused by slow drivers," he said panting. "Look at them! That nut over there! Look!" But he roared by so fast that we had not time to look, nor did we trust ourselves to look at the other vehicles speeding along with us. The expressway had been an excellent route a few years ago, but now it was out of date. Even on a Tuesday evening there were too many cars. Mr. Hofstadter showed his dissatisfaction by drifting up close to the rear of a car, breathing heavily, tapping on his horn, jerking his head back and forth in a tight series of disapproving, outraged shakes, and his hands gripped the wheel the way they might have gripped any weapon, with confidence and pride and barely restrained vengeance.

We sped along the expressway and out toward the suburbs, passing beneath sleazy viaducts and overpasses where Negro children dawdled, some of them kicking pebbles off onto the passing cars, and while the perspiration gleamed on Mr. Hofstadter's handsome forehead and his shoulders in their expensive tweed began to hunch up with cunning, we children tried to keep up our miserable conversation. I think it was Maureen who said, "Music is the only thing that can make you happy without qualification," or else I said it; and Gustave replied, his sentence peaking in the middle with the sudden swerve of his Father's excellent automobile, "Music bypasses the mind altogether . . ." We drifted on to talk of chess, but our desperate conversation inside the hurtling vehicle of steel and glass could not compete with the lusty dramas taking place on all sides of us. Poor children!

"There, so much for him," Mr. Hofstadter would mutter; or, "Like this—this is the way it's done!" He was not talking to us, of course. He was talking to the other drivers. A man in a car as fine as Mr. Hofstadter's gave him some trouble. They sped along side by side for a while, not glancing at each other, and when Mr. Hofstadter began to drift toward that car the car did not budge, no, not an inch, nor did anyone sound his horn, and Mr. Hofstadter laughed huskily and straightened out again, pressing his accelerator down to the floor. "We'll see, we'll see," he whispered. He finally did get ahead of the other car, but only after an interlude of sharp squealing brakes. "I was engaged in this three-dimensional chess game," Gustave said nervously. "My opponent is a member of London Teen-Mensa . . ."

After a few confused moments we flashed under an overpass, and just at that moment some kids dropped something over—a length of pipe, maybe—and it hit the windshield of a car alongside us. The car immediately swerved and fell back. Mr. Hofstadter accelerated. Maureen and I looked out and saw the car bounce up on the shoulder of the expressway, veer along at a tremendous speed, and crumple against a series of posts.

"Oh, look! Look at that!" I cried.

"Filming," said Mr. Hofstadter.

The accident was already some distance behind us.

"What?"

"It's a rehearsal. Television show," Mr. Hofstadter said and kept on going.

Gustave had told me once that his father had been born on a yacht on the Detroit River, one sunny Sunday many years ago. The birth had been the result of a grand slam dealt to his mother by a kindly hostess, and so Mr. Hofstadter had come into the world a few weeks early, lusty and bawling and ready to go. He hasn't stopped yet. He's still going strong, I know, since a recent *Time* showed him in a photograph with several fierce sheiks, aging but still handsome. And Gustave, if you're interested, is already a senior at Harvard, excelling in mathematics, and Maureen is studying in Bristol, and they're all growing up, going along their ways, "getting along," but I, I sit here at the end of my life. Now I have my meals sent up from a roachy delicatessen because it's easier that way and I can avoid the unfriendly stares of people in this neighborhood. It's strange how people end up, how different their destinies are, though at one time in their lives they've been together in a hurtling automobile just a few feet or a few seconds from death.

5 REVIEWS OF *Expensive People*

Everyone imagines with horror the opinions of others, but few people are unfortunate enough really to know what these opinions are. We are all paranoid, all self-loathing and vaguely doomed, but only writers and other exhibitionists are told the terrible truth about themselves. Ordinary people never know anything. They suspect but do not know. Years pass. Nobody gives a damn, nobody is watching. They die. They are forgotten. I, Richard Everett, will die and be forgotten and never know the truth about myself, if there is "truth," and so . . .

And so I have made up some truths. Last night I made them up. I should keep them for an Appendix to this book, but I am greedy and impatient and masochistic, and so here they are. The posthumous future doesn't seem quite real to me, but I suppose it will come. Can it be possible that you are reading this book in 1969, or later? This moment seems so real to me, so gluey and sluggish, that only a great effort of will can get me past it. I won't be alive to see the actual reviews of my exhaustive work, and no doubt that's just as well. But I imagine they will take these forms:

New York Times Book Review:
It is sheer cant (though speculative) that the product of a mad, feverish mind must be in it-

self mad and feverish, as if the mind, like Kant's kneecap, could bend only one way. This dogma seems possible only when the "voice" of the madman is so hysterical that it engulfs— one might say *drowns out*—the legitimate feverish voice of the writer. Verbal felicity or verbal awkwardness aside, the essential rhetorical pose of *Expensive People* is perhaps more mad than simply feverish, more sentimentally eclectic (in the *kitsch* sense) than tragically enlightened. . . .

Time Magazine:
Confused and confusing tale of a child with a famous madcap socialite mother and a dear doddering foolish father, set in that well-covered terrain, Suburbia. Everett sets out to prove that he can outsmartre Sartre but doesn't quite make it. It is all great fun though. As there should be, there are Problems with Mother. But these are probably resolved as the novel progresses. Hijinks galore, but, like a damp firecracker, most of them smolder rather than explode. There is a hint of patronage in all this (we are asked to believe the author is only eleven!), as there is in the best of documentaries about Eskimo or New Zealand customs. Of course it has all been done before, and with superior skill, by John O'Hara and Louis Auchincloss, and if and when Everett learns the lyric cry of rapture and horror which these authors call forth he will perhaps be worthy of our attention.

The New Republic:

Expensive People has as its verbal mode the reduction of a generation's anguish to the insufferable lyricism of one child; as the talisman of at least one plane of its purported operations, it exhibits vast mountains of junk (middle-class acquisitions, symbolic of life), about which its child-narrator turns dizzily, dreaming not simply the manic dream of the middle-class (which never wakes in this novel), but also the manic dream of the would-be novelist who would reduce complex sociological material to a thalamic crisis. For the mythic-sexual-sociological dimension is what Everett desires, though he fails utterly in his inability to get very far beyond common psychosexual boundaries into realms of metaphysical and cultural-philosophical recognition. The whole point of the doomed child is his legendary quality: exemplary of the American confusion between orders of being, of our perpetual conversion of sexuality into one kind of art and the consequent depletion of the sexual by being turned into emblem and shady metaphor. This entire problem was taken up only two months ago by the "Faintest Idea" troupe, who are running an amateur living theater in San Francisco, and their insistence upon definite ritualistic analogues and socio-emblematic drama have, in my opinion at least, cleared up this issue once and for all. Their shattering play, *Genghis Proust,* which takes place on a pitch-black stage, has been reviewed at length earlier in

F*

The New Republic, and I need say no more about it except to underscore my feeling that only at such points of moral infinity can this new energy find its proper mode in the creation of revolutionary substance. *Expensive People,* traditional as Charles Dickens, is therefore an irrelevant exercise. . . .

Hanley Stuart Hingham, a famous critic, writing in any one of the literary quarterlies:

And now we turn from Nabokov's scintillating anal fantasies to the crude oral fantasies of one Richard Everett, in a first novel called *Expensive People.* Worthless as sociological material (Everett shows a most naïve admiration for the Businessman, suggesting he's never met one), ludicrous as drama (any alert reader, thumbing through the book, will be able to predict the sorry outcome), embarrassing as prose (I'm the only reviewer content with the assertion that the author is an eighteen-year-old madman, I'm sure), *Expensive People* is nevertheless valuable as a fabulous excursion into the realm of the orally obsessed. Food abounds in this memoir. Sex is metamorphosed into the more immediate, more salivating form of food, so that it can be taken legally and morally through the mouth. But, as if to deny this surreptitious gratification, the novel is also filled with vomit. Those of us who have read Freud (I have read every book, essay, and scrap of paper written by Freud) will recognize easily the familiar domestic triangle here, of a son's homosexual and incestuous love for his father disguised by a humdrum Oedipal attachment to his mother. Author Everett, obviously an amateur, failed to make the best use of his oral theme by his crudity of material. He should have had the crazy young hero gobble down hotdogs, ice-cream cones, ladyfingers, all-day suckers. Instead, Everett doesn't bother specifying the food imagery. It is this lack of skill that sets him apart from Nabokov, whose every sentence is calculated, whose every image calls up at once from the deepest reservoirs of our souls Freudian responses of the sort that make Great Literature.

6

Gustave told me later that the evening of the chamber music concert had been an unusual evening for his father. "He was tired when he flew in from Spain, and he probably should have rested," Gustave said meekly.

I want to describe Gustave again, since he looked so much like me. You probably don't know what I looked like. He was a small, slender child with a patient and ageless face, serious eyes, a thin, serious mouth, and glasses with pink transparent frames; his narrow shoulders had the look of carrying enormous invisible burdens. Children like this are given to sudden eruptions of shrill, nervous laughter, after which they lapse into the silence that seems characteristic of them. We metamorphose into middle age without much strain, and the silence of our childhoods turns into a certain fussiness in old age about food, drafts from windows that only seem to be closed, and changing times.

Gustave told me that his father had done a peculiar thing that night: when he drove up the Hofstadter driveway he deliberately ran into the garage door, which was closed. The door was usually operated by electricity, like all Fernwood garage doors, but something had happened to the mechanism in the automobile, and when Mr. Hofstadter turned up his driveway and pressed his button, nothing happened. In Fernwood (I should have mentioned this earlier) all garage doors slide meekly up when their owners' automobiles turn in the driveway. They just do. Children don't question this; it is a fact of ordinary life. But the seeing-eye mechanism broke down that night and Mr. Hofstadter's finger was impotent on the button, but keep going he did, his gaze steady and cold on the garage door, and he ran right into it going ten miles an hour and crumpled the garage door and the front of his car. But he seemed satisfied, Gustave reported, for the first time that day. He went right inside the house and upstairs and to bed, where he slept soundly.

Something strange happened in my own life, with my own father. When Father arrived home the next day he asked me about the concert. We sat, two rambling, happy bachelors, in the Family Room, which we had never used, gazing through a big plate-glass patio door onto a patio, which we had never used and were never to use, and Father asked me closely about Mozart. I noticed that Father wore a new suit, not yet rumpled. He was not

164]

a handsome man but there was something attractive about his face, or perhaps his expression. You could tell by looking at him that he *wanted* to be good, and wasn't wanting almost enough? (In my desperate reading in preparation for this memoir I came across the heresies of one Flavius Maurus, who believed that the only Good was in desire and not in act, since purity can exist only in the mind. In his religion, wouldn't Father be saved?) I feel the itch to describe my father on all these pages, to get him down good once and for all, but do you know it's almost impossible? I always kept imagining that he wasn't really my father and another man would take his place. I was crazy. This big, lumpy, strong man with his tobacco-stained fingers and his habit of twirling wine about in wine glasses with a loving, precise skill was my father, all mine, and in a way he may be your father too. Let's all share him! And if you are a father yourself, you'll see yourself in Father. One cannot imagine him as a child or a young man, since he has been full-grown for so long, with his past as compact behind him as his wallet, which is filled not with money but credit cards, slim and flat, stuffed in his back pocket, his past so very slim and flat itself that for all practical purposes it did not exist. And his future? Imaginable only as an extension and inflation of his present.

He said, "I always did admire Mozart but you know I haven't had the time to develop that side of myself. I'm going to set aside two hours of each day, from now on, to catch up on things. Dickie, have you done much reading in Sartre?"

"I guess not."

[165

"Yes, well. Sartre is well worth reading."

"We read something in French class once, just an essay. It was sort of hard."

Father brightened at hearing this. "Yes, well, kid, everything worthwhile is difficult, as Plato said. Or did Plato say everything difficult is worth while? It's the same thing. But I think Sartre has something to say and I'm going to give him the benefit of the doubt. I'm going to give him the time to say it to me."

He smiled and seemed to be awaiting my approval.

I filled in great gaps of time by sleeping and eating, lying around the house. Sometimes I would be awakened by Father's striding into the room, all set for our daily afternoon walk, or ready to drive us to a Little League baseball game some friends' kids were in. He had a full life, Nada or no Nada. Father had instructed Florence to take the mail in before I got hold of it, so I didn't know if Nada was writing to him or not. She had stopped writing to me. There was something mysterious going on. I felt strange and inert, like a sleepwalker, and even when I did want to wake up I couldn't. I couldn't make myself rise out of sleep. Sometimes it frightened me, because I thought I might die, and the only thing to do was to think about something, some single, crucial *thing* that could draw me out of this paralysis. So I contemplated my toothbrush, which was far away upstairs, and imagined its appearance until my heart pounded with renewed vigor and I had to run up to my bathroom to check that trivial object. So far, so good. Or I doubted the reality of Florence, our good maid, and had to run to see her. Or I tried to reconstruct the room I had spent eighteen months of my life in back in Charlotte Pointe, imagining each wall, window, the furniture, the

166]

ugly tile, the apple tree outside. It took such enormous mental efforts to raise me out of my lethargy.

And another mysterious thing: Father began taking me to foreign movies. Films. We sat through a three-hour technicolor extravaganza of fantasies, enormous idealized bodies of males and females, and though I liked the splash of color well enough I didn't have any idea what was happening. And we saw a peculiar black-and-white film in which a couple pursue a disappeared girl over an island and a mainland, for hours, days, weeks, but fail to find her, and so it went. Despite my boredom I remember being struck by a sense of gritty, relentless futility in that movie, precisely the same futility I myself lived in. Afterward Father said, "Antonioni captures perfectly the malaise of the modern world, don't you think?"

"Huh?"

"His searching people, his ruins, his sand, his . . . well, you know, all the gadgets and stuff. Don't you think he captures it?"

"I guess so," I said. I was a little worried because one of the rambling, cheerful bachelors seemed to be changing.

Even his healthy outrage seemed to be weakening. When Florence tsk-tsked about the current newspaper drama—a girl of eleven abducted by a madman who was finally shot down by police—Father did not respond as usual with a hearty yelp of hatred, saying that it was the worst thing this state had ever done to revoke the death penalty; he seemed hardly to have heard. "Don't know what the world's coming to," Florence muttered, making our breakfast, and Father, who was glancing through the *Wall Street Journal* on one side of his plate and the *Partisan Review* on the other, did no more than agree vaguely as he chewed his toast.

7

At last he explained everything. He came home early one day and shortly afterward a man in a run-down truck brought Father a FOR SALE   INQUIRE WITHIN sign for the front lawn. We were moving again!

"We'll see how crazy I am to try selling it myself. We'll see." Father chuckled.

He had Florence clean the house inch by inch, and install flowers on the foyer table, the dining-room table, and the marble-topped table in the living room. Florence wore a dainty apron and a lace cap, and I was dressed in my Johns Behemoth blazer, my hair slicked down onto my forehead so that I looked like an English public-school boy, or someone's idea of one. I sat idly in the den, at the grand piano, and when would-be buyers were shown through the house I glanced at them, nodded stiffly, and turned back to my music. Father had other tricks too. He did not seem to be selling anything. He stressed the tight market, the difficulty of attaining a mortgage unless (and here his eyes would move kindly but realistically to the visitor's face) the borrower was quite well-off. And the maintenance of a house like this was high, he said, and mentioned prices that were absurdly low. "You will want the lawn serviced, of course; I think that's sixty a month." Or "The man with the little snowplow charges twenty dollars a winter to clear the walk."

And did it work? Of course. The house was sold in the first week for $88,000, a fine profit. He sold it to a family named Body who were moving up from Cleveland; the man was in advertising and needed a good-looking house. The wife hesitated over the circle driveway, thinking that it was "almost too much," but in the end she gave in; all women like things that are almost too much.

8

Moving did not upset me. Instead it made me feel slower than ever, bogged down, helpless. I sat around and watched the movers pack lamps and dishes, stuffing in newspapers skillfully and endlessly. The movers were competent men. I thought dreamily that they might pick me up and stuff me in one of the boxes, lined with newspaper, and ship me off to the new house. Florence was out in the kitchen, helping with the good china. She had never met Nada but she tsk-ed and clucked over the beautiful china and kept saying that she "would not be responsible" for what happened.

Didn't she know that no one was ever responsible for anything?

One by one things were packed up and packed off. There went Nada's table, there went the chair Father called "his" though he never sat in it. From upstairs came a procession of things that should have looked familiar—"my" own furniture. "My" things. I watched them with interest. Everything was so friendly. We owned all these things. They did not cause us pain and they had hardly cost us any money. Up from the basement came another procession of "our" things—washing machine, dryer, lawn furniture, a glass-topped table with elegant curlicues of iron, "my" old bow and arrow set, "my" badminton set, boxes and boxes of nameless things that must have belonged to us. Bundles and cartons. Suitcases that had been packed for the last move and had not yet been unpacked. Were we saying good-by to Nada in this sneaky way?

Florence said, "Richard, why are you crying?"

"I'm not crying," I said.

I was watching the big orange moving van drive away. It drove slowly up Burning Bush Way and took off in the direction of "our" new home, which Father had already bought. Another home, another town. My bones creaked and got me to my feet. I had to get ready because Father was coming home soon and we could start off in the car for our new life. Father had been invited by a certain highly successful firm, BWK, to take over one of their divisions. He explained his new job to me, but I hadn't listened carefully enough. I was having difficulty hearing, or maybe it was difficulty seeing. I couldn't match the sounds of words with the funny movements made by the speaker's lips. Even when Florence talked there was something odd. Her words came at me faster than her lips seemed able to shape them. A hodgepodge of sounds and ringing noises buzzed in my brain. I felt as if I·were asleep even when I was awake, and because

I was asleep everything was a dream and anything could happen.

Oh, we are so strangely matched with our dreams! We are so strangely suited to them, no matter how obscene or hilarious they are, and no matter how angrily we deny them. Yes, we always deny them. Looking back on Fernwood, now, as I write this memoir, I can see that Fernwood itself was a dream, and everyone in it dreaming the dream; all in conjunction, happy, so long as no one woke up. If one sleeper wakened, everything would have been stretched and jerked out of focus, and so . . . the end of Fernwood, the end of Western civilization! One would as soon trust Charles Spoon (that immensely talented designer of automobiles now applying to design another kind of weapon) with the life and death of Western civilization as one would trust people like Nada and myself with dreaming the good happy dream of Fernwood. We were failures. And so . . . were we saying good-by to Nada, sneaking off? Were Father and I packing up the stuff of our dream and taking it to another setting, where it could flourish safely away from all memories of that woman who kept waking and disturbing everyone?

Because—and this is the only truth I know about my mother, a most sorry truth—she wanted only to live but she didn't know how, that was why she made a mess. Messes are made by people who want but don't know what they want, let alone how to get it. And all the messes she made!

Father came, there were good-bys with Florence (three separate ones, awkward and moving), there was an exchange of money, the keys were dropped off at an attorney's office, I was entrusted with the road map, which looked like the plan for the intestines of a giant insect, and off we drove into the sunset. Father drove well, just like Mr. Hofstadter. He did not look back. I did not look back. But I could see in my mind's eye the placid winding streets (ways, lanes, drives) of Fernwood leading back farther and farther into the dimness of the past I had already spent here, from January to April of an uneventful year for Fernwood but a year to end all other years in my life.

I said to Father, "Are you going to write her and let her know where we're going?"

Father chuckled and said, "Tend to the road map, buster. You're the navigator for this run."

Two hours later, lonely for companionship, I said, "What kind of work will you be doing now, Father?"

"Cut out that Father business, I'm your Dad. Daddy," he said cheerfully. "It's a line of work you'd be interested in yourself, son. Top-security business, of course. Our new product is something that . . . well, I can't explain to you in any detail (not that I think you're a Red spy, kid!) but I can say generally that it has the appearance of our regular product, which has a certain superficial resemblance to the product of my former firm, a platinum-covered wire, but there are immense differences! A most intricate thing indeed. Our research team has been working for years to perfect a certain device that . . . well, has immense value in determining the security of America. Do you understand?"

My interest rose. "Is it a bomb then?"

"A bomb?" He laughed. "Look, kid, maybe and maybe not. On the day you get cleared I'll tell you. Okay?"

"Do you think I'll get cleared too?"

"If you keep your nose clean. If your mother keeps her nose clean."

"What?"

"Kid, I almost lost my top clearance because of your mother. But no more of that. Forget it."

"What about Nada?"

"Forget it, kid," he said.

He was jolly and restrained, like a magician with birds tickling him inside his clothes.

And so we drove on into the night and did not stop, for my father (and probably yours too) likes to drive straight through. "Drove straight through," he'll say modestly when he reaches his destination. "Straight through" from Fernwood to our new town, which was called Cedar Grove.

"That name sounds kind of familiar," I said.

"Ha, you're a riot, kid! You know very well that we lived in Cedar Grove once before."

"Is that right?"

"Ha, ha! I think you were about four or five. Yes, Cedar Grove is a fine place and we're headed for a fine new life because, you see, Dickie-boy, I have got a rather pleasant financial reward in connection with my switching to BWK. But of that no more need be said." And he wouldn't say any more either, because he was a little embarrassed over his success. He liked to talk about other men's successes and bring in his own by implication; he was modest, modest. So he chattered on about his new product, and the tie-in with the government, and the cultural advantages of Cedar Grove.

There was something boyish and giddy in his talk. He frightened me. But he was not frightening—there **was** nothing frightening there, it was his cheerfulness itself that terrified. I had the idea that I was trapped in this car with someone who wanted to destroy me, not by crashing the car or turning to me but just by talking, chatting, confiding, laughing, chuckling, patting my skull. He loved me. It was clear that he loved me and I loved him. Why was I so afraid of him?

I have on one hand this agreeable, well-appointed father, and on the other hand my morbid and obviously unnatural fear of him. I am unable to justify one by the other. They remain forever apart, and if I could get them together by telling you the tale of my dog Spark I'd do that, but when I tell that tale I either laugh miserably or cry hilariously.

I think, while Father speeds into the domestic American darkness, toward Cedar Grove, I will tell you the tale of my dog Spark after all.

9

When I was very little Father and Nada gave me a nice Christmas present: a little dog named Spark. Spark was a dachshund, which word was pronounced not "dash-hound," as the maid and the lawn men pronounced it, but in a fast, angry, wheezing way, like a sneeze. Father and Nada always said it correctly, and so did their friends. Spark did not know he was a dachshund, but his great sorrowful eyes seemed to indicate some misery or humiliation.

"Isn't it a lovely doggie?" Nada cried.

She hugged Spark and me together, entwining her

arms about both of us. In the background, sketch in a Negro maid smiling maternally, with what in hand (for she must be busy)? Oh, a rag, a bottle of Anglo-Saxon Furniture Polish. What kind of day? Misty, mild; spring. Nada dressed in a beautiful new suit, new gloves and purse in hand, ready to press the button and raise the garage door and drive off, destination unknown. Yes, I can see her there. In a minute she will leave.

Happy days are all one big blur of confusion, but so are unhappy days; in my sordid life, all days were blurs of confusion. But this was a happy day and blurred as usual with my shouts of joy and Spark's little whimpers and his fuzzy, downy stomach (more downy than the soft blond down on Nada's arms) and his caramel-candy-colored coat. He was delicious enough to eat! I hugged Spark in my clumsy arms and helped him wave good-by to Nada, who drove out and away, and I didn't turn aside from his wet leaping tongue.

And then . . . Not a minute later there was an aqua laundry truck.

In the driveway, from out of nowhere, and a man with a cap on his head looking down, cigar in hand. Yelps, whimpers. The maid came running behind me and screamed. Then she came running back and grabbed my arm and said, "Richard, you better get inside here fast," and I tried to get away to see where Spark had gotten to, but she took me back to the Family Room and turned on the television and that was that. I asked her for Spark and she said, "He's restin'," and turned the television volume up higher.

Nada came, and Father came. They looked at me from the doorway of the Family Room. Father had his arm around Nada's shoulders. They were saying something and their faces were sad, but though they were looking at me I could tell I wasn't supposed to hear them so I didn't hear anything. I was not a spy in those days.

We went out for a nice dinner, and I said, "Where's Spark?", and Father said cheerfully, "Spark had to go to the doctor. You know, like you did. Dr. Pratt."

"How come?"

"Spark needs his measles shot."

The next day when I woke up there was no Spark to be scolded at for making a mess in the kitchen, or rolling around whimpering on the floor. Nada stayed home. She made fudge, but it was too salty so I had to eat it all myself. At noon Father's car drove in, and I looked close and saw that Father was in it, and he jumped out of the car with a big happy hello for us, and along with him was Spark.

"Back safe and sound from the doctor—got his shots and he's set for life," Father said.

Spark yelped and whimpered and ran at Father's legs. Father had to pick him up and give him to me. Spark did not seem to know me, but after a moment he began to lick my face. Nada hugged us both, and when I looked at her I saw that she was so strange and beautiful. "Spark says he don't like doctors, just like me," I told her.

"He *doesn't* like doctors," Nada said gently.

And Spark and I played in the back and nearby stood Father and Nada, watching. They were happy. Father had his arm around Nada's shoulders.

Then one day about a week later (I am guessing at the time) Nada and Spark and I went for a walk. Nada wore slacks and had a scarf around her head. It was a blowy, happy day. Spark and I ran along, yipping and dashing, Spark's short little legs chopping as fast as they could and me falling down once in a while, and when I did I didn't bother to cry.

Nada said, "Wait for me," when we ran ahead to the corner, but Spark didn't hear her and kept running on with his little legs pumping. Off over the curb he went, and in the air for a second, and still running, and I was right behind him, and Nada said more sharply, "Richard, wait!", and I made a lunge to grab Spark's little tail but it was too late. Out of nowhere came an aqua truck, not a laundry truck this time but a delivery truck, and its brakes squealed and its body shuddered and swerved, and there was a scream of surprise from Spark and a scream of anger from Nada, who cried, "Oh, no!"

The delivery man stood talking to Nada. Spark was somewhere on the other side of the truck, but he was quiet, and Nada wouldn't let me go see him. I cried. Nada was crying too, but she was angry. The delivery man was not crying and he was not angry, he was like men are: they get things done. "Well, all right, you take that dog to the doctor," Nada said. "To the doctor. And when he is well you will bring him back again. Do you understand?"

"Yes, ma'am," the delivery man said.

They both glanced at me to see if I heard.

So Nada dragged me home. I cried for a while but then forgot why I was crying. She made fudge. We watched the Mickey Mouse Show together.

That day there was no Spark, and the next day no Spark either. I asked the maid where Spark was, was he at the hospital? She said he was getting fixed up and he'd be back. And the next day at noon Father's car

[177

turned up the driveway, and Father got out a little rushed and dropped Spark at my feet and said, "Good Christ, I should be at the airport right now," and said good-by and backed out again. There was a bad moment when Spark seemed to be running under the back wheel, but somehow he didn't run under it, or Nada's scream scared him out, and I chased him into the evergreens and picked him up. He was a lot bigger than he was two days before. His coat was not so soft. He whimpered and lunged in my arms, trying to get away.

"Spark don't like me any more," I said, weeping.

"*Doesn't* like you," Nada corrected me, trying to pet Spark's bony, nervous head. "Bring him inside and we'll feed him. He's been at the hospital for two days. After all . . ."

So we brought him into the house and he made a puddle right away on the kitchen floor, which the maid had just cleaned, and Nada said something she sometimes said to Father. We fed Spark and spent all day petting him and trying to make him stop whining. He wouldn't play, and I told Nada I didn't like him any more, and Nada told me that I had better like him if I knew what was good for me.

We had Spark for several years, then when we moved to Charlotte Pointe he had a nervous breakdown and never recovered.

That is the tale of my dog Spark.

10

We arrived somewhere late at night. I remember lights, car doors slamming, the scuff and scrape of luggage. Then bed. An unfamiliar pillow, but I slept my familiar heavy sleep.

I woke to hear Father arguing with someone. He was in the motel bathroom talking in a fast, furious voice with someone unknown. "Genêt is not sensational," Father said angrily. "You argue as if you were unaware that the *cas Genêt* has been studied by Sartre and other intellectuals. It's all sewed up." I dozed off again, and someone outside the motel-room door was scraping his luggage along. Two children argued bitterly. I woke up, startled, and it was dawn. I was alone in the cold motel room, and it occurred to me that perhaps it was I who had been left behind, not Nada.

The bathroom was empty. Father had never been there, of course; Father had his own motel room. When he came in to wake me he had already shaved, showered, and combed down the thinning hair on the left side of his head. He was ready to go. "First we eat and exercise our stomach muscles," he said happily.

We ate in a glass-enclosed coffee shop attached to the motel. A waitress in a uniform too yellow brought us food. I had an enormous appetite in spite of being so tired, as if someone else had charge of my stomach. Father ate well as always. There were a few travelers in the coffee shop, crabby husbands and bright-eyed wives, businessmen reading newspapers. From a radio set atop a shelf by the cash register came morning music interspersed with advertisements for the cure of thinning blood and chronic backache. It was a cheerful, sunny place, and when we left, the waitress giggled at some witticism of Father's and spiked our green-and-white "breakfast check" onto a sterilized nail on which many another check had been impaled.

"Things starting to look familiar yet?" Father said as he drove us closer and closer to Cedar Grove. "Ahhah, hah—look at that. New bank! Remember any of this?"

I stared out the window at the slow-passing sights, which were the sights of Fernwood. A bank with white shutters and white trim, pretty orange-red brick, evergreens framing everything; a shopping plaza empty of cars this early in the morning; across the way the Common, a big square area of green with library, courthouse, and post office, all of them constructed from the same mountain of buff bricks and according to the same plan. A feeling of lassitude overtook me, as if I were indeed coming home.

"Just like coming home, eh?" Father said.

We drove along. My eyelids were grainy, as if a few specks of sand had somehow worked in under them. The silence between Father and me was gettting awkward, so I said, "Have you read Genêt?"

He looked at me sharply. "Have you?"

"No."

"Yes, I've been reading Genêt," he said, a little relieved. "I was just discussing his works with Mr. Body the other day. You were in the den. Did you hear us?"

"I guess so."

"I don't recommend that writer for you, buster, not right now," he said comfortably.

We turned off onto a handsome boulevard shaded by elms. Some of the elms had yellow tags on them, but Father did not notice. Father's car sped along silently. It was strange how being awake did not make much difference. It was like being asleep. Dimensions were blurred and edges softened and even Father's cheerfulness was easy to take. He meant no harm, after all, no matter how much harm he caused, and in Flavius Maurus' heaven he would have been sainted.

"Look at that house! God," he said admiringly.

I didn't know which house he meant. It seemed important to me that I know, but already we were turning and entering a new street, and up before me arose more houses that looked different but were really familiar. I wondered if I should play the thinking game, to save myself from paralysis. I had to get awake enough for when Father finally stopped the car and pointed out our new home to me. What if I sat there all day, paralyzed? I tried to think of my mother, but at the very center of my vision there was nothing—a burned-out spot as if the mere thought of her had annihilated part of my mind.

"Here we are, buster. What do you think?"

We were driving up a hill. A driveway up a hill. Blacktop, but not overly black and vulgar: a worn smooth, conservative black. Sloping lawn, evergreens— some spiked up proudly against the house, others flattened out and creeping against the ground like sculpture. And the house—the house was (so I learned later) French Normandy, with a hint of a courtyard on one side, material that looked like hard-baked clay held together with strips of dark wood; wrought-iron gates, a tree growing placidly up near the doorway, everything lovely, lovely. It was a lovely house, and Nada would have wept to see it. Father said to me, "Buster, what's wrong? You're not *crying,* are you?" I astonished and dismayed the poor man at times. No, not crying, not crying! I was all right, I told him.

We bounded out of the car. He was like a magician showing me a galaxy of tricks, optical illusions—look at this, it all belongs to us! We live here! Ail this lawn, kid, and back here is a swimming pool, which we didn't use at the other house; see here, see the landscaping, see the bathhouse, see the bird bath, see the little grotto where all of us can have hotdog roasts and your little friends can join us, and here's a dog house in the exact shape of the big house, goddam cute!

Maybe Spark can come back, I said to Father, but this was too cruel, you don't talk to your father like that. He stared at me and told me that Spark had died, didn't I know that? (Evidently he had no idea how old an eleven-year-old child was.) I knew it, I told him, but sometimes I forgot.

Father led me around to the front walk, a lovely flag-stone walk. Silvery delicate bushes, just greening up (it was late April), and look at those rhododendron bushes —five hundred dollars' worth, for sure! Over there shaggy, golden forsythia, and everything lovely, lovely. My eyes throbbed with such sights. You would know, waking in such a world, that happiness is to be inhaled with the misty fragrance of the flowers, but at the back of my mind a voice began to chant at the same time that Father chattered about the house, so as to drown out his voice, You won't outlive this house, buster! This is the last one. You've had it. So many houses, so many miles, so many maids, plumbers, lawn men, snowplow men, so many doggies, so many parties, so much eavesdropping behind doors, sofas, over telephones, through laundry chutes, furnace vents, air-conditioner vents, so many roasted cashews, so many silver trays, so much hatred, so much love! You have had it.

Father rang the doorbell, silly, happy Father, and, shifting his weight from one big foot to the other, he chuckled just to be out here in the warm Cedar Grove sun. We heard someone coming, another maid I supposed, and then the door opened. The door was a most complex arrangement, very heavy; you must imagine a regular door and overlaid upon that a big greenish pane of glass and overlaid upon that a marvelously intricate pattern of wrought iron, half green (as if with age) and half gray, the pattern in the shape of a limp delicate vine, and blinding in the sun a nice vulgar brass doorknob—and when this vision was pulled aside there stood Nada herself!

She hugged me, and Father towered over us, clearing his throat, terribly moved and embarrassed and overjoyed. Nada kept saying, "Richard, I'm so sorry . . . Richard, how are you? How are you?"

"He's just fine, he eats like a little pig these days. Let's get inside where we can have some privacy," Father cried, red-faced.

Nada tried to gather me in her arms but I was too big. The three of us scuffled inside together.

"Everything's fine, just fine, absolutely first rate," Father cried.

Nada bent down to stare into my face. "But how are you, Richard?"

My heart was pounding heavily. I wanted to get rid of it, get free of its terrible rhythm, so that I could breathe the lovely perfume of her skin and hide in her arms, hide from everything. I had difficulty breathing and could not speak.

"Richard?" Nada said. "What's wrong?"

Father thumped my back. "He's just a little surprised, sweetheart."

"You mean you didn't tell him?"

"Well, you know—"

"You didn't tell him about me?"

"Just a little surprise for the kid," Father said, rubbing his hands and looking busily around. "Ah-hah, I see the painters finished in here. Very nice. Very good taste."

Nada touched my forehead. With her cool, soft hands she framed my face and looked at me. "Do you hate me?" she said.

"Don't talk morbid, please," Father said, turning back suddenly. "Richard is just a little surprised, as I said. I didn't mean to upset him."

I was embarrassed that they could see my heart thudding so violently in my chest. Nada said, "Richard? Are you all right?", and I managed to nod. She embraced me happily as if I'd given the right answer. "Do you love me? Do you forgive me?" she said.

I told her yes.

"Do you love me?" she said fiercely.

I said, "Yes, Nada."

"Oh, Nada," she said, laughing, "we should get rid of that foolish name. It was the first thing you said and I wanted to hang onto it, but it's foolish, your father is right. Richard, I will never leave you again. Never. You know that, don't you?"

I nodded again and let my eyes close.

11

In a day or two we had a ceremony and baptized the new house. This lovely, lovely house that Nada loved so much! "And your father picked it out himself. Your wonderful father!" Nada said. Oh, he was wonderful! There were big white flowers for Nada every day. Then the movers arrived and the furniture procession began again, inward this time, and rooms filled up slowly and the garage filled up with boxes and the basement with furniture that wouldn't be used (Nada wanted many new pieces of furniture), and when everything was settled we had our ceremony. Nada lay on the French love seat that now found its resting place in the hallway, and Father sat at one end so that her long lovely legs could lie across his lap, and I sat, like a little prince, on a stool at their feet, and she wore a green velvet dressing gown, and her hair was long and silky down to her shoulders, and she held the plastic Princess telephone in her graceful fingers and prepared to make calls. I had on my lap the two telephone books.

In the background was a strain of violin music— Father had requested Mozart. The records were in a jumble and I put on Bartók, knowing Father wouldn't notice the difference. Close about us was the perfumy but civil odor of white roses, Nada's favorites.

First of all Nada asked me the number of the Cedar

Grove Employment Services and she called to request a maid, and before she hung the plastic Princess phone up again a mysterious person was being contacted and would be on her way to us. The first call had been a success! What now? I said the groceries, but Father overruled me by saying, "Better send over a plumber for that bathroom." And I looked up another number for Nada and she called Cedar Grove Plumbing, and sure enough, in a few minutes someone else was on his way over.

"And now what?" said Nada. She was regal and soft as any queen. Father couldn't help but stroke the tassels of her robe.

"The lawn service," I said.

"The lawn service it is," Nada said briskly. She dialed the magic numbers and in no time was connected with the Cedar Grove Green Carpet Lawn Service. "Labyrinth Drive, *in* the village," Nada said. "*Oh, what do we want, darling?*—my husband says everything. Mowing, fertilizing, shrub and tree spraying, weed and insect spraying. Yes, what? Yes, fungus prevention, everything, edging, thinning, rolling, flattening. The usual. Everything."

"Now the Gas Company," Father said wisely.

And Nada called the Gas Company.

"And the Insurance Company."

And she called the Badger Insurance Company.

"And Vernon White, to let his secretary know I'm here."

And she called Vernon White, her hair falling over the side of her face.

"The garbage disposal is broken," I said.

"Ah, yes, the garbage disposal." Nada sighed. She

thanked me by touching my hair briefly, then called the Cedar Grove Garbage Disposal Service.

"And better call the sanitation department. There's a lot of junk out front," Father said, playing with Nada's silky green tassel.

And Nada made that call.

"And all that junk in the basement—better call the Good Will."

And Nada called the Good Will, to get rid of our junk.

"What about the swimming pool?" I said.

"Too early to clean that yet," Father pointed out kindly.

"There's something dead in there, birds or something," I said. "I looked under the canvas."

"They'll keep," Father said. "Too early for the swimming pool."

We all thought for a moment, and Nada said, "I was thinking about school for Richard. St. Ann's?"

"What's that, not Catholic?"

"Well, yes. It's a junior and senior high."

"Catholic, Nada?"

"I was just thinking of it."

"Well, honey, I'm not so sure about a Catholic school."

Nada smiled at once. "If you aren't sure, Elwood, then I'm not sure either. Cedar Grove Junior High, then?"

"Absolutely!"

And I looked up this number for her, and she called the school and made an appointment to bring me in. "Yes, he wants to attend summer school," Nada said.

When she hung up Father said, "What about the bank?"

And Nada called the Cedar Grove Bank of the Commonwealth.

"A dentist for buster here?"

And she called a Dr. Bellow and made an appointment for me.

"Eyes examined too," Father said, grinning at me as if I'd tried to put something over on him but hadn't been quick enough. "He needs the works."

So Nada called the Cedar Grove Eye Clinic and made another appointment.

"What about that scabby rash on your feet? Do you still have it, Richard?" Nada said. I had to admit I did. She pursed her lips and looked sorry and said, "Then we'll take you to a skin doctor too." She called a "skin doctor" and made another appointment.

"And reservations for dinner tonight, at the Roman Wall?" Father said.

"Absolutely," Nada said and dialed that number.

"Don't forget the Electric Company," Father said.

"Not at all," said Nada, "and while I think of it, the Water Company." In no time at all she had made both these calls.

"And the Telephone Company!" Father laughed.

"That's right too," said Nada. She dialed the proper number and smiled at us. "How many rooms in our house? I'm not sure, we've just moved in. Five, six bedrooms, I think. What? Oh, we want three or four phones. No, none in the basement. But I don't *work* in the basement, of course not! Yes. All black. Yes, black, we want to save money. Black." She hung up. "They're such talkers," she said, rubbing her offended ear.

"Why not buzz Armada and tell her you're in town?"

"Oh, Elwood, she wouldn't be home!"

"You could try."

"Later. And anyway I want to spend more time at home. With you and Richard. I don't want to be going out to lunch all the time."

"Ah-hah, I thought of another one: window washers. The windows are absolutely filthy."

"Right," said Nada grimly.

When she had finished with that call I said, "Now the grocery store," but Father outbid me by saying in a loud voice, "Now the drugstore. Send over some aspirin. The most expensive kind."

And she called the drug store.

"And the hi-fi up in the Family Room doesn't work," Father said.

Nada called a television and phonograph repair shop.

"And my lawyer, what's-his-name, Voyd, Maxwell Voyd, to get a little money out of the man who sold me this place. There's some wiring that doesn't work."

"But no one will pay, now. Isn't it too late?"

"We'll see," said Father.

So I looked up Mr. Voyd's number for Nada.

After that call Nada said, "Before I forget, an appointment for myself, to get my hair cut! Look how long it is!"

And she called the Cedar Grove House of Beauty.

"Ah, while I think of it, we need new keys for all the locks," Father said shrewdly.

I looked up the number of Cedar Grove Key Makers and Nada called them.

"Now the groceries?" I said.

"That pane in the Family Room that's broken, better call about that," Father said.

And Nada did that.

"Someone to clean out the chimneys?"

"Absolutely."

"To fix the slate on the roof?"

"Right again."

"Someone to install the chandelier from the other house?"

"Yes, right."

When she finished with all these calls she lay back and pretended to be exhausted. Then she said, "Now, Richard, look up the number of the Continental Market Basket and we will have some groceries!" And she called this exquisite store. "Yes, please, we have a charge account from years and years ago. I want it reactivated. Mrs. Elwood Everett. Yes. Will you please send me over some groceries? It's 4500 Labyrinth Drive, yes. We would like, please, three wonderful steaks, the best you have, and a large jar of bamboo shoots, Huang Brand, and three packages of hors d'oeuvre shells. The kind that look like snails, yes. And from your bakery counter, while I think of it, a nice loaf of French bread and a lemon meringue pie. Is it on special today? That's fine, and—*what, honey?*—my husband says to send us a case of shrimp, the big king-sized kind, and a case of boned turkey, any brand, and a case of—*what?* —Cheerios. Will they keep? And a case of Wash-Wight for the dishwasher—*that reminds me, Elwood, the dishwasher isn't working right*—and a plastic thing of sponges, you know, all different colors, and some steelwool things for cleaning out. Yes, pots and pans, and my husband says a case of Sylvan Ale, and a case of good cooking sherry, I'm not familiar with the brand names, and a case of red catsup, and a case of Big-Bite Peaches. Oh, moderate-sized cans, I should think, and a case of tabasco sauce, any kind, a case of noodles, that's the kind about the width of a pencil. Yes, that kind, and send us, please, a case of Midget-Treat Pickles— *Elwood, just for you!*—and five gallons of ice cream, different flavors. What's on special, vanilla? All right, all of vanilla, and three heads of lettuce and half-a-dozen nice bananas, not too ripe, and—*what, Richard?* —oh, God, yes, milk, plain milk, white milk, and a dozen eggs medium-sized—*what, Elwood?*—oh, large size. Grade AA, yes. And please send us a case of toilet paper, some pink and some yellow, and a case of tissue, any brand, but pink and yellow, to go with the bathrooms, you know, and a case of Shine-Eeze Floor Polish, the big bottle, and some Teutonic Stewed Tomatoes. No, absolutely no frozen things. In cans if you have them and if not, not. Fine. And two packages of butter. And salt, one container. Yes. Yes. I think that's all. No, don't bother repeating it, just send it over. Thank you so much."

When she hung up Father said, "Nada, you're so wonderful!"

She showed us the tip of her pink tongue and laughed. "I'm back home again and I'm never leaving. Never again!"

12

In a week the phone began to ring, Nada began to chat brightly in her old suburban style, people dropped in for cocktails, Nada dashed out in a brilliant pink dress to meet Elwood at someone's house for cocktails, people arrived and took them to the Old Mill Country Club, the delivery boy brought flowers for Nada's first dinner party, a box that was Nada's new late-spring suit, another box that was a surprise for me (not much of a surprise, just a Madras jacket).

One evening at dinner Nada and Father had this conversation:

"We'll have to have the Veals over," Father said.

"The Veals, honey?"

"I know how you feel, but—"

"But Elwood, the Veals are dead. They died in that awful plane crash, didn't they?"

"What? Dead? No, Tashya. I just met them the other day at Vernon White's, didn't I mention it?"

"Not the Veals, Elwood. You didn't meet them, they're dead."

"Who says they're dead?"

"Everyone said what a shame it was, don't you remember?"

"But they're not dead, I just met them! I just met them."

"Are you sure it was the Veals?"

"Of course. I think it was Thelma and Artie."

"They might have relatives—"

"But this looked like the Veals. You must remember them—middle-aged and sort of athletic? Always tanned?"

"Yes, but—"

"Well, we should invite them over. Thelma was very nice to you."

"But they're dead."

"I don't think so."

"Are you positive?"

"Tashya, I *think* so. I'm not positive, of course, but I *think* they're alive. Maybe we should wait a while before having them over though."

"It might be better."

"Still, I think—"

"I'm not sure myself, but . . ."

13

One day I went down to the library and there on the steps, clucking at some pigeons, was a boy who looked rather like myself. Skinny, hollow-chested, in a plaid shirt and wearing pink transparent-rimmed glasses. I looked again, and it was Gustave!

We greeted each other warmly. "I didn't know you were moving here," I said.

"I didn't know you were moving at all," said Gustave.

We were so overjoyed at meeting that we went immediately to his house and began a long, ingenious game of chess. Oh, it was wonderful, wonderful! I hoped we would never stop dreaming this time.

14

On another day I entered the library and found what I was looking for: a copy of *The Quarterly Review of Literature* with one of Nada's stories in it. I will reproduce for you here this story, which I have read and reread now some twenty, thirty times.

THE MOLESTERS

I .

I am six years old. There, at the end of the porch, is the old lilac tree. Everything is blurred with misty light, because there was a fog the night before and it is lifting slowly. I am sitting on the porch step playing with something—a doll. It has no clothes and is scuffed. It is neither a boy nor a girl; its hair was pulled off; its body is smooth and its eyes staring as if they saw something that frightened them. In the lilac tree some blackbirds are arguing. Not too far away is the cherry orchard; the birds fly over from the cherry trees and in a minute will fly back again. My father has put tin foil up in the trees to scare the birds away, but it doesn't work. If I lean forward I can see the brilliant tin foil gleaming high up in the trees—it moves with the rocking of the limbs, in the wind. My father has gone to work and does not come home until supper. The odor of supper and the harsh sound of my father's car turning into the cinder drive go together; everything goes together.

I climb up into the lilac tree. The first branch is hard to hold. The birds fly away. The doll is back there, by the steps. My grandmother gave me that doll, and the funny thing about it is this: I never remember it or think about it until I see it lying somewhere, then I pick it up and hug it. There is a little chair in the lilac tree made by three branches that come together. I like to sit here and hide. Once I fell down and cried and Mommy ran out onto the porch, but that was a long time ago when I was little. I am much bigger now. My legs dangle beneath me, scuffed like the doll's skin. My knees are marred with old scratches that are about to flake off and one milky white scar that will never go away.

My mother comes outside. The chickens run toward her even

though they know it isn't time to be fed; they come anyway. My mother puts something up on the clothesline. The clothesline is always up, running from tree to tree.

"What are you doing?" Mommy says. I thought she couldn't see me but she can.

"Can I go down to the crick?" I ask her.

There, in the grass, her feet are almost hidden. The grass is jagged and seems like waves of water. "Tommy isn't home," she says, without looking around. She finishes hanging the towels up —she has clothespins in her pocket and they make her stomach look funny. "Why do you always want to play there? she says. "Can't you play up here?"

"Tommy can go down anytime—"

"Tommy's bigger, Tommy doesn't fall down." She looks past me. There is something soft about her face—nothing bad stays in it. When I was little I kept going back into the kitchen to make sure she was there and she was always there. The big kids teased me and said she was gone, but she was always there. She would pick me up with a laugh.

I take the path through the field to the creek. There is more than one path: a path from our house and the Sullivans' house, and a path for fishermen who come from the road. Our path runs along flat but curves around, and there are prickly bushes that scratch you. By the creek the path dips downhill and goes to the bank. The fishermen's path comes down from the road, alongside the bridge. Fishermen leave their cars up on the road and come down the path, slipping and sliding because it is so steep. When fishermen come we have to leave. Mommy says we have to leave. One of the big boys threw stones in the creek once, to scare the fish away, and the fisherman ran up to the Sullivans' house and was mad. He was from the city.

The creek has a smell I like. I always forget it until I come back to it; there it is. There are big flat white rocks by the shore, covered with dried-up moss that is green in the water but white outside. This is what smells. It smells dry and strange; there is something dead about it. There are dead things by the creek. Little fish and yellow birds and toads; once a garter snake. The fishermen throw little fish down on the stones and let them rot. When

the fishermen are from around here we can stay and watch—
they're like my father, they talk like him. When they're from the
city they talk different.

Everybody has their rocks. Tommy's rock is the biggest one and
nobody can sit on it but him. I have a rock too. I sit on it and
my feet get in the water by mistake. That's bad. My mother will
holler. I try not to let them slip in but my rock is too little, I
can't sit on it right. I let my feet go back in the water. I like the
way the water feels.

I have a dam made out of stones, between two rocks. When I
look around I see the fisherman behind me.

He has a strange dark face; I saw someone like him in a movie
once. He has a fishing pole and a paper bag and some things in
his pockets. His hat looks dusty. "Do you live up there?" he says.
He has a nice voice.

That makes me think of my mother. I don't know how to talk
to grownups. They talk too loud to you, and something is always
wrong. I don't say anything to him. There are two crabs behind
the dam, little ones. Their bodies are soft to touch but they'd bite
you if they could; their pincers are too little. Tommy and the
boys use them for fishing, instead of worms.

"Do you live close by here?"

The fisherman is squatting on the bank now. His hat is off and
next to him. He has dark hair. I tell him yes. My face is prickly,
because of him looking at it. There is something funny about him.

"How old are you?" he says.

They always ask that. I don't answer but let a stone fall in the
water to show I'm not afraid of him.

"Are you fishing?"

"No."

"What are you doing?"

He is squatting on the bank and calling over to me. A grownup
would just walk out and see what I had, or he would walk away;
he wouldn't care. This man is squatting and watching me. The
bank is bare from people always standing on it. We play here all
the time. When I was little I could look down from higher up
and see the boys down here, playing. Mommy wouldn't let me
come down then. Now I can come down by myself, alone. I am

getting big. The bank tilts down toward the creek, and there are a whole lot of stones and rocks where the creek is dried up, then the water begins but is shallow, like where I am, but then farther out it is deep and only the big rocks stick up. The boys can wade out there but not me. There are holes somewhere too; it is danger-ous to walk out there. Then, across the creek, is a big tangle of bushes and trees. Somebody owns that land. On this side nobody owns it, but that side has a fence. Farther down where the bushes are gone, cows come down to the creek sometimes. The boys throw stones at them. When I throw a stone it goes up in the air and comes down right away.

"What have you got there?"

"A dam."

He smiles and puts his hand to his ear. "A what?"

I don't answer him, but pretend to be fixing something.

"Can I come look?" he says.

I tell him yes. Up there, nobody cares about what I do, except if I break or spill something; then they holler. This man is dif-ferent. He is like my father but not like him because he talks to me. My father says things to me but doesn't talk to me, he doesn't look at me for long because there are too many other things going on. He is always driving back and forth in the car. This man looks right at me. His eyes are dark, like Daddy's. He left his hat back on the bank. His hair is funny. He must have been out in the sun because his skin is dark. He is darker than Tommy with his suntan.

"A little dam," he says. "Well, that's real nice."

The crabs are inside yet. He doesn't see them.

"I got two crabs," I say.

The man bends down right away to look. I can smell something by him, something sweet. It makes me think of the store down the road. "Hey, look at that—I see them crabs. They'd like to bite a nice little girl like you."

I pick up one of the crabs to show him I'm not afraid. I am never afraid of crabs but only of fish that they catch and tear off the hook and let lay around to die. They flop around on the grass, bleeding, and their eyes look right at you. I'm afraid of them but not of crabs.

"Hey, don't let him bit you!" The man laughs.

"He can't bite."

The crab gets away and falls back into the water. It swims backward in quick little jerks and gets under a rock. It is the rock the man has his foot on. He has big black shoes like my father's, but caked with mud and cracked. He stands with one foot on a rock and the other in a little bit of water. He can do that if he wants to, nobody can holler at him.

"Do you like to play down here?"

"Yes."

"Do you go to school?"

"I'm going next year."

The sun comes out and is bright. When I look up at him my eyes have to squint. He is bending over me. "I went to school too," he says. He smiles at me. "Hey, you got yourself dirty," he says.

I look down and there is mud on me, on my knees and legs and arms. It makes me giggle.

"Will your mommy be mad?" he says. Now, slowly, he squats down. He is leaning over me the way some of them in town do, my mother's people. You can smell smoke or something in their breaths and it isn't nice, it makes me not like them. This man smells of something like candy.

"Little girls shouldn't get dirty," he says. "Don't you want to be nice and clean and pretty?"

I splash in the water again because I know it's all right. He won't holler.

"Little boys like to be dirty but little girls like to be clean," he says. He talks slow, like he was doing something dangerous—walking from rock to rock, or trying to keep his balance on a fence.

"You've got some stuff in your hair," he says. He touches my hair. I stop what I'm doing and am quiet, like when Mommy takes burrs out. He rubs the top of my head and my neck. "Your hair is real nice," he says.

"It's got snarls underneath. She has to cut them out."

"It's real pretty hair," he says. "Hey, you know in the city little girls have two daddies. One goes to work and the other stays home to play. Do you know that?"

Something makes me giggle. His hand is on my shoulder. He has dark, staring eyes with tight lines around them. He looks like he is staring into a lamp.

"Would you like another daddy?" he says.

"I got a daddy."

He touches my arm. He looks at me as if he was really seeing me. He is not thinking about anybody else; in a minute he won't stand up and yell out to somebody else, like my mother does. He is really with me. He puts his finger to his mouth to get it wet and then he rubs at the dirt on my arm. "I wouldn't never spank no little girl of mine either," he says. He shifts forward. His legs must ache, bent so tight like that. "You think they'd spank you at home for being dirty?"

"I can wash it off." I put my arm in the water. When you knock over a stone in the water a little puff of mud comes and hides the crabs that jump out—that saves them. When you can see again they're all hid.

"Maybe you better get washed up down here. I sure wouldn't want you to get spanked again," the man says. His voice is soft, like music. His hands are warm and heavy but I don't mind them. He is holding my arm; with his thumb he is rubbing it. I look but can't see any dirt where he is rubbing it.

"Hey, don't touch your hair. You'll get mud in it," he says. He pulls my hand away. "You can wash right here in the crick. They won't never know you were dirty then. Okay? We can keep it a secret."

"Tommy has some secrets."

"It can be a secret, and we'll be friends. Okay? Don't you tell anybody about it."

"Okay."

"I'll get you all nice and clean and then we'll be friends. And you won't tell them about it. I can come back here to visit sometimes." He looks back at the bank for something. "I got some real nice licorice in there. You like that, huh?"

I tell him yes.

"When you get cleaned up you can have some then. I bet you like it."

He smiles when I say yes. Now I know what the smell is about him—licorice. It reminds me of the store down the road where the licorice sticks are standing up in a plastic thing and when you touch them they're soft. They stick to your teeth.

"Little girls don't know how to wash themselves," he says. He pats water on my arm and washes it. I sit there and don't move. There is nothing that hurts, like there is sometimes with a wash-cloth and hot water. He washes me slow and careful. His face is serious; he isn't in a hurry. He looks like somebody that is listening to the radio but you can't hear what he hears.

He washes my legs. "You're a real pretty little girl," he says. "They shouldn't spank you. Shouldn't nobody spank you. I'd kill them if I saw it." He looks like he might cry. Something draws his face all in, and his eyes seem to be going in, looking somewhere inside him.

"But I'll get you clean, nice and clean," he says. "Then you can have some licorice."

"Is it from the store?"

He moves his hand on my back, slow, like you pet a cat. The cat makes his back go stiff and I do the same thing. I understand what it is like to be a cat.

"Do you want to walk in the water a little?"

"I can't do that."

"Just here. By these rocks."

"They don't let me do it."

I look at him, waiting for permission. My shoes are already soaked. But if I play out in the sun afterward then they will get dry.

"Sure. They ain't nowhere around here. *I* say you can do it," he whispers. He leans back and watches me. Because he is so close I am safe and it's all right to wade in the water. Nobody else ever sat and watched me so close. Nobody else ever wanted me to walk in the water and would sit there to catch me if I tripped.

"Is it nice? Does the water feel nice?"

The water comes up to my knees in the deepest place. I can't go out any farther than this. I was swimming somewhere, but not here; we go to a lake. There they have sand and people lying on blankets, but here there isn't anything except stones. The stones are sharp sometimes.

After a while the man stands up. His face is squinting in the sun. He walks alongside me, watching me; his feet will get wet. Something makes me yawn. I feel tired. I look down and see that I am making clouds of mud underwater.

"You better come out now," he says.

When I step out on the stones my shoes make a squishy noise. It makes me laugh to see the water running out. Inside my shoes my toes are cold.

He takes my hand and walks with me back to the bank. His hand is very warm. "You had a real nice time out there, didn't you?" he says. "Little girls like to play in the water and get clean."

He wets his finger and rubs something on my face. I close my eyes until it's clean.

The licorice stick isn't as good as the ones at the store. I want to take it back home but the man says no, I have to eat it down here. I keep yawning and want to go to bed. When I play in the water I get tired, the sun makes my eyes tired.

The man washes my hands with creek water, his own hands wet and rubbing with mine like he was washing his own.

"This is our own secret and don't never tell anybody," he says.

He wipes our hands on his shirt. He is squatting down all the time to be just as tall as I am. He has a black comb he combs my hair with, but there are snarls underneath and he has to stop. He pulls the hairs out of the comb.

"Now you have another daddy, and don't never tell them," he says.

When I turn around to look at him from higher up on the path, he is bending to get his fishing pole. I forgot about looking at the pole and want to run back to see it, if it's a glass pole like some of them, but now he looks like somebody I don't know. With his back to me he is like some fisherman from the city that I don't know and am afraid of.

I I .

I am six years old. At this time we are still living in the country; in a few years we will move to the city, in with my grandmother. But now my father is still well enough to work. My brother and his friends have gone on a bike trip. They have mustard sandwiches wrapped in wax paper and emptied pop bottles with water in them. I went out to the road and watched them ride away. Nobody cared about me; the boys call me baby if they are nice and push me away and tease me if they're bad. I hate my brother because he pushes me with his hand, like people do in the movies when they want to knock somebody out of the way. "Move it, kid," he says and pushes me. If I run to Mommy it won't do any good. He is four years older than me and so I can never catch up to him.

The day is hot. It's August, in the morning. The high grass in the orchard is dried up; the birds are always fighting in the trees; the leaves churn to show their sleek black wings. Tommy has a BB gun and shoots the birds sometimes, but when they hear the noise they fly away; birds are smart. The cat ate one of the dead birds and then threw up the feathers and stuff, right on the kitchen floor.

I am playing with my doll. Inside, Mommy is still canning cherries. On Sundays Daddy sits out front under the tree and tries to sell baskets of cherries to people that drive by. You can't go out by him and talk because he is always mad. The kitchen is ugly and hot. There are steamed jars everywhere, and bowls of cherries. Once I liked cherries, but the last time they made me sick. I saw a little worm in a cherry, by the pit. Twenty-five years from now I will drive by cherry orchards and the nausea will rise up in me; a tiny white worm. My mind will always be pushed back to this farm, and there is nothing I can do about it. I will never be able to get away.

Today is a weekday. Later on I will learn the number of it, from hearing so much about it. But now I know nothing except there are two or three days until Sunday, when Daddy stays home and sits out in front and waits for cars to stop.

My mother comes outside to see where I am. She wears an old dress with cherry stains on it. The stains make me look at them, they remind me of something. Of blood. She has her hair pushed back. Her hair is streaked up in front, by the sun, but brown everywhere else. There is a picture of her when she had long hair; she isn't my mother but somebody else. Around the house she is barefoot. Her legs look strong; she could probably run fast if she wanted to but she never wants to. Everything is slow around her.

The chickens are nervous, picking in the dirt and watching her for food. They jerk their heads from side to side. If she raises her hand they will flutter their wings, waiting to be fed.

My mother comes over to me where I am sitting on the branches, She brushes my hair out of my eyes. "Can't you wait for Tommy to come back, to go down there?" she says.

"I want to play with my dam," I tell her. I lean back so she can't. touch my hair. When she works in the kitchen her pale hands are stained from cherries. I don't like them to touch me then. When she gives me my bath they're like that too. I don't always like her. I can like her if I want to, but I don't have to. I like Daddy better, on purpose, even though Mommy is nicer to me. She never knows what I am thinking.

"I can take you down in a while, myself," she says. "Okay?"

I stare down at nothing. My face gets hard.

"What the hell is so good about playing in that dirty water?" she says.

This makes my heart beat hard, with hating her.

Her eyebrows are thin and always look surprised. I see her pluck at them sometimes. That must hurt. She stands with her hands thrust in her pockets, and her shoulders slump. I always know before she does what she is going to say.

"All right, then, go on down. But don't get wet."

I run around back of our orchard and through the next-door neighbor's field. Nothing is planted there. Then a path begins that goes down the big hill to the creek. In August the creek is shallow and there is filth in little patches in it, from sewers up creek. Fishermen fish anywhere along the creek, but there are some spots they like more than others. We always play by the rocks. There are also pieces of iron lying around, from when the new bridge was built. I can't remember any other bridge, but there was one.

I have my own little rock, that Tommy lets me have. It is shaped like a funny loaf of bread and has little dents in it. It looks like birds chipped at it, but they couldn't do that. When I come down and run through the bushes, some yellow birds fly up in surprise. Then everything is quiet. I walk in the water right away, to get my shoes wet. I hate my mother. Yesterday she was sitting on Daddy's lap; she was barefoot and her feet were dirty.

They told me to come by them but I wouldn't. I ran outside by myself. Down at the creek I am happier by myself, but something makes me shiver. It is too quiet. If I was to fall in the water and drown nobody would know about it or care.

A man drowned in this creek, a few miles away. It was out back of a tavern. I heard my father talk about it.

When I look around there is a man standing on the bank. His car is parked up on the road but I didn't see it before. The man waves at me and grins. I can see his teeth way out here.

"Real nice day to play in the water," he says.

I narrow my eyes and watch him. Something touches the back of my neck, trying to tell me something. I start to shiver but stop. He reminds me of the man that drowned. Maybe his body wasn't taken out of the creek but lost. This man is too tall. His arms hang down. He has a fishing pole in one hand that is long and gawky like he is. There is something about the way he is standing —with his legs apart, as if he thought somebody might run and knock him down—that makes my eyes get narrow.

"You live around here?" he says.

He takes off his hat and tosses it down as if he was tired of it. Now I know what he is: a colored man. I know what a colored man is like. But this one isn't black like the one my grandmother pointed out when we were driving. This one has a light brown skin. When Tommy gets real brown he's almost that dark.

"How old are you?" he says.

I should run past him and up the hill and go home. I know this. Mommy told me so. But something makes me stay where I am. To make Mommy sorry, I will stay here, right where I am. I think of her watching me, standing up on top of the hill and watching and feeling sorry for me.

"I'm six," I tell the man. With my head lowered I can still see him through my lashes. My eyes are half closed.

Everything is prickly and strange. Like when you are going to be sick but don't know it yet and are just waiting for something to happen. Something is going to happen. Or like when there is a spider on the ceiling, in just the second before you turn your head to see it. You know it's there but don't know why. There is something between us like a wet soft cobweb that keeps us watching each other, the colored man and me. I can tell he is afraid too.

"What are you doing?" he says. He squats down on the bank. He puts the fishing pole and the bag behind him. He looks like a dog waiting for his dish; he knows he can't come until it's ready. I could throw a stone at him, and he could reach out and catch it with a laugh.

"Can I come look?" he says.

He gets up slowly. His legs are long and he walks like he isn't used to walking. He comes right out to where I am and looks at what I have: a little dam made with stones between my rock and another rock. The water is running slowly through it. Nothing can stop that water. There is scum on it, greasy spots, and I touch them with my finger even though I hate them.

"I got two crabs in here," I tell the man.

I can hear him breathing when he bends down to look. A smell of licorice by him—and this makes me know I should run away. Men smell like smoke or something. They smell like beer, or the outside, or sweat. He is different from them.

"A crab would like to bite a nice little girl like you," he says. Right in the middle of talking he makes a swallowing sound. I keep playing in the water just like I was alone. I seem to seem my mother coming out on the porch, frowning and making that sharp line like a cut between her eyebrows. She looks down and sees my doll on the steps, by itself. If she would come down to get me I would be all right. But she won't. She will just go back in the house and forget about me.

Now the colored man squats besides me. He is still taller than I am. I am sitting with my feet in the water, and it makes me think of how the water might stop me, pulling at my feet, if I wanted to run. The water is quiet. If an airplane would fly past we could look up at it, but nothing happens. After a while the man starts to talk to me.

He says I have mud on me. Yes, this is right. It is like in a dream; maybe he puts the mud on me somehow when I wasn't watching. I'm afraid to look at him, but his voice is soft and nice. He talks about little boys and little girls. I know he is not a daddy from the way he talks.

"Your hair is real nice," he says.

As soon as he touches me I am not afraid. He takes something out of my hair and shows me—a dried-up leaf. We both laugh.

He is bending toward me. His eyes are funny. The eyelid is sleepy and would push down to close the eyes, except the eyeball bulges too much. It can't see enough. We are so close together that I can see tiny litle threads of blood in his eyes. He smells nice. Dark skin like that is funny to me, I never saw it so close. I would like to touch it but I don't dare. The man's mouth keeps moving. Sometimes it is a smile, then it gets bigger, then it changes back to nothing. It is as if he doesn't know what it's doing. His teeth are yellowish. The top ones are big, and when he smiles I can see his gums—a bright pink color, like a dog's. When he breathes his nostrils get small and then larger. I can almost see the warm air coming out of him, mixed with the smell of licorice and the dark smell of his skin.

He touches my shoulders and arms. He is saying something. He talks about my father and says he knows him, and he would like to be my father too. But he is not like any of the fathers because he talks in a whisper and nobody does that. He would not hit me or get mad. His eyelids come down over his big eyes and he must see me like you see something in a fog. His neck has a cord in it or something that moves; my grandmother has that too. It is the only ugly thing about him.

Now he is washing me. His breath is fast and warm against my skin. "They'll spank you if you're not clean. You got to be clean. All clean," he says. When he pulls my shirt off over my head the collar gets stuck by my nose and hurts me, but I know it is too late to run away. The water keeps coming and making a noise. "Now this. Hold on here," he says, with his voice muffled as if it was pushed in a pillow, and he pulls my shorts down and takes them off.

I can't stop shivering now. He stares at me. His hand is big and dark by my arm. I say I want to go home, and my voice is a surprise, because it is ready to cry. "Now you just be nice," he says. He moves his hand on my back so that I am pressed up by by him. I wait for something to hurt me but nothing hurts me. He would never hurt me like they would. His breath is fast and

206]

he could be drowning, and then he pushed me back a little. "Why don't you walk in the water a little?"

His forehead is wrinkled, and in the wrinkles there are drops of sweat that won't run down. I wouldn't want to touch his hair. He stares at me while I wade in the water. Everywhere he touched me I feel strange, and where he looks at me I feel strange. I know how he is watching. I can feel how he likes me. He would never hurt me. Something that makes me want to laugh comes up into my throat and almost scares me.

The sun is hot and makes me tired.

He takes my clothes and dresses me on the bank. He is very quiet. He drops my shirt and picks it up again, right away. Then with his long forefinger he rubs my arm down to the wrist, as if he doesn't understand what it is. His hands are real funny inside —a pink color, not like the rest of him. His fingernails are light too but ridged with dirt.

"Don't leave yet," he says. "Please. Sit and eat this with me."

When we eat the licorice he seems to forget about it, even when it's in his mouth. He forgets to chew it. I can see something coming into his eyes that makes him forget about me; he is listening to something.

We have a secret together that I won't ever tell.

When I come home Mommy is still in the kitchen. But everything looks different. It is the same but different. The air is wet. The way Mommy looks at me when I come in is different. She is smoking a cigarette.

"For Christ's sake, look at your shoes!"

She might be going to hit me, and I jerk back. But she just bends down and starts to unlace my shoe. "Just lucky for you these are the old ones," she says. The top of her head is damp. I can see her white scalp in places right through her hair. "Come on, put your foot up," she says, tugging at my shoe.

When the shoes are off she straightens up, and her face shows that she feels something hurt her.

"What the hell is that?" she says.

My heart starts to pound. "What?"

"On your teeth."

She stares at me. I can see the little lines on her face that will get to be like Grandma's.

"I said what is that? What have you been eating?"

I try to pull away from her. "Nothing."

"What have you been eating? Licorice? Who gave it to you?"

Her face gets hard. She leans down to me and sniffs, like a cat. I think of how I hate her because she can know every secret.

"Who gave it to you?"

"Nobody."

"I said who gave it to you!"

She slaps me. Her hand moves so fast both of us are afraid of it. She makes me cry.

"Who gave it to you? Who was it? Was it somebody down at the creek?"

"A man . . . a man had it—"

"What man?"

"A man down there."

"A fisherman?"

"Yes."

Her head is moving a little, rocking back and forth as if her heart began to pound too hard. "Why did he give it to you? Were you alone?"

"He liked me."

"Why did he give it to you?"

Her eyes are like the cat's eyes. They are too big for her face. What I see in them is terrible.

"Did he . . . did he do anything to you?" she says. Her voice is getting higher. "What did he do? What did he do?"

"Nothing."

She pulls me in from the door, like she doesn't know what she is doing. "God," she says. She doesn't know I can hear it. "My God. My God."

I try to push against her legs. I would like to run back out the door and away from her and back down to the creek.

"What did he do?" she says.

I am crying now. "Nothing. I like him. I like him better than you!"

She pulls me to the kitchen chair and knocks me against it, as if she was trying to make me sit on it but forgot how. The chair hurts my back. "Tell me what he did!" she screams.

She knocks me against the chair again. She is trying to hurt me, to kill me. Her face is terrible. It is somebody else's. She is like somebody from the city come to get me. It seems to me that the colored man is hiding behind me, afraid of her eyes and her screaming, that awful voice I never heard before. She is trying to get both of us.

"What did he do? Oh, my God, my God!" Her words all run together. She is touching me everywhere, my arms, my legs. Her fingers want to pinch me but she won't let them. "He took your clothes off, didn't he?" she says. "He took them off. He took them off—this is on backwards, this is . . ."

She begins to scream. Her arms swing around and one of the jars is knocked off the table and breaks on the floor. I try to get away from her. I kick her leg. She is going to kill me, her face is red and everything is different, her voice is going higher and higher and nothing can stop it. I know from the way her eyes stare at me that something terrible happened and that everything is changed.

I I I .

I am six years old. Down at the creek, I am trying to sit on a rock but my feet keep sliding off. Am I too big for the rock now? How big am I? Am I six years old or some other age? My toes curl inside my shoes but I can't take hold of the rock.

The colored man leans toward me and touches my hair. "I'm going to be your new daddy," he says.

The colored man leans toward me and touches my shoulders. His hand is warm and heavy.

The colored man leans toward me and put his big hand around the back of my neck. He touches me with his mouth, and then I can feel his teeth and his tongue all soft and wet on my shoulder. "I love you," he says. The words come back inside my head over and over, so that I am saying that to him: "I love you."

Then I am in the water and it touches me everywhere. I start to scream. My mouth tries to make noises but I can't hear them until somebody saves me.

"Honey, wake up. Wake up!"

My mother is by the bed. She pulls me awake.

"What's wrong, honey?" she says. "What did you dream about?"

In the light from the lamp her face is lined and not pretty.

I can hear myself crying. My throat is sore. When I see her face it makes me cry harder. What if they all come in behind her, all those people again, to look at me? The doctor had something cold that touched me. I hated them all. I wanted them to die.

But only my father comes in. He stumbles against the bureau. "Another one of them dreams, huh?" he says in a voice like the doctor's. He is walking fast but then he slows down. The first night he was in here before my mother, to help me.

My mother presses me against her. Her hands rub my back and remind me of something . . . the creek again, and the dead dry smell and the rush of terror like ice that came up in me, from way down in my stomach. Now it comes again and I can't stop crying.

"Hey, little girl, come on now," my father says. He bends over me with his two hands on his thighs, frowning. He stares at me and then at my mother. He is wondering who we are.

"We better drive her back to the doctor tomorrow," he says.

"Leave her alone, she's all right," my mother says.

"What the hell do you know about it?"

"She wasn't hurt, it's all in her head. It's in her head," my mother says sharply. She leans back and looks at me as if she is trying to look inside my head. "I can take care of her."

"Look, I can't take this much longer. It's been a year now—"

"It has not been a year!" my mother says.

My crying runs down. It always stops. Then they go out and I hear them walk in the kitchen. Alone in bed, I lie with my legs stiff and my arms stiff; something bad will happen if I move. I have to stay just the way I am when they snap off my light, or something will happen to me. I have to stay like this until morning.

They are out in the kitchen. At first they talk too low for me to hear, then louder. If they argue it will get louder. One night they talked about the nigger and I could hear them. Tommy could hear them too; I know he was awake. The nigger was caught and a state trooper that Daddy knows real well kicked him in the face —he was kicked in the face. I can't remember that face now. Yes,

I can remember it. I can remember some face. He did something terrible, and what was terrible came onto me, like black tar you can't wash off, and they are sitting out there talking about it. They are trying to remember what that nigger did to me. They weren't there and so they can't remember it. They will sit there until morning and then I will smell coffee. They are talking about what to do, what to do with me, and they keep trying to remember what that nigger did to me.

My mother's voice lifts sleepily. "Oh, you bastard!" she says. Something made of glass touches something else of glass.

The rooster out back has been crowing for hours.

"Look," says my father, and then his voice drops and I can't hear it. I lie still with my legs and arms stiff like they were made of ice or stone, trying to hear him. I can never hear him.

". . . time is it?" says my mother.

The room is starting to get light and so I know everything is safe again.

15

The first time I read "The Molesters" I had to leave the library at once. I felt uncanny. The air seemed to be rocking about me. I hurried through the shopping area of Cedar Grove as if under a spell, and for a while I stood at the corner near the Montclair Hat Shoppe and waited in terror for something to happen.

Nothing happened.

The story seemed to me very confusing but "artistic." Was it confusing because it was artistic, or artistic because it was confusing? I have since then stolen that copy of *The Quarterly Review of Literature* from the library, and to my shame be it said that I stole other copies of the issue from other libraries, I don't know why. I have seventeen copies here in my miserable room. They are all precisely the same.

The story takes time to figure out, but finally you see that:

1. There is only one man by the creek, only one man, and he happens to be a Negro. A Negro molester. (But rather gentle for a molester, I think. Is this Nada's sentimentalism?)

2. The title refers to more than one molester; hence we see that all the adults are "molesters"; they molest and are adults; they go about their business of adulthood, which consists partly (it would be selfish to say *wholly*) of molesting.

3. The child, who is much like myself, is telling the story to herself in various stages, unable to allow herself the full memory at first. It is too terrible. She gradually works up to it, is finally flooded by it and annihilated, so that the story ends upon an act of molestation. Clever Natashya Romanov, the author, who becomes herself one of the poking, prying molesters!

4. In symbolic terms: the child is myself, Richard Everett. Nada wrote the story to exorcise the guilt she rightly felt for abandoning me so often.

5. Nada, in three forms, as three adults, recognizes herself as my molester and acknowledges her guilt.

Have I seen something forbidden? Have I made an error?

About me on that fateful Cedar Grove day traffic moved on, traffic lights changed and changed again, people moved by, idle and ambling and attractive. I reached out to touch the brick of a building and the brick was rough, yes, and the sensation sped through my finger-tips and into the depths of my body, assuring me of one thing: I was alive.

Molesters are all about us.

What can I do to be saved?

If the child-hero of the story cannot understand what has happened to her, how are the rest of us to know? I include you, my readers. How will we know what mad acts were performed upon us, what open-heart surgery, what stealthy home brain surgery? Can we trust our well-meaning memories, our feeble good natures, which want to remember only the best about our parents, which brush aside ugly thoughts?

. . . Is this an ordinary disintegration, a routine text-book case, or is there something woeful and transcendent about it? Imagine Hamlet stunted at eleven years of age —do I claim too much for myself? Am I classic or trivial? Am I archetypical or stereotypal? Is all suffering too familiar?

Think of the power of words, my readers! Everything depends upon the style, the tone, the exact gesture, the divine play of words. Those anemic written signs Nada played with, having the power to raise up in me a seizure of trembling of the sort I hadn't had since the Johns Behemoth orgy in the Record Room—what a secret is behind them! There are some of us, sick people and mad-men, who should not be shown symbolic matter. Pictures, designs, words, are too much for us. We fall into them and never hit the bottom; it's like falling and falling into one of your own dreams. We make too much of things, we sick people and madmen. Words mean too much to us. You think only food excites me, my readers? You think all the food I devour (those disgusting bones

[213

over in the corner, those heaps of emptied tin cans!) means anything to me? Not at all, not at all—bulk to induce sleep and peace, nothing more. I am going to eat my way out of this life, like Nada's noble kinsman. Food means nothing but words mean everything! You see how I have become my mother's son.

Without her writing she would have been just Nada in the kitchen, Nada in her bathrobe upstairs, Nada on the telephone, Nada here, there, hugging me, turning vaguely from me—just that dark-haired lovely woman with the slightly knobby knees and wrists who, when she was in a hurry, walked along in a girlish, bobbing way with one hand bent sharply at the wrist as if to show that awkward little wrist bone. Yes, I would have loved her the way I loved Father, though probably more than I loved Father, but when I could read what she had written, creep and crawl and snuggle inside her brain, I began to see that the Nada who lived with us was just another visitor in our house, not as real or as colorful as Mrs. Hofstadter. That Nada was pretending. Wasn't she always saying to Father, "I admire you, I don't understand you so I admire you," and wasn't she always growing vague, remote, her gaze drifting away to the ceiling, and who was this Sheer? What could he give her that we couldn't? No, the woman I called "Nada" (that stupid name, she was right) was just a liar. She cheated all the time.

You who've never read the secret words of the familiar, domesticated people you love, you who've never snuggled into their brains and looked out through their eyes, how can you understand what I felt? It's as if I had opened a door and saw Nada not as she wanted to seem to us, but Nada as she really was, a stranger, a person Father and I did not know and had no connection with.

We are accustomed to people existing in orbit around us, and we dread thinking of their deaths because of the slight tug we will feel when their presence is gone—we'll be drawn out closer to the frigidity of darkness, space, death. We are accustomed to these smaller planets always showing the same sides to us, familiar, predictable, secure, sound, sane, accommodating, but when I looked through Nada's eyes I knew that I had been tricked, that she showed only her narrowest, most ignorant side to me, and that she had cheated me all my life.

Did I still love her?

I loved her more than ever, of course. Mothers who cringe and beg for love get nothing, and they deserve nothing, but mothers like Nada who are always backing out of the driveway draw every drop of love out of us. What's awful is that love is an emotion you can't do anything with. It has no value. We who love hopelessly are like noblemen in exile, an exile with no kingdom to look back at, to remember. Our beloved exists within the perfect halo of her own consciousness, selfish and adored, protected from us by the very violence of the love we feel. Is this a boy's love for his mother, you're wondering? Eh? Oh, let it be anything—any kind of love! I had enough love for any kind! I could outlast lovers, husbands, pals—and let me mention my most formidable rival, a woman with handsome olive skin, eyes slightly slanted (make-up? Oriental blood?), who wore dark wool, heavy jewelry, and had advanced degrees in European history. She had been Nada's friend for a few months one winter. I remember them laughing softly together, that coy, sly tilting of their heads that meant secrets, intimacy, a closeness Father never knew and I certainly never knew, as I hulked about in the den,

pretending to be looking for a book. Dr. Lippick, goddam you! But she disappeared finally, I don't know how,
drawn out into someone else's orbit or knocked askew
by someone in Nada's orbit, for Nada was always moving
on, you know, like any major constellation, driving onward toward whatever it was she believed she was seeking, and along with her went satellites and particles of
dust, among them myself.

I said I was a nobleman in exile and that's garbage of
course, it's sentimental bombast, and it isn't true either
that I had no kingdom or memory of one. My kingdom
was the place we were going to enter finally, Nada and
I. Together. Time was passing us, like a gentle spring
breeze that has come from some innocent cove thousands
of miles away, and overtakes us, and passes us by. I
had to get us safely into that kingdom.

Was it that day or another day, after reading "The
Molesters" again, that I made my purchase? Let's say
it was that same afternoon. At about one o'clock I read
the story, and at two o'clock I went into a small shop
called Ax's Sporting Goods. I asked the man shyly about
a rifle. He chuckled the way Father did and asked me
how old I was. I looked at some rifles, touched them,
smelled them. A rocking, nauseated sensation rose in me
but I recognized it—it was familiar, it didn't alarm me.
It wasn't a bad feeling. It was like coming out of a drug-
induced sleep: waking is painful but you want it badly.
You want it more than anything in the world, though it's
easier to sleep; you could sleep forever and spend no
energy. Ah, if I woke I would do many things! I would
grow into manhood and be a son worthy of my mother!
If I woke . . .

In the end I went down the street to a drugstore and

there bought a magazine called "He-Man Guns." In the back of the magazine (which was partly a comic book) I found the grubby little ads I craved: "Are Guns Your Hobby?" "For Target Practice." "Halt!" "New Amazing Ballpoint Pen Gun $3.98!" "German Sniper Rifle Used by Mad Fanatic SS Men—Limited Number!" "Assemble at Home—Be a Sharpshooter! Protect Yourself at All Times!" Crummy drawings of rifles, machine guns, pistols, revolvers, bazookas, cannons, anything. "Own Your Own Cannon! Powerful Enough to Down a Tank!" Why not own your own tank too? But no tanks were for sale in this magazine.

Read my desperation in the rapidity with which I settled upon one of these ads, distinguished in no way from the others, bought some envelopes in the drugstore and took out one of them, made out the coupon at the bottom of the ad, and actually slid into that envelope along with the coupon several handfuls of dollar bills Father had given me off and on, forgetfully, spasmodically, the way he sometimes offered people chewing gum or free tickets he'd been handed himself, forgetfully and spasmodically, everything accumulating in his pockets. And I bought a stamp in the stamp machine, was cheated of a penny, and addressed the envelope in my boyish block letters, and mailed it down at the corner. It took no more than five minutes and I was on my way.

part III

1

A friendly pilot skimming low over Cedar Grove would see as much of it as anyone else, but once in a while there are little cracks that let light through. One day I was downstairs doing my math homework (I was enrolled in a double-session geometry class at school; it was mid-July of an unforgettable summer) when Nada came into the den. She was chewing on something. She sat on the sofa and for a moment said nothing, was probably not even looking at me. Then she said, "How old are you?"

I looked up, surprised. She was chewing on a piece of celery. "Eleven," I said.

"Eleven," she said vaguely, as if counting mentally on her fingers to make sure I was legitimate. "You know, Richard, I'd like us to talk but there doesn't seem to be anything to talk about. Have you noticed that?"

"I don't know," I said.

"Do you have friends? What do you do? What are you always reading? Would you like to go to camp this summer? Your father said you might be interested in the Little League team, is that true?"

"I don't remember saying that."

"I'm sure you don't. He must have imagined it," Nada said sarcastically. She finished the piece of celery and wiped her fingers lightly on the sofa covering. "What have you been reading lately, Richard?"

I laid down my pencil reluctantly. What if I told her I spent my time reading the things she had written, understanding nothing except to know that the sympathy she showed in her stories must have used up all the sympathy she had in her? You would think nothing would be easier to get than sympathy from Natashya Romanov, but here was Natashya Romanov herself, in yellow silk slacks and a yellow and green blouse, staring at me as if I had just crawled out of a crack in the wall.

"Science-fiction stories," I said.

She looked disinterested at once. "Richard, did you miss me while I was gone?" she said. "Why didn't you answer my letters?"

"When?"

"When I was gone, silly. When I was gone."

It pleased me to be called "silly" by her. "I was busy with school."

"Oh, that ridiculous Johns Behemoth, that disgusting Nash! But did you miss me?"

"Sure."

"Did your father take away the letters I wrote to you, or did you see them?"

"I saw them."

"Are you telling me the truth?"

"Yes, Nada."

"He wanted to come between us, but it's over now and I don't blame him. Your father and I are friends now. Everything is forgiven."

"Father was very nice—"

"He wants you to call him Daddy."

"*Daddy*—"

"But call him anything you want. I don't care."

"He was very nice, he took me to the movies and bowling. He was nice all the time," I said miserably.

"Did he drink much?"

"Drink?"

"Richard, you don't really know your father. He's a man you haven't met yet. Don't let him fool you."

"Yes, Nada."

She stared at me. "What the hell do you mean? You sound as if you're imitating someone. What is it? Are you imitating the person I'm supposed to think you are? Who do you talk to? Listen to? How will you grow up normal if you keep listening to the wrong people? I know you were eavesdropping on me the other day when I was on the phone. I heard you upstairs, my little friend, but I was too polite to accuse you." She had been speaking seriously, but now she laughed. All of Nada's words were canceled out by her destructive laughter. She gave me the same sideways look a boy had given me the other day, except that boy had been wearing a sweatshirt with JESUS SAVES on its front and dark sunglasses, so that as a matter of fact one shouldn't have expected a "look" from him at all.

Out in the hallway, at the bottom of the door that led to the basement, something moved suddenly—a tiny face and paws emerged for an instant and then disappeared.

It was not enough to wake me from my stupor so I said nothing to my mother. Maybe I had imagined it anyway. Nada talked on and I noticed that she had taken on a new style of talk, this "my friend" business, and that this meant she had herself taken on a new friend. When she fell silent I was afraid she would leave, so I said quickly anything that came to mind. "Mrs. Hofstadter cut Gustave's fingernails and toenails the other day, with a clippers, and she almost severed his little toe."

Nada frowned. "You say the wildest things, Richard."

"It's true. Mrs. Hofstadter has been acting funny."

"You're too critical of adults," she said. "Anyway, my little friend, if a mother wants to clip off her son's little toe, or indeed his big toe, who has a better right?"

"Don't you like Gustave?"

"Of course. He's nice." She stretched out her legs and sighed lazily. "What say for a treat, friend? Should I drive us out to Ho-Jo's and get you a cone, or would you like to go down to the cellar and stick your head in the freezer? There are some vanilla cones down there."

"I don't want to go down in the cellar."

"Why not?"

"There are some mice or something down there."

"Oh, you're crazy!" She laughed. "We don't have mice here. What do you think this is, a slum? We could drive out to Ho-Jo's then."

"I'm not hungry."

"Why, mice out there too? Mice everywhere?"

"I'm not sure if it's mice."

Nada straightened. She had heard our maid, Libby, who was in the kitchen doing something; some pans clattered. "That woman can't suppress her unconscious hostile feelings," Nada said. "Listen to her banging around!"

"She's nice."

"Oh, everyone's nice."

There was a moment of awkward silence. Then the telephone rang at Nada's elbow. She said, "No, I'm sorry, I wish I were Natashya Everett but you must have the wrong number. No, I wish I *were* that woman." She hung up and winked at me.

"Seriously, Mother, there are mice or something down there—"

"What's this, now you're calling me *Mother?* Weaned at last? Don't give me that solemn weepy look through your glasses, my friend, I don't particularly care to be called *Mother* by anyone. I don't respond to it. I'm trying to hold my own and that's it. No *Mother,* no *Son.* No depending on anyone else. I want you to be so free, Richard, that you stink of it. You're not going to blame me for anything."

"Who should I blame then?"

"Nobody."

"Not even Father?"

"Especially not him."

"Isn't there anybody?"

"My own father, my drunken madman of a father," Nada said, but without her usual melodramatic conviction. It was plain that she regretted having hung up on that call. "If you don't be quiet I'll buy a Home Clipper-Cutter from the Discount Mart and cut your hair here at home and 'almost sever' your ears, little chum. You and Gustave both." She reached over and stroked my hair.

She was right, it did need to be cut. Father took me out on Saturdays when he had his own hair cut, but sometimes he was far away and forgot about me; it was possible for me to go a long time without having a haircut. Like most things about me, my long hair did not quite matter.

"You know, Richard, once I spent two days tracking down a single lie of your father's. Two days of my life. And I discovered that he hadn't lied, no, but when he told the truth he told it in such a way that one thought, Good Christ! That *must* be a lie. That's your father."

"Nada, what is an *abortion*?"

She sat up and her hand moved away from me. There was something too casual about her expression.

"An abortion, if you must know, is something that fails to come off. Let's see: we plan on Father grilling steaks for us tonight, but at the last minute Father fails to come home. Hence, the steak barbecue is *aborted*."

"Is that what it means?"

She was silent for a moment, not exactly looking at me. It was never possible to tell what she was looking at or thinking. After a moment she said, "What say we drive out to Ho-Jo's then, pal? Stuff ourselves on some cheap tasty food? Father will be gone tonight and tomorrow night, so we can eat anything we please and at any time we please."

"You never tell me the truth, Nada," I said bitterly.

"Oh, you're making me tired. Leave me alone, you little pest."

The telephone rang and she picked it up at once. "Yes, hello. Yes," she said quickly.

Sunk in my lethargy, I watched her and thought how strange it was that she was my mother, that there was so much that should be said between us but which would not be said. The time in which to say it was running out like that breeze drifting gently past us as she dawdled and talked with that Other Person . . .

"Oh, I can't talk now, don't annoy me," she said in the same voice she had used with me. "When, tonight? No, not tonight. Tomorrow. Yes, he won't be back. Look, I can't talk now. I've told you not to call me. Yes. Good-by."

"Who was that, Nada?" I said.

"Don't Nada me, you little fake," she said. She rose lazily, happily. Her voice was slightly detached, as if she were still on the telephone. "Look, are we going out to dinner or what? Why do you sit there?"

But we never got out to dinner that night: a strange thing happened. Libby slipped down the three steps that led to the back porch, spraining an ankle, and we had to tend to her. We had been about to leave when this happened, and dutifully we came back. That's how it is in ordinary life. Scenes move toward sensible conclusions, then someone slips and falls and ruins everything. Now, years later, I still nurse an unreasonable hatred for Libby.

2

She was a greedy woman, my Nada. You know the story of the old grouch Juvenal eating until he was sick, out of pure spite at the heaven of sensuality he could not enter, and if you know that you also know the story of Laurence Sterne and Charles Churchill come to London (but not together), lunatic, depraved gluttons of clergy-men whose only aim in life was to devour as much of anything as was available!—and all of history gives us these weird writers whose scribbling must in itself have been a kind of grossness, but not enough to satisfy, coming to London or Paris or Rome or New York, any-where, to fill their stomachs and brains with whatever was handy. But even as Juvenal vomited as he ate, so Nada did vomit back out much of what she took in so eagerly; and even as Sterne and Churchill met their ends in excess, so did Nada invite her finish by an excess of greed.

On the evening following Libby's fall Nada went out at about five. She said, "Richard, will you be all right? I have to see someone."

I heard her drive out and watched the yellow car dis-appear down Labyrinth Drive and wondered whether I should follow her on my bicycle; but no, you don't do that. And at five-thirty what should turn in our drive but another yellow car? It was Father come home a day early.

He drove up but did not drive the car into the garage. I noticed that. I was sitting in the kitchen, in the darkened breakfast nook, waiting. I heard Father's car pause, stall, stop. I heard him sit there for a while, looking in at the empty garage. Finally he got out and came to the backdoor.

"Father?"

He stumbled up into the kitchen. "Oh, it's you," he said. There was a moment when his smile did not work, then it worked. He rumpled my hair as if this were an obligation to me. "Nada not in just now, eh? Is she shopping for food?"

"I don't know."

"Did she say where she went?"

"I don't remember."

"Yes, hmmm," he said meaninglessly. He wandered into the dining room and turned on the lights. I followed him into the hall, then into the living room. This living room was rather long. You could not be certain, standing in the doorway, if the room was really empty or not. There was always the feeling that someone was sitting down at the other end, screened by a giant plant or disguised simply by distance. In the instant before Father switched on the light I thought I saw someone sitting by the fireplace.

"When did she leave?" Father said.

"A few minutes ago."

"So late? Very strange," he said. We wandered back into the hall. Father switched on another light, and we heard the scratch of tiny nails down at the far end of the hall, by the basement door. "What in good Christ is that?" he said, genuinely astonished.

I ran to open the basement door, and we saw two chipmunks dashing madly down the carpeted stairs.

"What's that?" Father cried. "Rats? Mice?"

"Chipmunks."

"But what are chipmunks doing in here? In our house?"

"They must have gotten in by mistake."

Father was panting hoarsely. We listened and heard the scratching of tiny, frenzied toenails downstairs, then something happened to Father. He grunted and took off his suit coat and thrust it at me. "I'll get 'em," he said. "Little saucy bastards!"

He ran downstairs two and three at a time, a big,

heavy, sweating man, and at the landing he grabbed the broom Libby had left and, wielding it like a great weapon, made his way into the main room of the basement. Three chipmunks scattered, panicked, and Father started after them with the broom raised and his chest sending out great bursts of rage. "Hyar! Hyar!" he cried, like a mythical Texan routing a maverick steer.

I sat at the foot of the stairs and hugged my knees. I watched. Father rushed at one corner, swinging the broom, and slapped it down hard. The chipmunk flew out to one side and, its tiny legs pumping wildly, ricocheted off the wall and fled in another direction.

"Hyar, you little bastard!" Father yelled. His eyes bulged as he brought the broom around in a great muscular arc, this time scooping the chipmunk off the floor and slamming it hard against the wall. It fell with a soft plopping noise, and he hit it again and again with the flat of the broom, grunting. "Oh, you little bastard," he said softly, in just the same tone Nada had once used on him.

Then, flushed with victory, he turned from the lifeless and battered chipmunk and rushed into another corner, where another terrified creature darted out blindly—and he swung the broom around again in a most skillful, graceful arc, at the last moment scooping the broom up in the air so that he could bring it down flat on the chipmunk. And again. And again.

After a few threshing minutes he got the third chipmunk, and then, panting wildly, he whirled around to see yet another chipmunk making its cautious way in from the laundry room. Stupid rodent! Father yelled and rushed at it and chased it back into the laundry room. I did not follow. I heard the broom fall again and again.

My heart beat calmly and regularly, O my readers, and I will not be so sophisticated as to deny that I felt sorrow for those poor beasts, and something beyond sorrow.

When it was over, Father appeared again, with the broom up over his shoulder like a musket. "Good Christ, what a workout," he said, wiping his forehead. "That did me good. That really did me good." He glanced at me and said, "You want to help me get rid of them?"

"I feel a little sickish."

"Oh, sickish! Buster, you're always sickish! Poor kid."

He pitched the broom into a corner and it remained standing, as if by magic, then he turned and contemplated the battlefield with his hands on his hips. The three mangled and crushed chipmunks lay curiously close together. "Hah, hah," Father murmured, rubbing his hands vigorously, "we'll just clean up this little mess and that's that." But when he bent to pick the first chipmunk up, delicately by its tail, an unfortunate thing happened: the tail broke in two close to the body and what was left of the chipmunk fell to the floor. "Dirty little bugger," Father hissed. It is no credit to me that I did not offer to help him. I thought of the newspaper in the corner before he did but hadn't the heart or the stomach to speak. I wanted to sit still, very still. But Father finally thought of the paper by himself and unfolded it near the chipmunks and kicked them onto the paper, gingerly enough. Then when he had them he folded the paper up neatly and took it to the incinerator.

"Will this stuff burn, Dickie?" he asked, grimacing over his shoulder.

3

And did they fight that night? No, indeed, because Father did this: he emerged from his triumph with the chipmunks, washed his hands, had a bit of Scotch, sat in the living room for two hours, and finally said, "Richard, I will make a deal with you. I will take you out to all the Little League tryouts you want, I'll pull strings to get you on the team, if you'll help me with this. You see, I don't want to upset your mother, so I think I'll spend the night at a motel. Then I'll come home tomorrow as planned, right? And she needn't know . . . well, she needn't know what you know. I mean, that I was . . . home tonight. Will you help me?"

Yes, it was pathetic to watch, because he was still rather flushed from his workout and at the same time a chill had come over him. Poor Father! He looked like the mad maniac who had kidnaped a child in Vermont, held her captive and "molested" her for five days, and was finally shot down by police, a state militia, and many private citizens on foot. The whole story was in the current *Post,* a first-person tale told by the child herself of the peculiar apocalyptic mutterings of the madman, of the many times he did "it" to her, and how close he came to killing her! A most chilling tale indeed, and it did your heart good to see the child's newly curled locks and smile for the photographers, and to know that she had received many thousands of dollars for her exclusive story. But the photograph I speak of is the madman's:

some daring cameraman got a shot of him just as he turned to meet a barrage of shotgun pellets and bullets, and his glittering, twisted, wet look was just the same as Father's look, though Father must not have really expected bullets to come tearing into his chest.

"Is it a deal, buddy?" he said nervously.

"Sure, Dad."

We shook hands on our Secret.

4

Father said I was always sick and and I want to defend myself. I wasn't always sick. There were many days when I was well, ordinarily well, and many other days when I was well enough to drag myself around. On other days I suppose I was "sick," but not really ill. There is a difference.

I hope you won't think that I ever played sick, begging a quiet morning home from school with Nada. It was not necessary for me to play sick, though I played many things. I played healthy, for instance, which could be a tiring task, and I played an eleven-year-old with some success. But I never needed to play sick because sickness, or a mild queasiness, was my natural state. After I confessed to my crime at least one doctor, attracted as they all are by the most choice exhibitions of corrupt flesh and spirit, made a study of my various diseases and ailments and termed me a "medical catastrophe." Another doctor, a psychiatrist, declared that I was a hopelessly neurotic/psychotic hypochondriac with some respectable overtones of the Kress syndrome—that is, some real disorders. Still another physician, a Dr. Saskatoon, combined the two diagnoses and pronounced my physical organism to be supplying my mad mind with the basis for its madness or, on the other hand, my mad mind so despised itself for lying (no one believed my confession, of course) that it summoned up physical disorders to punish the body. I like that theory! I like the eerie, primitive magic behind it—the mad mind "summoning up physical disorders" as if by telephone. Dr. Saskatoon was a genial and intelligent man, and his professional decline saddens me.

And what precisely were my troubles? I will list them in an order dictated by a poetic association of ideas. My readers, I suffered from chronic toothache, mysteriously begun and mysteriously ending. I suffered from twelve-hour flu, four-day flu, two-week flu, and common intestinal flu that could shoot incredible pains through my abdomen for half an hour, then vanish. I suffered from watery eyes, sore eyes, sensitive eyes, weak eyes—and all the same two eyes, of course. I suffered from mild and severe headaches, sometimes simultaneously (the mild ache throughout my brain and the severe one above my left eye). I suffered from frequent sore throats, from various kinds of asthma (I was allergic to cats, to chicken and turkey feathers, to pollen, poppies, birds' nests, fox stoles, etc.), from rashes both scabby and flaky, from bumps, itches, and undefined swellings. I suffered from all kinds of colds: head, chest, stomach, muscle, anywhere. My eyes watered and my teeth chattered. I was subject to severe shivering fits in the winter if I went outside too scantily dressed. I coughed, I hacked, I sneezed. I was always falling down too, even at the age of eleven. As a smaller child I always had bruised and

234]

scab-marred knees and elbows. I could fall from tricycle, wagon, tractor, pushcart; I even fell out of my baby buggy once when no one was looking. I could fall while standing flat-footed on a sidewalk, don't ask me how. I fell down stairs and stumbled up stairs. I fell over my own shoelaces, tied or untied. But nothing ever hurt me, much. It was as if my bones were too unshaped, too limp and malleable, to break.

And I had the usual boring run of diseases. Measles, chicken pox, mumps, scarlet fever, rheumatic fever (a mild case). I almost died with one attack of flu, however. Something had been wrong with my tonsils, and I think my appendix flared up once, years ago.

Now I am a bundle of worse troubles, but I don't go to doctors and I don't know what's wrong. I don't care to know. By body is just a vessel or instrument I am using, as this typewriter is an instrument I'm using, and when I am finished with this memoir I will be finished with this body. That's all.

5

Sometimes I could hear the invisible grit in the air singing around my ears, sometimes not. I was a good student at Cedar Grove Junior High Summer Session. I studied math. My mathematical steps were always sensible, though my conclusions were often wrong. It was as if, led to the very brink of the inevitable, my pencil somehow swerved and whimsically snatched at an impossible answer.

I think I woke up totally at times. I don't know. Squealing brakes warned me to jump back up on a curb, yes, but whether this qualifies as "waking" me I'm not sure. There were pressures that kept me tired and dopey. For instance? Walking into a room in which Father and Nada were and having them stop at once their conversation to smile dazzlingly at me. That pushed me down a little. Nada had moved out of the big bedroom again and left Father there alone, retiring as she always did to her "study." Four days in a row she asked me what I was studying in summer school, and Father kept mentioning the Little League as if it were something I should be teasing him about, nagging him into taking me. I didn't mind this because at such times my gaze would meet Nada's and we would share a silent contempt for such nonsense—imagine *me* acting out the farce of childhood athletics!

Precarious as they were with each other, their good spirits bubbled over onto everyone else. Many people visited them. I won't bother with the list of names; it's different from the Fernwood list but only superficially. One interesting man stands out: Mr. Body. You have heard the name Body before (the advertising man who bought our house in Fernwood), but this is another Body family, unrelated, I'm sorry to say. I'm sorry because I like unity of one kind or another, however foolish or arbitrary. Mr. Body loved to sit in Nada's gold Queen Anne chair, cross his legs, and talk about the loss of freedoms in America. "Soon they'll be taking away from us the right to bear arms, to protect ourselves with rifles," he declared.

Everyone agreed with Mr. Body, even when they

weren't listening. Everyone agrees with everyone else in Fernwood, or Cedar Grove, wherever we are.

And there was another interesting man, one who did not fit in, one whose coming was contrived and suspicious: an old friend of Nada's. He was a professional intellectual whom Nada had brought to town, under the auspices of the Village Great Books Discussion Club. Each year a speaker came to speak at their luncheon, the good literary ladies' luncheon. They had money, and in the past they had flown out to them James Dickey, Bennett Cerf, a very top narrative-writer for Walt Disney, even Paul Goodman, even Pearl Buck, and many others. But this year Nada had snagged for a mere $500 the editor of *The Transamerican Quarterly,* who was also a book reviewer for *The New York Times Book Review,* and also the somewhat notorious and flamboyant "film critic" for a prestigious men's magazine to which Father subscribed. I missed his name, though I believe it ended in a complicated swish, a "-sky" that was not Polish but Russian-Jewish.

He was a house guest of Nada's, a fact that agonized me, and a scant two hours after his arrival by jet there was a cocktail party for him, with all the literary ladies and their unliterary but very friendly husbands—the élite of Cedar Grove—present in his honor and anxious to make him feel at ease; even Mavis Grisell, in town to visit her sister, was present with her winning, girlish smile. I, Richard, was allowed to parade around with plates of hors d'oeuvres (tiny smoked oysters, tiny anchovies, shrimp with shrimp sauce, glazed crackers, cheesed crackers, cheesebits, onionbits, flaked, blown, browned, and homogenized potato chips, and of course roasted cashews), and I took advantage of my role to observe this stranger from another part of my mother's life. It was so rare that I was allowed to peek into that life.

Let us draw nearer to this man. He was in his forties but not young—I have to add that "but," for in Cedar Grove all men under sixty are spry and young, demons on the golf course (until that fatal day at the ninth hole) as they are behind desks and alighting from jetliners; in the intellectual world they evidently head downhill fast after forty. This editor had short, thin, wirelike hair that stood up straight from his skull; his hair was blond. His face was an aggressive blank to me the first time I served him some smoked oysters (he scooped up several and ate them greedily), but the second time around I was able to look at him more closely. Face an oblong, rather bony, and eyebrows gray and patchy; a band of small pits along his cheeks (acne scars, smallpox? not important anyway). His skin was sallow and heavy. An argumentative nose; jaw darkened as if with shadow or a bluish beard about to pop out at any moment. His voice was rapid and assured, and his eyes were nervous, darting, and critical. He began to talk at once about the hypocrisy of American society, and he ate large, soft shrimp from a plate beside him as if to emphasize his words.

"Our culture, my friends," he said, "is based upon competition and greed. Who can deny this? It is inhuman, totally inhuman. It is terrified by love— not just sexual love, my friends, but all love. Paradoxically enough, or rather not paradoxically at all, this culture is obsessed with brutality: in its fixed aesthetic forms, the police state and the television set."

Mavis Grisell clinked her Egyptian jewelry in agreement; she was always agreeable. Nada sat a distance away and crossed her legs. Her vagueness that evening puzzled me, and it was only years later that I realized she took Cedar Grove so unseriously that even her old friend, placed in it, became unserious; she hardly listened to what he said and therefore had no idea that he might be insulting her guests. Of course her guests had no idea either.

"Very interesting point," a man in a dark suit said with enthusiasm. This was Mr. James Bone, a manufacturer of garage doors.

The editor popped a shrimp into his mouth and his jaws ground with vehemence. "Certainly it's *interesting*! It happens to be true. America, my friends, is based upon money. And money is based upon man's natural selfish desire for power. So we may say that the basis of our evil is the selfish desire for *power*."

Mrs. Bone, a writer of "light verse" for local newspapers, said politely, "I read something like that just this week in *The New Yorker*, an essay by a Negro, I think—"

"Power is deadly, disintegrating," the editor interrupted. He accepted some mushrooms on sticks passed to him on a silver tray. "We have lived for so long, my friends, in the shadow of propaganda put out by the West that we have no conception of objective truth." He swallowed the mushrooms with a mouthful of Scotch. "Consider yourselves, frankly. Today I flew out here from New York City, a fantastic but utterly real city, totally integrated, totally alert. I flew out here and in two hours I can see that the suburbs of America are doomed. I am, frankly, amazed at the artificiality of this suburban world. Your very children look artificial, do you realize that? Type-cast, healthy, well-fed, tanned children with no cares, no problems, no duties, no responsibilities, no sufferings, no thoughts, children out of a Walt Disney musical! And these children are your products, my friends. Think of what you are creating!"

I had the idea that Nada glanced at me, vaguely, but I might have been mistaken.

"That's fascinating," a woman said. "Is it tied in with your work?"

He wiped his mouth. Excited, passionate, a little overwrought—was it the liquor, or the airplane flight, or the prospect of his speech the next day? (for, alas, he gave a very poor, shaky, nervous speech and disappointed the Cedar Grove ladies)—he began glancing apprehensively around the room. "Did you speak ironically?" he said to that lady.

"Did I what?" she said graciously.

"Ironically. Did you speak ironically?"

"My heavens no. I don't know how to speak ironically," she said, surprised.

He grinned at her, then stopped grinning, then glanced around for Nada. Nada was scratching the base of her head idly, off in a corner. Silence fell.

"Some of us have been meaning to ask," another lady ventured shyly, "whether there is much intellectual excitement in the New York world? Do you think that we in the Midwest are missing much the best part of life?"

"Is this the Midwest?" he asked vaguely. "Oh yes. No. I don't know. Of course we go to boxing matches in New York. That sport is marvelous. It's so contained. Within a comparatively small area, it tests manhood and skill. It . . . it's very much like writing. I had a work-out the other afternoon with Norman Mailer—"

"Ah yes," said a gentleman, "didn't he write. . . ? And then didn't he go downhill afterward?"

"John, for heaven's sake," said a woman, "don't you know they all go downhill? After all! Didn't Tolstoi go downhill after *War and Peace* and *Anna Karenina*?"

The gentleman turned seriously to the editor. "Well, I'll put that up to *you*. Did Tolstoi go downhill after *War and Peace* and *Anna Karenina*?"

The editor was taking another drink. "I think he did. Yes, I believe so," he said gloomily. After a few minutes of silence he began again, as if from another angle, telling us about his latest discovery, a disturbed and alienated young man who wrote film reviews for various New York publications. This young man had just made an underground movie called *Dentist* which was forbidden exhibition even in a *private* East Village hangout . . . a fantastic event, unparalleled, a raw comment upon the psychosociological inertia of contemporary America . . . and a very gifted young man too . . .

Unfortunately, just then Father arrived from the airport ("Held up by fog!" he explained), rushed and happy, and strode into the living room already agreeing with the editor.

"Yes, yes, interesting, fascinating!" Father declared loudly.

The editor got to his feet and they were introduced. Father chuckled with sheer good feeling. "Yes, very fascinating words I heard just now!" he said, looking around the room. Everyone agreed. He drew up a chair and sat facing the editor as if he'd flown in from Holland just for this talk.

The editor returned to his subject but something had gone out of his spirit. Father sat facing him, shifting his buttocks and agreeing, "Uh-huh, uh-*huh*," and with every grunted agreement the editor weakened, losing his grip on his sentences, stuttering over the phrase, "the whitewashed society and its brainwashed morality." Everyone else listened in the way Cedar Grove people listen to all things—immensely polite, enthusiastic, generous, showing interest especially around their mouths. Finally Father eased sideways into the conversation by saying, "Now, what you've said about freedom is, you know, one of my favorite topics of conversation. I've spent many hours discussing it with various people. However, as our Yugoslav man says, one cannot always define such things—freedom for me might not be freedom for you—so in the meantime what's left?"

He had taken on a slight "British" air, just as Nada, when excited, took on a "Russian" air.

"Freedom through legislation . . . or . . . or revolution," the editor stammered.

"Ah-hah, it was some Founding Father, I believe, who said, this wonderful man said, *Who cares about understanding the world? We're going to change the world! Yessir,* and we Americans have changed the world forever, you can bet your last dollar!"

The editor stared at Father. There was a moment of silence, then Mr. Bone said amiably, "Elwood, was it by any chance Thomas Jefferson who said that?"

"Probably," said Father.

The editor looked around. He began to say something, then thought better of it.

By the time dinner came and went the editor was inclining his head toward Father and flushing with agreement, yes, uh-huh, his hand with its pointless circular gesture adjusting itself to Father's more masculine sweeping gesture, which reminded you of nothing so much as a jetliner taking off for London in the early gray light of the American continent.

Much later that evening, when all of Nada's guests were gone and only she and the editor and Father remained downstairs (Father had fallen asleep in his chair), and I was at my drowsy perch on the stairway landing, the editor began to speak to Nada in . . . in a certain tone I had been dreading. "Natashya, this is fantastic. This. Him. What is this, where are we?"

"Not so loud," Nada said.

"Is this a location in space or a condition of the brain?" the editor said drunkenly. "This? All this? Who is that man? Years ago I knew you, and since then *this* man appears, *this* mansion of a house, and a child! Natashya, are you quite serious about all this?"

"Of course I'm serious," Nada said vaguely.

"And the child too?"

"Of course."

"You've had a child, you, you've become a mother? Is it possible?"

"Will you shut up about that?"

"But you, you're not even a woman, I mean, you're *in essence* not really a woman, and yet you've had a child. It's monstrous . . ." He sighed heavily. "Natashya, you frighten me. I'm a wreck. That man there, that massive man, he frightens me. He unmanned me tonight, he devastated me, and do you know why?"

"You're drunk."

"He devastated me because he is not contemporary with me. No. That man, what's-his-name, Elmwood? Elwood? That man is out of Charles Dickens and he should not exist today, Natashya, not as your husband, you know that very well. Don't look so disgusted, of course I'm drunk. Natashya, I see you've sold yourself and well done too, but don't you sometimes feel rotten about it? You're a beautiful woman, Natashya. I will always regret turning down that novella of yours. You were very spiteful about it—it broke off our friendship. You took everything too seriously in those days, but, my friend, imagine a reader struggling through the thoughts and impressions of a fourteen-year-old girl who has become demented! Imagine! You expected too much of your readers in those days, Natashya. Now you've loosened up and wised up. The other day I read your story in galleys at *Esquire*, and it's very nearly a *New Yorker* story—think of how far you've come!"

"Jesus Christ," Nada said in disgust.

"But a husband out of Charles Dickens—"

"He is not out of Charles Dickens but out of Proust, you bastard," Nada said.

"Well, anyway I haven't read either of them. Look, Natashya, I'm not as nervous as I seem. My hands shake like this after midnight. No, don't laugh, I am being quite serious . . . even tragic. I think I must have been in love with you at one time. Because other women remind me of you. I have an extraordinary fixation upon beautiful women! But then I read those novels of yours, and all those stories, you dumped thousands of pages on me and I couldn't possibly . . . couldn't get through them. Does your husband always sleep so peacefully? What is his secret? I have insomnia every night. Why is there such terror in him, in his weight? Even asleep he looks like a torpedo, or like a certain kind of deadly fish. Tell me, how much money does he make in a year?"

"You'd better go up to bed, you're drunk."

"But I have something to say to you. I won't pretend I came all the way out here just to say it . . . I'm honest . . . actually I need the money and five hundred dollars is a lot to me, I'm broke. But I wanted to see you again, Natashya, and tell you that I think of you often, and I admire you . . . but must you publish all the time, must I see your name everywhere and feel like puking, Natashya, when I should admire you? Look . . . I will tell you about the most beautiful evening of my life."

"Really? What was it?" Nada's voice had become rather eager.

"Don't mind my hands' shaking like this, it's the hour, and also I feel very sentimental. Look . . . you must promise not to tell anyone about what I'm going to say."

"Of course I promise."

"You know my life. A rotten childhood, like everyone's, the years at Harvard . . . the early years fighting for the integrity of *The Transamerican,* rescuing it from the Trotskyites . . . Jesus, what I've given of my life to that magazine! And last year the paid subscriptions, library and individual, went down to eight hundred! And my writing, always my own writing, that took years off my life, my translations of Rilke . . . and my first marriage . . . and . . . and the twins . . . this is very maudlin, Natashya, and I forbid you ever to put this in a story, in fact I beg you, for both our sakes—"

"But what happened? What was this wonderful event?"

"It was in New York last winter. By then I had made it, you know, all the years of struggle added up, my anthology of radical essays was reviewed by Harry for the *Times Book Review,* and by Linda for *The Nation,* and Joey Kay was all set to do it for *Newsweek* when he got sick . . . well, anyway, I had made it to the top, I was invited to six parties a week, to ten parties a week . . . and . . . and—"

"And you were a judge for the National Book Awards, you bastard," Nada said.

"And, Natashya, listen to me. I'm not drunk, I mean I am not simply drunk . . . with alcohol . . . I am drunk with this memory. I was invited to Pandora Bright's apartment. You know, she owns a television station and some magazines, in fact, she owns my magazine. She owns everything. And there, there at a late supper, at a large gathering of only the best people in the city, there I was introduced to Princess Margaret, who was visiting Pandora that week . . ."

There was a dramatic moment. The moment passed in silence.

"You what?" Nada asked.

"My dear, I was introduced to Princess Margaret! *I*, Moe Malinsky, the ordinary, insignificant, intellectual Moe Malinsky, *I was introduced to Princess Margaret!*"

The *Transamerican Quarterly*, with which some of you are familiar, is an excellent magazine, I believe, though reading it gives me a headache. I don't think I ever read it through, even in the old days when I suspected Nada of . . . I suspected the editor of . . . but never mind, that will come. The magazine gives you a general frontal headache, a dull glow of a headache that can't be concentrated upon and so can't be shaken, as you think, Just *what* is the New Radicalism?, after you've read fifteen smudgily printed pages. And what is "Action Theater," after all? (" 'Action Theater' tears away the walls of the bourgeoisie and destroys totally the idea of Theater; it is the only art form that will ultimately bring about the long-awaited synthesis of ethics and aesthetics . . .") Pieces on "Soviet Economic Growth" and "China: The Sound of Tomorrow," *de rigueur* and harmless enough; also, "An Open Letter to Our Young Friends of the New Left." Lyric reviews: "This young poet has vitality, wit, paradox, firm technical control— and yet—and yet curiously enough his poems do not succeed . . ." "It has become increasingly difficult for me to take American art seriously . . ." And on and on, uh-huh. The stories are all experimental, though not as good as Nada's (or am I prejudiced?), and you've all read the poetry:

> stroking her hair, singing
> the Teevee goes on, I weep
>
> Oh, she is sleeping!
> . . . I read late and reconcile
> Abraham Lincoln, the Talmud, and God.

6

And now it is time to tell about "A Doctor Looks at Love and Life For Teen-agers," and about my mad spell in the flower bed outside the Cedar Grove Bank of the Republic, and about Mavis Grisell's sister who cracked up in her new Lincoln, unable to get it out of a parking spot in the village and therefore driving it into the car ahead, jerking it into reverse and slamming it into the car behind, back and forth, back and forth madly, desperately, while a small crowd watched and a mother cautioned her son, "Don't say anything, she could sue" (actually, the sister's crack-up was Mavis' reason for coming to Cedar Grove), and . . .

Here is my problem: I am afraid to die, and when I finish this memoir I will be faced with suicide. I have made up my mind. There's no turning back. But still I am terribly afraid, which is why my memoir keeps going on, going on. But no matter. I had several other digressions in mind which I will not indulge in; I will be concise. The business about the doctor did not seem to me at the time to have anything to do with my behavior, but now, seven years later, I am not so certain. Though my criminal act was committed with all freedom, still it might have been influenced by one or two things in my environment. (It's difficult to analyze yourself.) I know I am completely to blame for what I did; I was free then and I am free right now. As Nada said, "I want you to be so free, Richard, that you stink of it." Well, yes, I do stink. And I am free also.

Well, one morning Father said to me on his way out, "Kid, I think I know what your trouble is. This moodiness, this out-of-focus look . . . no, don't be frightened, kid, just sit still . . . it's typical of young teen-agers, I mean, pre-teen-agers, I know all about it. I was your age myself once! Greg Hofstadter and I were talking yesterday at the club, and he said yes, now that I mentioned it, Gustave was the same way, all moody and bookwormy, doesn't want to go out and play, and we hit upon a solution. You and Gustave are going tonight to the high school to hear that Doctor what's-his-name give a talk. It's all very educational, buster, okay?"

He was backing out, his briefcase in hand, and he filled even that large doorway with his brimming holy energy. I said yes but he didn't hear me, so I said "YES" and he grinned and winked and was gone.

Nada said, "It's all right if Bébé doesn't drive you," but when Mrs. Hofstadter drove up that evening with Gustave, Nada was not even home to notice. I climbed into the car and said a polite hello to mother and son; Gustave and I were both a little embarrassed. It was clear that he did not want to go to this talk any more than I did. Mrs. Hofstadter chattered as she drove. She was a frail, stern-voiced partridge of a woman, always perfumed and attractive, but, unlike Nada, she looked as if she might come off in peelings with her clothes. I could not tell at once whether she was worse or the same as usual or slightly better. Gustave often reported her condition to me in a terse impersonal whisper, but tonight he was strangely silent and seemed to be paying no attention to his mother's chatter. She had a habit of driving in the middle of our narrow Cedar Grove lanes whether she was ascending a hill or not, and she had a habit of brushing rather close to parked cars, and she often glanced around into the back seat at me while she drove.

"There were these Egyptian sailors, you see, and they had been commissioned by one of the Pharoahs. I would date this at about 400 B.C. or maybe 400 A.D. They certainly had invented things in those days! You would be fascinated to learn about it, Richard! Well, the point of this was, that to disprove their findings the European navigators thought it was enough simply to measure their routes according to the existing maps, but—and this is the marvelous thing—the Egyptians were measuring according to *below the Equator*, and the Europeans were of course above . . . and so . . . it's a wonderful example of how we must not leap to conclusions."

I

"Yes, it is," I said shyly.

I felt my brain begin to click off, part by part. The low buzzing and ringing began. Mrs. Hofstadter chattered on, occasionally creasing her powdered neck to look back at me. We passed a drive-in restaurant in front of which sullen Negro women, of middle-age, were walking with picket signs. "That is one thing you would never see me doing, never," Mrs. Hofstadter declared. "I would never in my life carry a picket sign!"

"Mother, you're swerving to the left," Gustave said.

By the time we got to the high-school auditorium and sat down near the back, the talk was well under way. A middle-aged woman stood on the stage, looking out into the lighted auditorium. I heard her say the word "sex," and another part of my mind turned off, in a panic, but then it focused upon Nada and That Editor, and so I plugged myself in again to the good doctor and her talk.

" . . . And so, you see, there is this vast, marvelous area of human life called sex, and we know so very little about it, so very little! But I think that, after our discussion tonight, many of you will feel that the problems you have are not so gigantic after all. Many times a young person is like a driver in a new car, inexperienced and giddy with excitement. He is more interested in the looks and the speed of the car than he is in safety and the laws of the road, drawn up for him by his somber, well-meaning parents. Yes, some of your parents are well meaning!"

This brought forth a ripple of appreciative laughter.

"Now, I hope there will be many, many, many questions. I think that you must have many problems of your own or many curiosities about sex which you have kept back or expressed only to your peers. Are there any questions? Did any of you feel shocked or worried about what I said earlier? Do you think that such things should not have been voiced?"

An awkward moment. There were muffled whispers and the creakings of seats, then a girl put up her hand. You could tell by her taut, unworried throat and her confident voice that she was a Leader. "Dr. Muggeridge, may I ask a pretty far-out question?"

"My dear, nothing is far-out in the twentieth century," Dr. Muggeridge said, beaming. She was a handsome, muscular woman.

"Well, Dr. Muggeridge, I got to thinking that some of us are going to go home, and maybe our parents are . . . I mean . . . they might be mad when they hear about this talk . . ."

"Yes?"

"They might get mad or something because . . . well, you know . . ."

Everyone except Gustave and myself chuckled sympathetically. Oh, it was a warm, harmonious group! I felt my mind begin to drift slowly away.

"You know how parents are!" The girl giggled.

"My dear, I know only too well. I have had enormously pitiful conversations with pregnant teen-aged girls who waited far too long to talk over their problems with a responsible adult. Yes, I know, I know! But what can we do, we, all of us, toward educating the parents of teen-agers into discussing these things openly?"

A few seconds of excited silence, then another girl said, "Dr. Muggeridge, I think a talk like yours should be offered to our parents too. *They* need it even more than we do."

"Do you think that your parents are perhaps afraid?"

"Afraid?"

"Afraid of sex, themselves?"

Everyone hesitated at this. So Dr. Muggeridge went on in her gentle, kindly voice, "It may be that the parents of young people are simply afraid, and that they need help. I have often come to this conclusion in my talks with troubled teen-agers. *If* some understanding adult had only been available in time! But I can see so very few young people. Now that I am traveling on this lecture tour, and the tight demands of my television show, I'm afraid even these few teen-agers I could have helped personally will have to go without anyone to talk to. Incidentally, may I ask, how many of you here tonight *feel you can* talk openly to your parents about sex?"

Everyone looked stealthily around. One boy started to put his hand up, then thought better of it. Gustave and I sweated and did not look at each other.

"How pitiful!" Dr. Muggeridge cried. "How very tragic! Tragic! But surely some of you girls talk to your mothers, at least about mild problems?"

A few girls raised hands. "But not openly and freely, Dr. Muggeridge," someone said. Other girls agreed.

"And you boys, with your fathers?"

A few boys laughed. One boy said, "I'm afraid I can't talk with my father about anything."

"This is much more serious than I thought," Dr. Muggeridge said, shaking her head. "How do you account for this strange secrecy?"

No one knew.

"Well, fathers are like that," a boy said slowly.

"You mean they are difficult to approach? They are embarrassed?"

"They get all red and funny," a boy said. "You know. They start coughing and can't stop."

"And why is that, do you think?"

"Who knows? It's just easier to talk to a friend, or someone like you."

Dr. Muggeridge smiled. "Thank you, but flattery is out of place here. I wonder, have you ever thought that perhaps your parents don't discuss these enormously important and complicated problems even with each other? That perhaps they are simply afraid? There are extraordinary cases of non-communication between married people."

For some reason I thought of Nada a few years before, standing on the stairs with her back to Father, who was yelling certain names at her. (I was peeking around the dining-room louver doors.) But I shook this image away and uncrossed my legs.

Dr. Muggeridge was now saying, "And don't you think, then, that you boys and girls should feel free to discuss these matters with one another? Particularly those of you who are already quite intimate, or who are even thinking toward marriages. Yes, I know there are some of you here," she said, smiling, "and I know there are others of you who have had sex without marriage in mind, and I don't make any distinction between you. Wouldn't it be helpful for you to know as much as possible about each other, about your feelings and worries? Wouldn't this help communication later, when you're married? Then you could avoid the problems your parents have."

A girl said, "Dr. Muggeridge, can I say something? It's funny, but . . . but this talk tonight has done me a lot of good. It really has. My mother would never talk to me like this. It's a real experience."

"And this is the tragedy, boys and girls, the tragedy of non-communication. Think of our culture—the advertisements, the intensely stimulating movies, your popular dances and the clothes you wear. You must come to grips with this environment and conquer it; otherwise it will conquer you. We must demand of the adults of America that they face up to the realities of the world they have created. There is no room for squeamish hypocrisy. Did you know, boys and girls, that in any given group of young people a certain percentage of the girls will have unwanted pregnancies, and a certain percentage of all will have a venereal disease? Everyone knows that, but no parents will face up to the fact that *their* children may go into these statistics. Were I a parent myself, I would insist that my children come to me with any and all questions they have. There would be no red faces, no coughing spells, nothing except rational, wholesome talk. Sex is not a tabooed subject, boys and girls. It is not unhealthy and dirty. Sex should be discussed openly anywhere, in Sunday school, in classrooms, as well as in school lavatories"— (Laughter of a spontaneous sort) —"and even at the dinner table."

"But, Dr. Muggeridge," a girl said, "have you ever talked to adults on this subject?"

"My dear, I will tell you a secret," Dr. Muggeridge said sadly. "Whenever I offer a talk like this, it is precisely *those parents* who need it most who stay away. The open-minded parents who come are rarely in need of my advice—and, I must say, there are very, very few of these who do come. I think this points back to something we said earlier, the fear adults have toward sex."

"Oh, Dr. Muggeridge," a boy said, "they did show a movie at our school a while back. About reproduction and stuff like that."

"Shown to which grades?"

"Freshmen."

"A bit late, wasn't it?" Dr. Muggeridge snapped. "By that time many of you had no doubt conducted your own experiments—absolutely unknown to your parents and teachers, however."

A few faces reddened. I was leaning forward, my elbows on my knees and my hands encircling part of my face. Someone put his hand up, and I closed my eyes, forcing my mind off. At first there was nothing. Then I made out the image of Nada, a few years back. She and Father had given a party but it was one of their unwise parties, a mingling of Brookfield people and a few stragglers from somewhere else, an awkward group of people who were Nada's friends.

It had been a poolside party, and I followed Nada and a man (a "composer") around the side of the house and hid in some evergreens while I eavesdropped. And this talk stayed in my mind for many months: Nada told him that if he didn't like her guests he could go to hell, and he told Nada she had become a ridiculous person, and Nada told him in a furious whisper that he was a bastard, that his suit was cheap and ready-made and that every-one, everyone, had seen that his shoes were brown, in the first instant everyone had seen that, goddam them! She began to cry in ugly, jagged gasps. "What do you want from me?" she said. "I'm trying to survive. Should I sink down in the dump heap and suffocate, like my people, my ancestors, everybody's ancestors? Most of the world is swimming in a cesspool, trying to keep their heads up, and I'm sick of it, I'm sick of knowing it, God, how I'm sick of living and thinking and being what I am! But I won't live any other way. This is heaven. *This* is heaven, I've found it, they don't torture you or back you in ovens here, in 1960—what more can we ask? Our ancestors tortured other people or were tortured themselves, or both. Well, I am Natashya Everett and I am out of history, I'm clean of its stink and crap, and there is no one to thank for it, no one but myself and good luck. You son-of-a-bitch, to criticize me for being out of the crap pile! To criticize me for not suffocating in it!"

They were silent. Then the man (his face is a complete blank to me) slid his arm around Nada's shoulders, and she did a strange thing, she let her head fall back against him as if they were old, old friends, when I'd never even seen him before! And he seemed about to kiss her on the mouth, but she turned aside a little and somehow, perhaps with an indolent gesture of her hand, indicated that he should kiss her throat instead, which he did, while I stared from out of the evergreens and my eyeballs pounded. I was eight.

Gustave prodded me. "You all right?" he said. I blushed and nodded and sat back in my seat.

The discussion had ranged onto something else. A boy with purplish acne was saying loudly, "Yes, some kids at my school had pictures like that. When the teacher caught them she was afraid to do anything, she just hushed it up."

"Well, now, she was afraid, poor thing, to admit such things existed," Dr. Muggeridge said brightly. "Anyway, it's my personal feeling that anyone who resorts to pornography is a wee bit pathetic. What do you think? After all, normal people exercise their desires in normal ways. I think we should all be tremendously *sorry* for people who use pornography, just as we are for homosexuals and other perverts who are just plain sick people. Let's all help them, boys and girls, instead of pretending they don't exist! And you all know boys and girls your own age who are inclined toward abnormality. I don't mean just boys with dirty pictures but also the opposite, boys who show no interest at all in sex, and girls who show a morbid disinterest in boys. We have to admit our impulses and curiosities about this, or we are being hypocritical like most of the adult population of America. What do you think? You all, I suppose, know unfortunate boys and girls who have reached sixth grade already without admitting the slightest interest in sex, don't you?"

I shifted guiltily in my seat.

A girl raised her hand. "What about younger brothers and sisters?" she said. "What if you can see how your kid sister, for instance, is really out of it—I mean, she just doesn't know *any*thing—should you maybe talk with her and bring things kind of out in the open?"

"But how can you, if your *parents* are against it?" Dr. Muggeridge said.

This was true. There was silence for a few seconds, but not a dull silence. I could feel everyone thinking excitedly. Another hand went up and a girl said, "I guess the question most of us girls want to ask you, Dr. Muggeridge, is this—and I'm really serious—how do you tell a boy to stop being fresh?"

"Boys," said Dr. Muggeridge with a smile, "what would you advise?"

"Just say so," declared a boy.

"A slap wouldn't hurt either," said another.

"No, but some boys won't stop anyway. They just

won't stop," the girl said, red-faced. "Why are boys like that, Dr. Muggeridge? Sometimes they just get so *nasty*. And society never blames them either. It just blames the girl."

"Now you are talking, my dear, about the notorious double standard," Dr. Muggeridge said as if this were a favorite topic. "This means that society expects highly moral behavior of its young women and looks the other way when its young men do as they please. Of course this is grossly unfair. But our society is changing, as you know. I think this more than anything else is what is bugging your parents. They expect you girls to be dainty and pure, like their grandmothers. Even the most flagrantly immoral boys expect their wives to be pure when they decide to marry . . . finally!" (A ripple of laugher.) "But our society is changing so rapidly that there will be a time when girls will have exactly as much freedom as boys."

"Dr. Muggeridge," said a girl, "some people think that if you're going to get married it's all right—I mean, if you're engaged or going steady or something. What is your opinion on this?"

"My dear, you have misjudged me if you think I have any opinions on this subject other than the good healthy one of believing that problems should be aired. I would not dream of forcing my moral standards on anyone else. Some people will argue that engaged couples have every right to go to bed together, others argue that an engagement should be entered into only *after* this kind of experimentation. I do not give any particular advice. This sort of thing must be worked out between the two young people themselves."

"Dr. Muggeridge," said a girl, "what about a kiss on the first date? Is that bad, or what?"

"Some people go all the way on the first date," Dr. Muggeridge said. "It's just a question of quality, not quantity, don't you think so? Again, discussion is called for."

"Dr. Muggeridge," said a girl, "what about abortion? Do you think that's a good solution to an unwanted pregnancy, or what?"

"There are many opinions concerning abortion. The old-fashioned religious belief was that it was a crime, and it is still a crime in many states. However, if we look at the situation objectively and scientifically, it is clear that a couple, faced with an unwanted pregnancy, may make the decision themselves about what to do. I personally believe that marriage in such circumstances is a poor solution. For one thing, it would cut down severely on your youthful experiences in the world, to be married in your teens. Think of the fun you'd miss out on, the dates and dances! And it suggests that sex is something very, very serious and not just a normal part of life, something to enjoy . . ."

"Where are you going?" Gustave whispered.

"Out," I said.

I left the auditorium, which was so hot I felt sick. But outside in the corridor, and outside in the parking lot where I was sick to my stomach, it was just as hot. My clothes were drenched with sweat.

7

And my mad spell in the flower bed came about like
this: I was walking along in a ringing, singing daze of
dust particles, thinking of Dr. Muggeridge of the night
before and her upraised, kindly, blighting hand pro-
nouncing my doom, not to mention Nada or rather
Nada's absence when I finally got home (Mrs. Hofstadter had been an hour late and we had waited on the
school steps. She had burst into tears, seeing how wearily
Gustave got to his feet, and for some reason had begun
to attack my mother: "I don't know who Natashya is,
and nobody knows, nobody, and your father's family *do
not exist* in Philadelphia society no matter how much
money they have. And at one of your dinner parties I
saw lipstick marks on my glass, my supposedly clean glass
just brought in from the dishwasher . . .") when something happened to me. It was terrifying but somehow
wonderful. It was like a bolt of lightning (that marvelous
metaphor!) that flashed down upon me and would have
split my skull in two except for my knowing enough to
bend with the blow.

Some safety device in my brain melted away and let
all of paradise rush loose. I was on my way home from
school, which lasted most of the morning, and I was
crossing the village green and just passing the Cedar
Grove Bank of the Republic when this flash of lightning
freed me. You must understand that all morning, all

the night before, I had been in a kind of slumber. I could hear things well enough—sometimes too well—and I had been able to do an absurdly simple problem in division up at the board, but . . . but I had not been awake. Then, suddenly, I did awake. It happened that quickly. An overpowering fury rose in me, and I jumped into the flower bed so neatly kept up by the bank (a bed of pansies, snapdragons, little furry, fuzzy white border flowers) and began kicking at them. I kicked violently, madly, and as I kicked their tiny faces a feeling of soaring happiness filled my hollow little chest. I muttered something, but it was not "Take that! Take that!"; I don't know what it was. I couldn't hear myself, I wasn't interested in hearing myself, I was not aware of *hearing* anything. And then I was lying in the flower bed, groveling around and still kicking, fighting, scratching, even tearing with my teeth, the fury let loose in my body ringing in every muscle and giving me that holy strength that was not truly mine.

My panting sobs slowed and I heard someone whisper, "Let him alone, don't say anything. He could sue." A boy my own age was cautioning a younger boy. And behind and around them were many Cedar Grove ladies staring in amazement.

A young policeman came to the very edge of the flower bed and bent to look at me. "Did you lose something, son?"

I was still panting violently.

"What did you lose, son? Maybe I can help you. Money? Keys?" He was a cautious policeman; he knew enough not to touch me. I lay there, my heart pounding, and waited. The policeman motioned politely for everyone to disperse—"disperse" is the word he was thinking, I am sure—and I sat up, still panting, and finally I got to my feet.

"I hope it wasn't anything important," the policeman said.

I stepped out of the circle of ruined flowers. Someone from the bank was standing nearby, smiling. "It's quite all right, officer. Quite all right, just an accident. Did you find what you were looking for, son?"

I nodded and began to walk away. It seemed incredible to me that they would let me go . . . but yes, they did, they let me go! And though many clean people in the village noted my filthy clothes and tear-streaked, mud-streaked face, of course no one said anything. As I walked home the memory of that devastating flame began to fade and I lapsed once more into my slumberous state . . . until I found myself opening the side door of a house that wasn't ours but had once been ours (our former Cedar Grove house of years back), and this mistake kept me moderately awake until I got to our real home, which was the big long elegant one on Labyrinth Drive that seemed to promise so much.

Nada was not home. Father was not home. Libby was ironing in the basement—I could smell something scorching. I ran upstairs and went to my room, and from under my bed I pulled the soiled sheet in which my rifle was wrapped.

8

It was a deer rifle that I thought might blow up in my face if I ever used it. It had a telescopic sight attached to its barrel, and this was the most interesting thing about it. I lay on my bed and aimed the gun in various directions, just to be able to look through the telescope. The gun was a little heavy. Nothing about its sleek, cheap wood and its dull barrel suggested the power it had, and the secrecy of its power frightened me a little. The gun was such a still, quiet object.

I went to my window and looked out through the telescope. Everything was brought up close, but it was rather fuzzy. The lens might have been smudged from my wet fingers. I swung the barrel back and forth and saw ordinary Labyrinth Drive sights: the woman next door, pretty and hurried in white high-heeled shoes and pink suit, was instructing her colored maid in the art of watering roses—the woman tripped daintily to a bush, pointed, and the maid followed and squirted water on that bush from a garden hose, then they went to another bush, and to yet another. There was something beautiful about that sight. Then, across the street, the Cedar Grove Green Carpet Lawn Service was at work. The telescope didn't bring the men up close enough so that I could really see their faces. It brought them to me in a kind of haze, not quite real but not imaginary either, and it pleased me to think of how they existed both for themselves and for me, their spy. The Cedar Grove Green Carpet Lawn

Service was made up of a big foreman who did nothing but smoke and walk from one part of the enormous lawn to another, and a crew of surly, sullen white men who were too tanned to be happy, with overlong hair and sweat-drenched clothes. The foreman could talk to any housewife charmingly, but to his men he did not talk at all. It was clear that they all hated one another. I had to admire the foreman's empty, blank muscular face. It occurred to me that I could pull the trigger of my deer rifle and bring him down, but that would be cruel, and anyway I did not want to hurt anyone; I certainly did not want to kill, so I thought then—that day. I sat and watched a slow procession of trucks pass by: laundry truck, flower-delivery truck, TV-repair truck, liquor-store truck, plumber's truck, air-conditioner-repair truck . . .

And down the street was the Cedar Grove Sprawater Service, fixing someone's sprinkling system. All day, every day, these little trucks were parked in front of homes. But these men were too far away. I could not see them well, and probably if I pulled the trigger nothing would happen. I didn't know much about guns and I still don't. Do bullets drop fast? Should you aim higher than your target, and how much higher? The perfunctory instruction sheet that came with my rifle did not tell much. I turned the gun up into the sky and stared dizzily into nothing, nothing. It did not seem possible that anything would ever be within the range of my weapon, of any weapon of mine. Wouldn't the gun blow up in my face if I ever dared pull the trigger?

9

That night I heard them arguing, but I must have been a changed boy because I really did not creep out of my room to hear. I did not have to hear. Just as the telescope brought sights nearer to me, so did my strange new peacefulness tell me that I had heard this already, I did not need to hear it again. How could they surprise me? When I was a child I needed to hear every ugly word and, if possible, I needed to see Nada's face distorted with hatred and Father's with rage, but now, now at eleven, I didn't need to hear or see them any more. I knew.

It did me no good to play the Thinking Game at these times. The Thinking Game helped if I was sinking so deeply into inertia that I was afraid I might die, then I would seize upon some forlorn trivial memory, of a shoe, of one of Nada's rings, or of the sheet music on the piano (just which specific pieces were out?). But the Thinking Game was no good when Nada and Father argued, because I did not want to stay awake at such times. Better to sleep. Better not to hear Nada's upraised, horrified voice, which did not predict pain or even horror but only her own fury, and better not to hear Father's bellow, because in the end they would go off to bed, each to his own bed, and they would sleep while I lay awake.

10

The next morning when I came downstairs Nada was already up, wearing a flimsy yellow shift of a summer dress, her bare legs stretched out under the dining-room table. This memory brings to my mind exotic things— parrots, cockatoos, big bursting jungle flowers—because of the shiny green fabric, minutely textured, that covered the dining-room walls, and Nada's sunburst dress, and the peaches and bananas she was eating. She had quite a few long narrow sheets of paper out before her, which she touched gingerly with her sticky fingers. "Hello, honey," she said. "Going to school?"

It was Libby's day off, and Nada sometimes thrust toward me a conspiratorial, intimate smile on such days, but this morning she was distracted. I asked her what the papers were, and she said nothing, nothing important. Was it a story? I asked. "Oh, nothing. You won't be late to school, will you?" she said. She brushed her hair back sunnily and indifferently from her face, smiling at me with that smile that meant nothing. It was strange how this gesture reminded me of one of the pretty, confident high-school girls at Dr. Muggeridge's lecture, a girl I hadn't even remarked upon at the time and who was only summoned back by Nada.

So I went out to school, but somewhere along the way it occurred to me that I wasn't going to school that morning. I turned and came back by a side street, cutting through to the lane (not quite an alley) that ran behind the houses on Labyrinth Drive. The lane was lined with garbage cans, some new and some weathered, and one or two houses sported a mighty line of six, seven cans all their own! I am embarrassed to say that the Everett household could fill up no more than two healthy-sized cans in one week. Our house looked a little unfamiliar from this spot. I climbed up onto our back fence, which swayed slightly, and peered over onto our lawn. It was shaded, and the swimming pool glimmered a pale, delicate blue. Insects dotted its surface. The back of the long house was broken up into sections: a screened-in porch with lawn furniture, a glassed-in porch that was the Family Room and looked out onto a patio the former owners of the house had evidently thought highly of— there were hanging plants, hanging vines, flowerpots everywhere, which Nada hadn't bothered with and out of which now grew stunted little brown things. The patio floor was flagstone, larger than the kind I was familiar with, and around it were evergreens and a few rose bushes. The dining-room window was a kind of bay-window affair, but it was wasted because of the overgrown bushes. I could still see Nada in there at the table, and if I'd had my telescope with me I could have made sure.

I entered the house by the front door. Doors are always unlocked in Cedar Grove. Just inside the door I paused, listening: a sound of rustling paper from the dining room. She was still at work.

I tiptoed to the staircase and went upstairs. Nothing creaked. At the top I waited. I was good at waiting. A kind of sunny haze enveloped me, and I stood there waiting and not-waiting, thinking that Nada and I were alone in the house, all alone, and she did not even know it. I was in a kind of agreeable trance. Later, when I was to recount all this as part of my confession, they checked with my math teacher, Mr. Hale, and to my amazement he told them that I hadn't been absent that day! According to his records, this "Richard Everett" had had perfect attendance up until the time he stopped coming altogether. But I insist, my readers, that I was absent, yes, I was absent from class that morning and all but absent from even this perch at the top of the stairs, my mind was so drifting and wandering.

Then the doorbell rang, or rather tolled. I must have been waiting for this, for I came awake at once as if everything had been planned. I heard Nada's bare feet padding to the door, or rather I *felt* them, and I shivered to think of the faint little indentations her feet would make in the thick white rug. Then two voices mingled, hers and a man's. I believed at the time it was the editor Malinsky's voice (but it turned out that he had flown back to New York that morning). They went into the dining room; I saw their shadows pass, but I was too frightened to peek over and look down at them. Nada's voice rose with a pleasant irony upon the word "Elwood." The telephone rang. No one answered it. It rang and rang, and its ringing interfered with the wild beating of my heart.

I ran down the hall to Nada's room. The door was open. Inside was the unmade bed; its white cover had fallen half onto the floor and looked both flouncy and soiled. The floor was covered with a rather thin but still lovely Persian rug Nada had picked up somewhere, under some lady's influence, and the furniture had an unmatched look. Nada had always been influenced by other women, led astray to antique shops, auctions, following

268]

up Regency pieces because some emphatic lady had told her they were the finest, seeking out Country French frauds because someone's mansion was decorated in that style. Of course, Nada had no style of her own.

Everywhere there were books and papers. Off to the side was her "powder room," painted pink, and a big long closet filled to bursting with her clothes. I opened the closet door and the light went on. I went inside and hid among her fragrant, perfumy clothes, though some of the things should have been dry-cleaned, it seemed to me.

What instinct! Dr. Muggeridge had taught me more than I had realized. In a short while, a half hour, I heard them come into the room. Nada's voice was very close to the closet door when she said, "It's a pattern. Sometimes I'm drowning in it. It's all whirls and spirals, like a diagram of the ear."

"Anytime you want, you can get out."

"Oh, shut up, what do you know? What point is there living without being normal? A world like this is shit without money, don't be pretentious." Then she said something I couldn't make out, a phrase sharp and whiplike.

The man's voice said, "Natashya, that Russian of yours has always been a farce."

"Like everything else, then. Well . . ."

My sanctuary, my hiding place that was so clever, then turned into my prison. It happened slowly enough. I crouched in there behind something long and silky, listening, sweating, and it occurred gradually to me that I might be sick if I listened any further. No, I cannot type out what I heard and it isn't important, I mean not to you. To you nothing is important, this is just

[269

something to read and discard, but to me, even now I
writhe in agony and humiliation to have to remember,
but . . . I crouched in there with my eyes shut and my
hands pressed against my ears, but not hard enough, not
hard enough! I could hear much more than I wanted.
I pressed my sweaty palms against my ears so hard that
a ringing began that was like the ringing of a telephone,
and static sounded in my brain, and . . .

After a while I heard nothing. I let my aching hands
come away from my bruised, aching head, and for a
moment I thought I might be deaf, I heard nothing at
all. Then it came to me: voices. They were talking about
something, but very gently. I could not hear what they
said. Maybe they spoke in another language, the language of lovers, who could tell? Their talk drifted off,
drifted on again. It was all very gentle and casual. Then
there was a sudden sound of bedsprings and Nada said,
"Yes, please, it's blue, some frilly blue thing."

I knew the man was coming to the closet, and I began
to breathe fast through my mouth. My eyes narrowed.
I brought my hands up to my head again and crouched
down low. Have I mentioned that I spent all this time,
an hour or more, with my backbone hunched in two and
my thighs aching under me? Have you ever crouched
on top of a pile of women's shoes thrown all over a
closet floor, suffocating and writhing in shame, hardly
daring to breathe? Have you? Have you ever squatted
down just for five minutes, so that your legs ached
desperately beneath you and you wanted nothing, nothing so much as to stand up straight?

None of this flashed to me, of course. I thought
nothing. I was frozen with terror and baked with terror,

and only now in writing this memoir (God, what shame even to write it!) am I able to remember just what I felt. But then, back then, I had no time to think about anything. The closet door opened suddenly and the light came on. I was crouched back of her things, you know, and I hoped desperately that I would be hidden, but this abrupt, hurried man began going through the clothes hanging on the rack as if impatient of all that was offered him, and when he came at last to Nada's blue bathrobe he moved five or six hangers full of clothes aside, and there, there he stood looking down at me: a naked man with short, damp, curly hair on his chest, a face I had never seen before, eyes that were mildly incredulous. The most horrible thing about a naked man is his face. This naked man stared down at me, and I hunched down farther on my small mountain of shoes, my hands now on top of my head, staring up at him. A second passed. Then he yanked the blue robe off the hanger, the wire hanger nearly swung off, and he turned away and closed the door and the light went out. That was that.

11

In that way I became a Minor Character. I slipped out of focus. It's difficult for you readers to understand my becoming a Minor Character because 1) you can't imagine anyone except yourself being Major, hence my becoming Minor should be no great shock; 2) you don't believe a genuine Minor Character should exhibit so much anguish, pain, tedium. It's ridiculous, like a vehement pamphlet put out by an organization of white laboratory mice.

Anyway I, Richard Everett, became a Minor Character. This is the opposite of schizophrenia and yet closely related, according to Dr. Saskatoon: there is no splitting of the ego in two or three but a curious case of disappearance, like a snake swallowing itself or a pocket pulled out when there's no pocket there to be pulled out. (My digressions are getting more desperate: I have to fight back an impulse to type out a list of the things I ate this evening, so you can judge for yourself the depth of my degradation. But who wants to hear about Wong's Chop Suey in the can, of Teutonic Stewed Tomatoes, and canned spaghetti, crumbly cookies, greasy potato chips . . . and . . . everything else? A far cry from Nada to crumbs!)

But if I had it to do over again, and thank God I don't, I'd pay more attention to food. Hanley Stuart Hingham's advice is good advice, for though this is nonfiction, all writing is selection and I haven't selected the right details. I should have told you of the pies, both fresh and frozen, the custard cups, the ice-cream cones, the strawberry and cream tarts, the chocolates, the mints, the fine sweet cake Nada sometimes made (from a mix), the bottles and bottles of all those beverages you see tanned teen-agers holding aloft in advertisements, the meat, the potatoes, the gravy, the lobster, the shrimp, the chicken (fried, baked, stewed, barbecued, diced, quartered, fricasseed), everything—everything I stuffed into my voracious mouth from the time of my Disintegration until the time of my Death. I should have reprinted menus from Cedar Grove's most exclusive restaurants, and from the country clubs, and from Nada's kitchen, to give you not simply a sense of my sinking into a slough of food but an idea of social conditions as well.

But all these digressions are useless. I am running out of time. I am one of those people who talk faster and faster as the pain mounts in them. At first you feel shock, then sympathy, then you swallow a yawn, then you don't bother swallowing a yawn.

But listen . . .

12

That evening I did twenty math problems. You do not recall pure and useless math from your youth—the safety of step-by-step procedures, the baroque luxury of numerals slowly and lovingly shaped by pencil; these fade. But through the maze of slow-motion steps and half steps, a parody of my slowing brain, I kept seeing and hearing things I did not want to remember. No matter what they were, you can guess. I felt as if I were falling headfirst into the blankness contained by those innocuous drawings, but I could do little to stop the fall. I could reach out and grab a triangle's sides the way you grab the sides of a window to keep from plunging out. But none of this was enough.

I went into my bathroom and ran cold water. I put my hands under it, but that wasn't enough either (cold water closes the pores). So I turned on the hot water and let it run until the mirror was steamed; then I lathered soap between my hands and washed. I washed my hands and face and as much of my arms as I could manage without taking off my shirt. In the steamy window I could see this strange child gazing at me, nearsighted without his glasses, and I washed slowly and dreamily. There was no thought of what was coming next.

Then I went back into my room, which I haven't described and hardly remember now: a boy's room painted blue, with a vaguely nautical air about it. Out the window the evening sky reminded me of lavatories in public places: pale gray floors. Something seemed to be waiting to happen. They say of children like me, "But he was such a nice boy, so quiet and polite," but they don't go on to say something they've half thought: that children like me seem to be waiting, always waiting. Even now, I suppose, I am waiting, and it is clear to me that all of my childhood was a period of waiting.

After a while—I don't know how long—I pulled my rifle out from under my bed and went to the door. A quiet evening, both parents at home. Nada was down the hall in her room typing, and Father was two floors away in his basement "workshop." Someone had told Father once that busy executives should exercise their hands, so Father made bowling pins (or did he call them Indian clubs?), smooth, handsome things that sometimes stood up by themselves. If I dropped an anchor through this house it would sink forever before it would come into contact with my father. So I walked noiselessly down the hall to the back stairs, with the gun, not even sneaking and not even in a hurry, and no one was to see me go out or come back.

In the darkness I walked alongside the house with my rifle drooping casually before me. I walked like any hunter out for humble sport in any suburban darkness, and when I came to the fence at the back of our property I remembered to put the rifle down while I climbed the fence. That was instinct, perhaps. It was important that I didn't blow myself up yet, I knew. Though I wasn't really awake I knew this. I had a dull pain everywhere in my head and a sharper pain right behind my left eye. In short, I felt more or less normal. Once in the alley I began to walk faster. I had no idea of where I was going. It was a pleasant July night—July 23, 1960.

At the end of our block I crossed the street. Everything was quiet, empty. I began to walk faster. I felt vaguely harassed, as if I were late for an appointment. Above, the sky was still faintly overcast but a smattering of stars had appeared. Mr. Grenlin back at Johns Behemoth had told us that the stars did not exist but they did *represent*—they represented "stars" from the past. So you could really look into the past, after all, one of the boys had said. But Mr. Grenlin had replied, with Johns Behemoth's easy superiority, "You are only looking into a concept of the past which is *your* concept of the past, once you have been told that the stars do not exist as they seem to exist. But since you are only looking at your own concept, it's rather whimsical to suggest that you are looking into a past that is anyone else's past, let alone a historical past. Any questions?" No, no questions.

I came to a larger street and now I had a vague idea of my destination. This was Broad Road, and it divided the rather ordinary section of Cedar Grove in which we lived from an enormous area called Pools Moran (a name I do not understand) which was roughly equivalent to Fernwood Heights. As you crossed Broad Road your taxes mounted, and by the time you trod on the other side, the pebbles and grit beneath your feet were worth nickles, dimes, even quarters. I was running now. I turned up a lane called Melon Lane and yes, this was familiar, and inside my chest a pulse began to come alive. I was coming alive! Before me the lane turned and flipped like a lazy snake, and just around the corner would be the Bodys' estate, which Nada had pointed out to me several times. It was accessible from back or front because of the winding lane. Through a small pine forest, posted against trespassers, I could see the Body house and a glow of activity around the swimming pool. Though Pools Moran is supposed to be quiet, what a lot of noise came cascading through the demure night! Music and shrieks. There were many people around the swimming pool, some swimming. Lanterns strung around the pool were glowing like moons. It must have been a party given by one of the Bodys' college-age children. I walked quietly through the little woods with my rifle up to my shoulder, so that I could look through the telescopic sight. I saw energetic figures, three-dimensional shadows. The sight brought me up so close that I had no fear of being seen. My heart was pounding with excitement! I did not remember it having pounded so well since my mad spell in the flower bed, which had been a child's tantrum. Now it was pounding again and sending precious blood through my veins, and . . . I saw a woman patting powder on her face with a white fluffy puff, and as she did this she spoke sharply to a dog whining at her feet. The powder puff was very large and white; it was an effort for me to turn away from it. Someone was doing a trick on the diving board: a muscular young man who achieved a perfect somersault. A few girls applauded. By the steps to the diving board a group of young people were anointing a girl, who jumped up daintily onto the board, stretched her young body (which gleamed in the lantern light), and pointed with the tips of her fingers up to the sky. Her bathing cap looked made of gold. I felt the night air grow humid, just watching her. Then someone clicked a cigarette lighter and touched the flame to her ankle and she burst all at once into flames! And as I stared in bewilderment and from all parts of the patio came a wondrous murmuring, the girl walked on tiptoe to the end of the board, aflame, and did a perfect dive into the pool.

When her golden head appeared once more the fire was extinguished and only a few people applauded. I felt as if I had gazed upon something forbidden.

But it was not these people I seemed to want. I went quietly by them in the dark, jostled by friendly giggling girls who never noticed me; the rifle I carried was nothing alarming (it could have been a walking stick or something to pry a sunken bathing cap out of a drain). I made my way up the hill to the big house itself. Windows there glowed with light. The kitchen was filled with young people in bathing suits. Past the kitchen was a series of bathrooms evidently—the windows were glass bricks. Then a hallway with a great potted plant, then a darkened living room, then—and here my heart began at once to throb—then a kind of Family Room, and there sat Mr. Body himself. I understood that it was this man I'd been seeking.

Seeing him, I began at once to back up. With the rifle to my shoulder I was able to see Mr. Body clearly; he was reading a newspaper. My body tingled. This was real! This was reality! I could not have said why I was here, what Mr. Body meant to me, any more than I could have explained why, a moment later, my finger squeezed the trigger.

But I did squeeze it, and the gun went off. In the same instant, the windowpane that had protected Mr. Body from the night air smashed and I saw Mr. Body, that man in my telescope lens, dive to the floor. He was fast! He dived with as much skill as the man on the diving board. Again I squeezed the trigger, aiming not at Mr. Body but at the wall behind him. Another shot. Mr. Body's newspaper was scattered about him, and his big fragile head was bent to the floor as if he were about to burrow into it. I pulled the trigger again and yet again. Mr. Body lay very still, playing dead. No need for him to play dead, I knew better! But he waited, and I waited. A few seconds passed, and he made a tentative movement with one hand, perhaps symbolic, in the direction of the telephone, and again I squeezed the trigger and shot the wall.

Now I turned and started running down the Bodys' front driveway, past all the cars. You are surprised that no one heard me? But yes, of course they probably heard me; their ear devices registered the sound of the shots, but they didn't listen because why should they have listened? Rifle shots were not rifle shots to them but, at the most, firecrackers or a motorbike backfiring (if motorbikes backfire).

I ran and ran along Melon Lane. Lovely road! You must drive out to Pools Moran someday, twenty minutes from the heart of downtown but twenty light-years from its stench and poverty, and there stroll along Melon Lane some pleasant July evening. Feel the pebbles underfoot, smell the faint acrid odor of dust (the lane is unpaved). If you want to guess at my feelings, run along and pretend that all of Cedar Grove and Pools Moran are pursuing you. Though you know no one is there (as I knew), run faster all the same, delirious with joy, until your legs are carrying you faster than any skeptical gym teacher of your youth would have believed—and you will have some idea of what you are! Why hadn't I guessed at myself before this? What had I done to Mr. Body, what had I committed? I ran, and through my mind thoughts ran also, new, alarming, refreshing thoughts. But my legs carried me on without error, without any lapse in rhythm, carrying me forward, onward, back to Broad Road and across into the darkness of Cedar Grove, and in five minutes I was back home again at 4500 Labyrinth Drive, my home.

I slept well that night; it seemed to me that at last I had discovered myself.

13

The next morning, Nada knew long before the paper came what had happened over in Pools Moran. I heard her talking on the telephone and saying vaguely, "Yes, it's shocking, it's really shocking . . ." When the paper arrived Nada and I read it eagerly. I was a little startled at the publicity the event had been given. To me it hadn't seemed much, a rather private ceremony, but there was the big black headline on the front page: SNIPER MISSES BANKER. It was a while before I understood that the word "sniper" referred to me.

When Father came home he too discussed it with

Nada. He seemed excited and alarmed, gesturing so that his ice cubes clicked. "See what it's coming to, finally! The way the country's going!" he said.

"Yes," said Nada.

"Honey, you'd better be careful while I'm gone. Keep the shades pulled and everything. Okay?"

"Do we have shades in this house?"

"I don't know, I think so."

"Not downstairs."

"Upstairs then. Stay upstairs."

A few people dropped in for cocktails and they all discussed the sniper, who was eavesdropping on them from the stairs. I looked down to see Nada greeting new guests, arching her elegant backbone as she kissed the cheek of some female acquaintance, and I could see the tops of their silky hairdos and the lids of their eyes, which told me nothing. My backbone did not seem strong enough today to keep my body erect, so I sat on the stairs and lay back. I listened to their opinions shot back and forth. Father's loud voice triumphed finally. "It's the judges and the sleazy liberal sentiments that are ruining this country, and just as Tashya here says, it's a wonder things like that don't happen every day with things like they are!"

"Oh, how can you say that?" a woman said.

"I did not say that," said Nada.

"Well, it's a hell of a thing," said a man. "There's no protection, it's like a jungle—"

"Why shouldn't it be a jungle?" Nada asked.

Only her voice excited me! She seemed to be talking right to me, to my soul, as if she knew the sniper himself was eavesdropping on her.

"All the world and all of history is a jungle, when it

hasn't been a garbage heap or a graveyard, which comes to the same thing," Nada said. "Why not? What right do we have to complain? Are we better? What my people did to the Jews, what they did to one another, and what they're still doing—it's all a mess." Her "accent" was getting stronger and more vicious; her guests must have been astonished. "We think we are in a holy city here— what is it? Cedar Grove—and yes, yes that's true, this world we have is holy but let us understand that it will not last. It won't stop us from getting shot or dying in some other way. Of all people, we have no right to complain."

A few seconds of silence. Then a man said, clearing his throat, "Of course, with Anthony Body, there's that peculiar business of Armada's sister's estate, dragging on now for five years. And I think, I just think that *maybe* that might have some bearing on the—"

"Oh, how can you say things like that?" a woman interrupted shrilly.

Safe in my room, I read through all the papers that Father had brought home. My room was safe because Libby didn't come in it: I had explained to her that, as a punishment, I was to clean my own room from now on. So I was safe. I slept well again that night. I was buoyed about for a while on the surface of an immense dark ocean, then I sank very slowly to the bottom, where I drifted gently back and forth with the warm currents all night long. When morning came the sunlight shone murkily through the water but did not dispel it. What was wrong? I sat up in bed and was still sunk in water, but I was able to breathe and I felt a surprised smile spread across my face very slowly, the way smiles always move in water.

When Nada came in she declared me "sick" and said she would nurse me. I lay soothed by the warm currents of the ocean bed and by my mother's kindness. It seemed to me that both Nada and myself were being buffeted about by the waves, but Nada did not know what was happening and I did know. I said, "Don't be afraid of the sniper, you're safe here."

Nada laughed, and I said again, not knowing what her laughter meant, "Like Father says, if you stay up-stairs—"

"Like Daddy says," she corrected. Then she said, "As Daddy says."

14

I didn't need to wait for the paper to know that no further sniping had been done, but I was interested to see what progress the police had made. The county sheriff had nothing to say to reporters; he was cagey. Neighbors of the Bodys were interviewed. College friends of the Bodys' children gave their opinions. A few photographs. In short, nothing.

Without me they couldn't get along!

I waited cunningly for a day or two before I went out again, and this time I stayed close to home. I sprinted down our back lane only a few houses! I was pleased to see that many windows were shaded, that lights were burning around houses, set up in trees and above garages, to dispel the forces of darkness. But the darkness, which frightened others and had always frightened me, was now something into which I ran with great joy and longing, my face still smarting from the soap I'd used on it, and my eyes keen as they had never been in the daytime. Oh, what a failure I was as a daytime creature! How feeble, how despicable! Nada was a nighttime creature and never until now had I understood that. Night people don't stir to life until the sun sets or, at least, until shades are mysteriously drawn; in the daytime they pretend. My daytime self was a failure, no doubt of it, but my nighttime self was strong. If only Nada could see me now and realize what I was—not that feeble, sickish daytime child of hers, but a darker, more secret child of hers, a boy who belonged only to her and dedicated everything to her.

This time I paused, panting, by a wire fence. A few dogs barked—dogs always bark in upper-middle-class neighborhoods. Dogs own those neighborhoods. I saw a car coming down the street out front and waited, and, sure enough, it turned into the driveway of the house I was watching. I hid behind the garbage cans. The car's headlights flicked near me, sailing through the little curtained windows at the back of the garage, then there was the sound of one car door being slammed shut, then another. A woman's voice . . . a man's voice . . . a jangle of keys . . .

My heart was pounding once again, and when the people appeared inside the lighted alcove that led to the side door I was prepared. My rifle rested on top of the fence, aimed, and through the telescope I could see two ordinary, attractive, anonymous people who looked as if they were arguing. I aimed at an expanse of white wall near them and pulled the trigger.

This time I ran at once. There was nothing to wait

for. My heart—listen to it!—it pounded as if it might burst! What abandonment! The silence of the lane through which I ran fell back before me as if it were terrified of my power. I ran and ran, and in a sense I am still running, panting as I type out these words, recalling the night air and the terrible loneliness I had discovered, but a loneliness that made me know who I was. The loneliness everyone feels, suddenly, when he begins to think: and once you discover it you can't push it away. Only Nada and I lived in it, this loneliness, and never until that night had I sucked it happily into my lungs and guts and understood what it was.

15

But the next day when I woke I was in the daylight again. A daylight Richard. I dressed feebly and picked up my books and went down to breakfast. Nada glanced at me with moony, distracted eyes. Was she thinking about the sniper? Did he seem to her maybe a new lover, one of those men she met somewhere, somehow, and took home with her? But she only said, "You don't look well, Richard. Should I take you to the doctor?"

"No, I'm fine."

"You look pale."

"It's just the light."

She accepted this nonsense and continued her breakfast. I had cereal: it looked and tasted like wood shavings from Father's workbench. I poured milk on it.

"What's this?" Nada said, pulling my math book

to her. She leafed through it, nodded, and pushed it back. "Maybe you're working too hard and that's why you look pale."

"Did that man shoot anybody again?"

"Who, the sniper? I guess not. There's nothing in the paper."

"Why do you think somebody would do that? Is he crazy?"

Nada shrugged her shoulders.

"Wouldn't he have to be crazy to do that?" I said anxiously.

Nada, licking her lips free of sweet cantaloupe juice, was drawn to say after a reluctant hesitation, "What's crazy is that he shoots to miss."

16

And now things began to go fast. All my young life things had gone slowly, like leaden beetles, and suddenly at the end of that July they began to go fast. My daylight time was slow as usual, but my night time was picking up faster and faster, like a deranged heart. You see, my readers, I was suddenly joined by another sniper.

Ladies and gentlemen, another sniper stepped out of the light and into the darkness, following my lead!

It was now August 2, and by this date I had gone out a total of three times, very cleverly each time, and each time I had shot to miss and had indeed missed: a bloodless operation. But on August 2 I was joined by another sniper. That bastard hadn't my Cedar Grove touch. He was obviously lower class, a slob who shot an old man out on the sidewalk and hit him in the knee. As if I, Richard Everett, would have shot an old man in the knee! But while my stomach cringed at the thought of such vulgarity, my heart swelled with unreasonable pride to think that I had a follower, an imitator. The only problem was that the police made no distinction between us.

SNIPER STRIKES FOURTH TIME. "An elderly man, out for an after-dinner walk, was shot today by the mysterious sniper who has . . ."

I trembled with rage at their stupidity. Three of the stories on the front page dealt with "the sniper," but which sniper did they mean? The chief of police said that he did not think the sniper really intended to kill or even hurt; he was a sick person looking for help, and he would get help, yes, if he identified himself. A minister complained about the cancerous erosion of morality in public life: how could it *not* affect the unstable in our midst? It was time to "assess ourselves." The bosomy president of a Mother's Club demanded greater police protection and more convictions.

There were subsidiary stories, about suspects: men with lamentable records, men found loitering near the shooting scenes and unable to justify themselves, all adults, I'm proud to say, and all of them stripped and exposed to public view, so long hidden cleverly behind respectable faces and respectable homes (it turned out that an advertising executive, evidently a trustworthy man, had been arrested on a morals charge twenty years ago, what do you think of that? His photograph in the paper showed a most worried man.) And there were

286]

many telephone calls. I haven't mentioned my third time out, but it was an excursion to an ordinary Cedar Grove home, nothing sensational, the home of a couple named Mr. and Mrs. Frazer Crane. Now the Cranes were receiving peculiar telephone calls. "Next time I'll get you! I won't miss!" someone promised them. They reported jazzy music in the background.

Ah, yes, and what else? It was a circus. People were interviewed, men at lunchtime, and housewives, someone from the City Council; a psychiatrist (*de rigueur*), the police commissioner (who was indignant).

Libby was afraid to journey out to Cedar Grove, and Nada argued with her over the phone. "But I'm having guests tonight!" she cried. She slammed down the receiver and sat without speaking for some time. I approached her, but she did not notice me. I wanted to ask her what she was thinking about. Was she afraid of the sniper? But I would protect her from him. Yes, I would protect her. Or was she thinking of something else altogether—of her dinner party or of some man in another city, of another life free from me? Was she thinking of what her life might have been if she hadn't married Father, hadn't given birth to me? I was near enough to embrace her, but I was never near enough to know what she was thinking.

"You shouldn't give that party tonight," I said. "Mrs. Hofstadter has their house all locked up. She won't let Gustave go outside."

"Oh, Bébé's crazy."

"But we could stay home and sit upstairs and read or something. We could watch television—"

"We don't have television," Nada said.

"Yes we do," I said, but her gaze had already moved off me. She picked up the phone again and called someone else.

I went out to school. The awful sense of inertia and nausea that I had pushed back for so many days was pressing in on me again.

17

Nada had her party that night in spite of everything. She did the cooking herself. Could she cook? I don't know. She so loaded up her dishes with spices and sauces and wine that the essence of the thing was irrelevant anyway. Everyone complimented her just the same. Everyone complimented everyone else no matter what. But that night something was wrong, for Father was very, very late, and they dawdled through cocktails (nine guests, the odd one being Mavis Grisell, who was still in town) and talked about the rumors concerning an enormous million-dollar home in Pools Moran that had no furniture at all and only mattresses in the bedrooms, and they joked about the sniper, and still Father didn't appear, so they went in to dinner. I listened part of the time. I didn't feel well. In fact, I felt very sick, but it was not a familiar sickness. It did not seem to have anything to do with my body.

I dragged myself out to do a little spying, out of a sense of duty more than anything else, and came down to the landing. I could see and smell the dining-room candles, and the dancing flames reminded me of that lovely, mysterious girl on the Bodys' diving board. The guests talked quietly and politely. I had no fear, as they might have had, that the sniper might shoot in upon them. Or could the other sniper show up? Where was Father? Had Father been hit driving home, or was Father himself somewhere oiling his rifle, his tongue between his teeth?

But Father did finally arrive. I heard the front door being thrust open and heard next a quick surprised *oh* from our guests. Father strode into the dining room. I could look right down on him as he passed. He marched to the table and said, "All right, all right, just look! If you want to know what's going on, what she's really like, what she's got in her, just look! Look at this!" And he tore open his rumpled white shirt to display his naked chest (no undershirt!), and there on his hairy, beefy flesh were dozens of red marks.

"Heels, gentlemen! High heels, ladies!" Father cried. That old buffoon wept, prancing around the table with his fake wounds displayed, while everyone sat and stared. Even Nada was totally upstaged. "When a man is down his wife leaps upon him with her high heels, sharp high heels, sharp as daggers! Ice picks! She does a dance on him, yes, she dances on his body, on his corpse, and he has to lie there and take it . . ."

I don't know how the guests managed to get out of it, how Nada managed to sit there with that small fixed smile of hers. I ran back to my room. I had no stomach for any more of it. Father's drunken bawling went on for a while after the last guest had escaped, and then I must have fallen asleep. Later that night I woke to silence, except for a dog barking down the street.

And what now?

18

That bare chest reminds me of a snapshot I have here in my desk drawer. I can find it easily enough—there's nothing in the drawer except snapshots and a few notes.

Here it is. A photo of Father taken in Miami, many years ago. He is sitting squat on a beach blanket, under a lollipop umbrella, and that woman beside him must be Nada. She looks quite thin. Yes, this is an old snapshot, dated January 1948. Before my birth! Imagine Father and Nada, before my birth, in the Miami sun, and knowing nothing at all of what is coming: that's why Father is sitting so confidently, a cigar in his fingers, his big broad almost muscular chest posed for the camera, and Nada, dear Nada, is less confident, for she stares through her sunglasses at the camera as if it were a gun. Beside him, my mother looks small. I had never noticed that she was a small person; when I "saw" her in any public sense she was always in high heels. She is wearing a dark bathing suit, her hair is long. It makes me dizzy to think that the world of January 1948 was a world in which I did not even exist, I was not even a tiny seed in that woman's body—imagine me, not having existed! Imagine! I always start to weep, looking at this photograph. I hate my weakness but I can't help it. Because it is like staring up at the light from stars that are no longer there but have passed on in their mysterious orbits or exploded and turned to dust.

The universe is encrusted with the dust of things no longer with us.

19

Next day I went to school, and then I did an extraordinary thing: I went out to the Main Street of Cedar Grove, which was also the Main Street of the city, and took a bus downtown. Downtown I wandered around a while in my usual daze and went to see a movie. The movie house was ancient and very large, and its offerings were advertised by shabby posters set out upon the sidewalk. A few bums stood around. I went inside the theater, hoping for a pleasant, cool darkness, but it was an ordinary warm darkness filled with people who did not smell very clean. The first movie was in black and white; don't ask me what it was about. Soldiers, music on the battlefield, shots of airplanes dropping bombs. When someone died I did not know whether to despair or rejoice because I could not remember who were the Americans, who were the enemy. Another movie, in technicolor, dealt with the horrors of a mad doctor's laboratory, secret beneath his Tudor house. One scene showed a woman being nailed inside a barrel, I don't know why; much blood. And yet another movie came on —what a wonderful theater! It was an Italian movie with subtitles but I liked it best, not having to understand the words. Actors in muted shades of gray, silhouetted against cloudy skies, walking about on an island. Hair blew in the wind. Eyes squinted. It occurred to me that Father and I had seen this movie one evening a few light-years ago. But still I did not understand it.

When I came outside the sunlight bothered me. It was late afternoon, and the sun slants in an unpleasant way in our part of the globe at this time of day. I walked squinting past a newsstand and saw a headline that brought my eyes open wide: SNIPER CONFESSES. I stood trying to read the story while hands moved in, hurried and impatient, letting dimes fall in the slot and snatching out papers, and finally it seemed to me only right that I buy a paper myself, it was the only honest thing to do.

Then I took the paper out tenderly and unfolded it, and there it was: SNIPER CONFESSES. The sniper turned out to be a thirty-seven-year-old bachelor who lived with his parents and his older sister. They were all Baptists and, believe it or not, the sniper was characterized as a "devoutly religious man." He himself said, "I don't know why I did it. I don't know." His photograph showed an apologetic little man with wild eyes.

My brain reeled. I waited in a large, loose crowd for a bus, and inside I opened the paper and read feverishly. Yes, yes. But didn't they know he was lying? He had walked into a downtown police station to confess. His mother did not believe his story and refused to see him. His father and sister swore that he had been home when all the shootings had occurred. A neighbor lady said suspiciously, "He was always real quiet and kept to himself, but there was something funny about him . . ."

Nada wasn't home when I got there; neither was Father. Libby hadn't turned up for days. Nada was out for cocktails or in bed with someone somewhere, and Father was drinking or maybe not drinking at all, but freshly shaven, spruced up, sparkling and jovial at a board meeting—who could tell? I felt how alone I was in this house and how alone I had always been, whether out running down the lane or jostled about on a city bus or safe at home in my own house.

20

In Nada's room things were scattered. As usual, the bed was unmade. An odor of powder and ink distracted me from what I was trying to figure out: but yes, there it was—inside her closet lay a suitcase, opened, but with nothing in it. I was not surprised by any of this. It registered upon my mind that the suitcase was there and she had not left yet.

I went down to the basement and hunted up, in a cardboard box no one had bothered to unpack for the last two moves, a pair of Father's old hunting boots. Don't ask me what he was doing with hunting boots. I put these on right over my shoes and the fit was about right. I stomped around, testing them. Our basement was very large and rather damp, divided up into several sections: a kind of apartment, filled with unwanted furniture and various junk, a pool table with a stained top, and lesser rooms filled with things like a freezer, washing and drying machines, cases of food in tin cans. I saw no signs of life in the basement. A mist seemed to rise up about me, suggested perhaps by the damp air and a leaking pipe that had sent a rivulet of water across the floor. I went upstairs with the boots still on and had the idea that as I ascended I would be walking up out of the drizzle that surrounded me. But the drizzle was deeper than I imagined.

Now the next thing I did was to peek cautiously into the kitchen. No one was there. I went to get my rifle and returned to the kitchen, which I haven't described for you, but no matter, I am past describing it. I did not see anything as I sat out there. I could have been sitting in a country cemetery or down in a sewer, beneath a Christmas tree, anywhere—wherever I sat there was the drizzling vacuum. Consider me sitting there with my rifle, a child of eleven, pale, overwrought and yet curiously quiet, much too quiet, and you have penetrated one of the opaque secrets of life: how do these things happen? You ask with chaste dismay how they could have been allowed to happen, and this is the answer—just this simply!

But don't get the impression that I was thinking anything like that. I was not thinking at all. I was in a suspended state some call waiting, when they see it from the outside. I was "waiting" in the way the frog (a statue that was also a sprinkler) on the lawn across the street is "waiting"—that is, I just *was*. I wasn't existing in addition to anything else. And then, when the door did finally open (hours later), I remained in the same state as if I knew it wasn't yet time for me to act. My body has always known what it planned before my brain has caught on.

I heard Nada running up the front stairs. Was anyone with her? For some reason I did not think so. (This turned out to be right.) So I reached for the telephone with my cold steady hand and dialed Gustave's number. It never occurred to me that Gustave might not be in. I felt no relief or surprise when he answered, "Hello?", in his cautious voice. Always a shy child, I nevertheless blossomed like a depraved flower in the tension of this moment: you should have heard me talk to poor Gustave! I talked about my mother and father, their fight of the evening before. I talked about my math class. I asked him how he was, had he heard anything more about the sniper? And we chatted casually but aimlessly, the way children do over telephones, Gustave sighing occasionally to indicate that he had better things to do but not really wanting to hang up.

You are going to be skeptical about my timing. But the timing seems clever only because it turned out well. It might not have turned out well, whereupon it would have been bad timing, but, as you'll see, it turned out very well. At a mysterious instant I suddenly cried out to Gustave, in the midst of a conversation about math, "Did you hear that? Somebody shot a gun right nearby!" And I slammed the receiver down. And, losing no time, I ran out the back door with my rifle, heavy and ludicrous in Father's shoes, and around the house away from the driveway—which was too open—so that I could inch along between our evergreens and the wall of the house. Near the front, at the corner, I waited for only a few seconds, and then the front door opened and Nada appeared on the walk with her suitcase. Her car was parked out at the curb and the driver's door was half open. But of this I took little notice, and indeed I hardly took notice of Nada herself, as if she no longer existed for me, except to raise the rifle and fire at her, the barrel of the gun swerving up to bring the telescope to my eye as if some terrible force were sucking it from me. And I didn't need to see what happened because I knew.

At such moments you think of nothing. Nothing.

Things come at you—low-hanging branches, doors, and you duck or reach out your hand appropriately and take hold of them or fend them off. They come singly and so you can handle them. I ran back alongside our house, through the dense shrubs, to a spot that had caught my eye earlier: a long bank of shrubs that screened us from our neighbors, or screened our neighbors from us. The soil was dark and rich and moist; lawn men had tilled it just the other day. I stood on the lawn and plunged the barrel of the rifle into the soft soil, on our neighbor's property now, and nosed it in with desperate strength. In the end I had to scoop up dirt with my fingers to cover the gun, and then I had to pat and smooth everything over, but finally it was hidden, and then, still without thinking, I ran back to the house and sprinted into the kitchen where the telephone was ringing.

It was Gustave. He started to ask what was wrong and I screamed, "They shot my mother!" And again I left the phone, dangling this time, to run down to the basement, where I hit Father's boots together over a sink and got most of the dirt off, and tossed them back in the box. By the time I was upstairs again and ready to look out the front door I was really crying the way an eleven-year-old would cry. There was no stopping what happened to me after that point.

21

I suppose there is no need for me to say that when I pulled the trigger that time the world cracked in pieces around me? I did not come alive as I had in the past. No great heaving clots of blood rushed to my heart, to stir it into activity. I felt no surge of strength. What had been in the innermost hollow of my being dimmed to a spark, a pinpoint, and very slowly went out. Through the mist that rose above me I was able to make out certain faces, certain voices. Father, for one, and kindly official men who were policemen, though not dressed in uniform, nurses, a doctor. I must have been in a hospital. At times I drifted, free and helpless, at the bottom of the ocean, far from their ability to touch me, and at times I lay on a windswept desert far to the west of Cedar Grove.

Well, this memoir is about Nada, and with her death it comes to an end, more or less. Since I cannot do anything gracefully, you won't be surprised that the memoir keeps on for a few pages, and it isn't just that I am afraid to die. Why should I be afraid to die? I have nothing to live for, after all.

There is no point in a fake chronological report, because in the hospital I lost all sense of chronological time. Time was compressed and exploded in my brain. But outside me, in the real world, time did progress ordinarily, and someone must have called the police, after I pulled the trigger, someone did run up to her and to me, and out of the silent houses of Labyrinth Drive came maids and children, to watch the usual vehicles drive up and the usual uniformed people jump down. In my own delirium I caught sight of a boy of about four, crying hysterically; the Negro woman with him had to pick him up in her arms and run down the street to their house.

You'll notice how I refrain from mentioning my mother. I am not going to look at the center of that circle, any more than I really looked at it through the telescope. And, later that day, the final edition of the evening paper was quick enough to have as a headline, CEDAR GROVE WOMAN SLAIN BY SNIPER, and a photograph not of Nada but of our home, described as a $95,000 home in the heart of Cedar Grove, but the photograph was a poor one and did not do our house justice. A baroque X marked the spot where she had fallen. Subsequent editions followed with photographs of Nada, described variously as a "beautiful woman," a "writer of national reputation," a "figure in local society." But I don't want to go on with this. You can dig up those papers yourself.

22

Yes, she did die, and no, she won't be back again. It is as simple as that. I have used up years of my life trying to realize how simple it is. But let me call your attention to these photographs—quite simply stolen from Father, who forgot about them in a few months. They are photographs taken from Nada's room, pictures I had never seen, a little creased with my handling because I look at them constantly. The first one is of Nada as a young bride, and note the happy smile but the rather serious, suspicious eyes. Or am I imagining this? Her hair is fixed in a style that looks old-fashioned now. I like this snapshot very much though. Nada is wearing a spring suit and she is squinting into the sun. Perhaps it is Father she's looking at, Father with a loaded camera like a loaded gun, and if I could only reach out and warn her—tell her to get out, escape! But she squints and smiles forever at me, the son she is going to have and cannot escape having, as far from me in that snapshot as she ever was in life.

And look at this one—this is a surprise. When I first saw it I must confess I was very upset. It is a snapshot of a girl of sixteen or so, standing on a porch, a front porch of a frame house. But if you look more closely you see that the girl is Nada, and her hair is cut short, she is smiling too widely, and the shadow of the porch cuts very unprofessionally across her face. On the back of the snapshot Nada's mother had written in her cramped hand, "Nancy June 1945." But who is Nancy? And who is Nada's mother?

They came to the funeral and they stayed around afterward, Nada's parents. No, they weren't dead as I had always thought, and they weren't peculiar either; they were just ordinary people. Nada's father had worked in a rubber plant for many years and was now retired; he was a janitor in a parochial grade school. Nada's mother was a thin, sickish, whining, rather deaf woman who had Nada's hawklike nose but nothing else, nothing else! Their name was not Romanov but Ukrainian *Ro-*

manow, and it had not been out of political necessity that they had come to America but for ordinary reasons: not emigrés but immigrants. The father was neither madman nor genius but just an ordinary, very ordinary, apologetic, slow man with the slightest suggestion of a hump between his shoulders. Nothing more. I don't want to go into the details of those visits with them. Father handled it well enough, but it's better to forget about it. And Natashya was never Natashya but Nancy, Nancy Romanow, born and baptized and confirmed in the Catholic Church, and therefore, according to their notion, saved in spite of everything. The Catholics believe that one can make a swift last-second prayer of repentance or something, and Mrs. Romanow argued with us about this as if we were selfishly holding Nada's soul back from its rightful place in heaven.

This Nancy, this sudden intrusion of another person, was born in a small town in upstate New York with a ludicrous name: North Tonawanda. Yes, it must be an Indian name. I have lulled myself to sleep many a night with that name, which hints of mysteries and beauties that are no doubt betrayed by a sky full of smoke from rubber plants, but anyway, North Tonawanda was the town she was born in, and there she went to a Catholic grade school and a Catholic high school, and Mrs. Romanow said, "She was always a good girl, not wild, a *good girl,*" though her tone would change in a minute when she moved on to the subject of her good girl Nancy's running off to New York City. When Nancy at last bothered to write she explained nothing; she did not even ask for money, which of course meant the worst. Some time later she wrote her parents to announce her marriage and to promise them they'd be invited out soon, as soon as she and Elwood ("What a name, Elwood!" Mrs. Romanow said sourly) were settled, but of course no invitation ever came. So Nancy was a bad girl after all, and when she turned up as Natashya, slain by a sniper who was never to be apprehended, it would seem that North Tonawanda should have been the limits of her world after all.

Other snapshots I have here—let's see—this dog-eared one of an even prettier Nancy, who holds up her chin aggressively and is surely contemplating New York City and its wonders, the darkness of which will allow a re-birth and a rebaptizing—this Nancy is standing with an obscure and anonymous girl friend, both in white summer dresses and looking rather coy. This time the background is the side of a garage with a few scrawny rose bushes. No background at all. My mind swirls to think of the leap Nancy-Natashya made, from the bland wooden-frame world of North Tonawanda to the bland headi-ness of Cedar Grove. Wonderful! Wonderful! But look closely at the snapshot, look at the face that girl had. This is in 1946, so she's seventeen and ready to graduate from high school and take off, and look at the face she has already—fine, serious, intelligent, the lips coy and closed. How beautiful she is! Her girl friend is smiling and showing her teeth, but not Nancy. Nancy's lips are closed. I have such an urge, such a desperate urge, to go to North Tonawanda and look up this girl friend, talk with her, force from her all of Nancy's secrets . . .

You are wondering what happened after Nada's death? Well, nothing happened. This is a memoir and not a novel. I can't fabricate anything. The search for the sniper continued without success, dropping out of the newspapers with a stunning swiftness, and when I was well enough to talk I told Father that I had done it. I remember him bending to me, his ear moving toward my mouth—the pink swirls and coils of that ear—but he only laughed loudly, then he stopped laughing. He thought I was crazy. I told my doctor that I was the person who had killed my mother, and he too thought I was crazy, and I began shouting and screaming that I had done it, no one else, and everyone thought I was crazy, the bastards!

A detective came and listened kindly to me and made a pretense of taking me seriously. I was such a thin, wretched child, you see—in that hospital bed that was too big for me, fed intravenously, with my weak near-blind eyes and my bruised arms. I believe he wrote things down to be polite, information about the buried rifle and the boots. (The boot prints in the ground had been one of the police's strong clues.) But for some reason I never heard from the detective again, and when I questioned Father desperately about him, Father cleared his throat and said it was "Coming along, coming along."

What about the Baptist who confessed? Nothing happened to him either. He disappeared from the newspapers, and that was that. They didn't believe his confession either. They are very jealous and suspicious, the police. But to hell with him.

As soon as I was released from the hospital I made Father take me at once to the site of the shooting. I marched triumphantly to our neighbors' shrubs and went to what I thought was the correct spot and poked around and finally got to my knees and dug wildly, but I found nothing. Father watched me in silence. I said, "Please may I have a shovel, Father," and he brought me one but did not offer to help. I dug in the dirt but found nothing. Father said that the police had been in this, everywhere, digging up everything, but I ignored him, turning my sweating face to the ground that had betrayed me. How was it possible the gun was gone? Can you explain that? What happened to my rifle? And I hadn't even had sense enough to keep the box it had come in, but I had thrown that away immediately. Father all but picked me up under his arm and carried me into the house.

Did our neighbors find the gun and, not wanting to be involved, dispose of it themselves? Did one of the sullen, muscular men who worked for the Cedar Grove Green Carpet Lawn Service discover the gun and steal it?

I never found out.

We moved from 4500 Labyrinth Drive to another huose, about the same size but more expensive, with a living-room ceiling that was three stories high and quite a conversation piece, across Broad Road in the heart of Pools Moran. Of course we had to move. It wasn't just the memory of Nada, but Father was shoulder-tapped for a presidency, which he modestly accepted (the product was—still is—some sort of wiring, perhaps for detonators), and after his remarriage he spoke less and less of Nada, which was not surprising, until one day I thought I might as well steal those snapshots Mrs. Romanow had given him in a tearful moment of sentiment. So I took them out of his bureau drawer, and he never mentioned them, thinking, perhaps, that his new wife had destroyed them, out of jealousy for Nada. She had already relegated Nada's expensive French Provincial living-room furniture to the back part of the house and decorated everything with her own Spanish rugs, swords, and spears, her Oriental tapestries and Mexican church doors.

Are you wondering if you know the second Mrs. Everett? A week after my discharge from the hospital I was sitting in my usual daze out in the sun porch, fingering the part where the screen had rusted and broken (in an interesting pattern, a hexagon), digesting breakfast and waiting for lunch (and after lunch I would wait patiently for dinner), when Father came home at a surprising hour, eleven in the morning, and with him was Mavis Grisell, in a splendid new fall outfit and dusky-gold jewelry that clattered as she approached me. "Richard, Mavis and I have something to tell you," Father announced. I saw on Mavis' finger a diamond large enough to pierce your hearts, my readers, and I was silent in awe of that diamond and the fact of its being bigger, far bigger, than Nada's had been. My silence displeased Father, I think. He took Mavis out to the car and came striding back, a large, rather paunchy, but still attractive man, at whom I glanced in surprise as if I hadn't seen him before. He came right to me and said, "Look, you little brat, you neurotic little nut, I'm through with all this horseshit! Mavis is going to be your new mother, and if you don't like it you can go to hell! I've had enough of this lousy American father bit! I've had enough of smiling and gritting my teeth and taking it in the guts, from you or your mother, both of you, and from now on things are going to be different. It's no happy, forgiving Elwood *Daddy*—it's going to be your *Father* whom you are going to respect, buster, or get the hell out, I don't care how young you are or how nuts."

And I recognized then my real father, who was shouting at me out of that familiar man's face.

Yes, there was a series of psychiatrists. Father did that much for me, or against me. My favorite was Dr. Saskatoon, who explained gently to me that I had loved my mother so much, indeed overmuch, that I could not accept the fact of her death being caused by anyone except myself; a familiar delusion, he assured me. I had wanted, poor deluded brat, to be my mother's destroyer simply because I had wanted to establish forever a relationship between the two of us which no one could transcend, not even my father. "You have a very ambivalent, may I say rather negative, attitude toward your father," Dr. Saskatoon told me.

"Dr. Saskatoon," I would say, my teeth about to grind together in a spasm of shuddering, "Dr. Saskatoon, you don't understand what it is like to be free and alive when everything is finished—no, please let me talk," I would cry, shivering convulsively. "Nobody ever lets me talk and I have to say this—there's nothing more terrible than to commit a crime and still be free, there's nothing more terrible than to be a murderer without a murderer's punishment. Dr. Saskatoon—"

And he would say, "Richard, let me assure you of this: hallucinations are as vivid as reality, and I respect everything you say. I know that you are suffering just as much as if you had killed your mother."

And so in the end I stopped saying anything at all.

23

Because I stopped raving and weeping, I remained in the Normal World. You might have seen me, years ago, sitting sadly on a park bench, doing nothing. Not even waiting any longer. I was a quiet, bespeckled child growing into a quiet, bespeckled teen-ager (far removed from the happy, sweating hordes led by the music of Dr. Muggeridge's pipes!). I sleepwalked my way through the years, and as I slept I ate, and as I walked I ate, because there was this peculiar hollowness inside me that I had to fill—but that's just sentiment, ignore it.

So I am waiting out the last minutes of my life sentence of freedom, and outside on the street are—what now?—some kids playing. They don't act like kids though; their movements are jerky and brutal when they throw and catch their ball, and one of the children is smoking a cigarette, and the big one is always ready to punch the others in the arm or back—there he goes again, the little bastard! Ah, summertime here in the city! I pull toward me a few cans and my rusty can opener. Time to begin . . . Did I explain to you that I left home at sixteen and was not lamented, and Father sends me an allowance that is generous enough to keep me well stocked with food? Look at the size of this can of apricots! Enough to stuff a horse! Yes, my dear harsh Father appeared to me at last, after eleven years of disguise. But I did find him at last, and isn't that what we all crave, a confrontation with the truth? I was confronted with the truth. And I found my true mother, or one of her truer selves, that girl Nancy Romanow (younger than I am now), and of course here in my room are many of her stories, everything I could get hold of, and I read them and reread them and sometimes think that I am coming close to . . . something, I don't know what.

As for God—did I find God through suffering and repentance? Indeed not. I am afraid not. God came to me in a dream once disguised as Father and backslapping and loud as usual, but his slaps on my back were harder than need be. And that is the secret of the backslapper—he is really pounding you to death. In my reading I came across Freud's remark that everyone's notion of God is based upon his unconscious notion of his father. Well, I am stuck with a sadistic, happy, backslapping God and to hell with that.

And here are eight bananas, just flecked with brown and therefore ready to be guzzled, and as soon as you turn your back I will begin. The softness of bananas, the hardness of peanut brittle, the pliant cool sanity of lettuce! I have sauces and jams which I will pour over those pieces of bread and those cookies which have gone stale, never fear. This must be the end of the memoir. I excuse you at this point. My career as a writer now ends, and I don't have time to look through what I've written. Let it stand. I am being carried along on the wave of a most prodigious hunger. All I ask is the strength to fill the emptiness inside me, to stuff it once and for all!

That, and the fierce consolation of knowing that whatever I did, whatever degradations and evils, stupidities, blunders, moronic intrusions, whatever single ghastly act I did manage to achieve, it was done out of freedom, out of choice. This is the only consolation I have in the face of death, my readers: the thought of my free will. But I must confess that there are moments when I doubt even this consolation . . .